Praise for *The Perfect Father*

'I absolutely loved *The Perfect Father*! A real thriller of a ride with a twist I did NOT see coming'

Nikki Smith, author of *All in Her Head*

'Unpredictable, tense and engrossing, *The Perfect Father* will challenge your perceptions of parenthood and keep you hooked from the first page to the last'

Rebecca Fleet, author of *The Second Wife*

'Modern, smart and fast-paced, this thriller had me hooked from the first page'

Ruth Heald, author of *I Know Your Secret*

'I love Charlotte's dark, messy takes on modern relationships, and this is no exception'

Claire McGowan, author of *The Push*

'I loved this book. *The Perfect Father* is an emotional and intelligently written thriller. The twists are so expertly woven in that at times I had to pause to let them sink in. Highly recommended'

Elisabeth Carpenter, author of *The Woman Downstairs*

'Such realistic, well-drawn characters, gripping emotional plot twists (that also feel rooted in reality) and a really distinctive story style'

Nicola Mostyn, author of *The Love Delusion*

'*Doctor Foster* meets *Gone Girl*. Tense, twisty and deeply unsettling'

B P Walter, author of *Hold Your Breath*

Charlotte Duckworth has spent the past fifteen years working as an interiors and lifestyle journalist, writing for a wide range of consumer magazines and websites. She lives in Surrey with her partner and their daughter. You can find out more on her website: charlotteduckworth.com.

Also by Charlotte Duckworth

The Rival
Unfollow Me

THE
PERFECT
FATHER

CHARLOTTE
DUCKWORTH

Quercus

First published in Great Britain in 2020 by Quercus
This paperback edition published in 2021 by

Quercus Editions Ltd
Carmelite House
50 Victoria Embankment
London EC4Y 0DZ

An Hachette UK company

A CIP catalogue record for this book is available
from the British Library

PB ISBN 978 1 52940 8 300
EB ISBN 978 1 52940 8 294

This book is a work of fiction. Names, characters,
businesses, organizations, places and events are
either the product of the author's imagination
or used fictitiously. Any resemblance to
actual persons, living or dead, events or
locales is entirely coincidental.

10 9 8 7 6 5 4 3 2 1

Typeset by CC Book Production
Printed and bound in Great Britain by Clays Ltd, Elcograf S.p.A.

MIX
Paper from
responsible sources
FSC® C104740
FSC
www.fsc.org

Papers used by Quercus are from well-managed forests and other responsible sources.

For Sophy

NOW

ROBIN

Sorry.

The message to Esther was a mistake. But I meant it.

My cheeks are wet. I swipe at the tears, sniffing so aggressively my nose aches.

Sorry.

I am sorry now. Sorry I sent it.

Never mind. Too late. No going back.

Literally, no going back.

I stare at the clock behind the steering wheel. We're lucky, rush hour is at least forty-five minutes away, the traffic is light – or as light as it ever gets in this part of London. This traffic-clogged Petri dish of Boden kids and city fathers and yoga mothers that we call home.

How did I even end up here?

I glance in the rear-view mirror. Riley is staring out of the window from her car seat, taking in the parade of filthy shopfronts we pass. Soon we'll be on the A24 and then . . . what?

The ferry to France?

Or Gatwick? Riley's never been on a plane.

If we go to Gatwick we'll have to leave the car.

I sit back in my seat, my mind running through all the possibilities. The traffic lights ahead turn to green as I approach and I accelerate hard through them: 30 ... 35 ... 40 mph. I revel in the empty road ahead.

Just one more turn and then I hit the A24. Riley laughs as the car's engine roars. My fearless kid. I glance back at her; she's clapping her hands. Thrilled at the adventure.

We are a team. There is nowhere she'd rather be. No one she'd rather be with.

I hit 65 mph. The sense of freedom is exhilarating. The tears dry up.

Seventy now. I take my phone out of my pocket, fumble to switch it on. My battery has four per cent left. Just enough to look up ferry times.

France first.

France first, just to give us some distance, and then we'll make a proper plan.

ESTHER

Sorry.

That's all Robin's text message said. What does that mean? By the time I turn the corner on to our street, my hands are shaking so violently I'm not sure I'll be able to turn the key. Please God, please God, just let me find them at home as usual. Let him have sent that message to me by mistake. A stupid, thoughtless mistake. Or a joke. Yet another joke I don't understand.

We'll be laughing about it in a few minutes. Please, *please*.

I spent the entire journey here talking myself down from the edge, like the rational woman I am, reading over Amanda's reply to my message, telling me that she dropped Riley off with Robin just before 3pm. That he seemed a bit preoccupied, but no more so than usual. Nothing that gave her any cause for concern.

But . . . a bit preoccupied?

I phoned, said I was worried I hadn't heard from him and asked her to pop round to ours, to see if he was there, but she was at the swimming pool with Madeline and wouldn't be back for ages.

No matter how my mind torments me, there is one thing I know for sure: he would never hurt her. He adores her. He's looked after her since she was born, so that I could go back to work as soon as possible. Back to the career I love. Their bond is undeniable.

I push open our small gate – newly painted – and I run up our front path. The house is pitch-dark, but the front door is ajar. The panic sets in again, followed closely by anger. What the hell is he playing at? Why is the front door open?

I swallow the vomit that rises to my throat, as salty and disgusting as seawater, then I push the door open fully, fumble for the light switch and squint as the spotlights blind me.

'Rob!' I call out in the silent house. 'Rob! Where are you?'

My voice soon becomes a scream. I race from room to room, but there's no one here.

There's no one here.

I grab my phone from my bag and ring his number again, but it goes to voicemail, as it has done ever since he sent that text message. There's nothing too unusual about that – he often has his phone switched off.

I try to think. Where could they have gone? It's nearly 4.15pm. They might be at the park. They're probably at the park.

But it's freezing outside.

And why was the front door open?

I check the coat rack in the narrow hallway. Riley's coat is not there. Neither are her little boots. His shoes are missing. He has taken her somewhere. But where?

Why is he sorry?

I look around our shiny new house, remembering a time when I thought the extension project wouldn't end. It was meant to be a fresh start. It's not a big house, but it's big enough for the three of us.

But now. Now that it's just me, standing here alone, it feels too big.

Of course it's too big. Riley isn't here. Her absence is the biggest space of all.

I go through to the kitchen, wondering who to call. The police? Would that be an overreaction? What if that just made everything worse? And then my phone pings.

A message from my friend Vivienne, telling me that she'll have Robin 'disappeared' as a birthday present for me if I like? Her humour has always been the blackest, yet the timing of her message is unnerving.

I stare around at our shiny new kitchen, the immaculate white stone worktops gleaming at me. The space is cavernous, and it echoes. It's too empty. It's empty of everything: warmth, trust, passion. Just like our marriage of late.

I turn again and then I notice that the biggest kitchen drawer is open wide. The drawer in which we fling all the stuff that has no other home: batteries, key rings, paracetamol, old Calpol syringes, pens that have nearly run dry . . .

The doorbell chimes, catching me unexpectedly. Please let it be them. Please let it be him bringing her home.

I rush through the hall to the front door. But when I open it, I don't find my husband. Or my daughter. My tiny, vulnerable two-year-old girl.

Instead, there are two police officers: one male, one female, their breath misting in the cold.

Sorry, his text message said.

What has he done?

THREE YEARS
EARLIER

ESTHER

Pregnant.

This is what we both wanted, so why do I feel so shocked? Perhaps it's the fact that I had resigned myself to it never happening. To *this* never happening – this moment of staring down at the pregnancy test, and not just seeing the usual single line, staring sadly up at me.

Two lines. Two pink lines!

My eyes fall on the huge pile of paperwork we took home from the IVF clinic last week, sitting right opposite me on the coffee table. The complicated array of different options, and pricing plans and decisions that needed to be made: would I like my tubes flushed first as a precaution?

Suddenly, none of it is relevant any longer. We can burn it all: all the paper and the jargon and the decisions and the appointments.

'How?' I say. 'How is this . . . possible? After what they told us, after what they said . . . nearly two years! Two years of trying . . . why . . . how?'

I'm so bewildered by it all, so terrified that it's a mistake, that the test is faulty.

'I'll do another test,' I say. 'Just to be sure.'

But I am sure. I know it, I feel different. So different from all those months when I had held my hopes up as high as I possibly could, only to have them punctured by that single pink line again.

The second test confirms the first. I am pregnant.

All my dreams come true.

I sit back down on the sofa in the living room of our tiny flat, our pride and joy, the shared creation that we are both so passionate about. I pull the check blanket over my legs, a souvenir from our latest minibreak in the Highlands, turning the situation over in my mind. Robin sits beside me, still. So very still. It's unlike him; he's usually a ball of energy.

He hasn't said anything yet.

'Rob . . .'

I think about his reaction when I showed him the pregnancy test, trying to work out what the facial expressions meant. I'm nearly thirty-eight. We've been together for five years. The most unlikely of couples. Me, Mrs Sensible, with my first-class English degree and reluctance to drink more than one glass of wine at any occasion. Him, Mr Reckless, smarter than me but not academic, quick-witted and sociable, the non-stop talker, the life and soul of a party who can never have 'just one'.

Opposites attract, I always say to people. We bring out the best in each other.

We got married two years ago. Just woke up one freezing Saturday morning in February and marched down to the registry office and did it. Dragged two witnesses in their fifties

12

off the street – they were less enthusiastic about it than we'd hoped, and we laughed about them afterwards, how unromantic their souls must be. Swore never to end up like them. Came home and interspersed making love with eating Ben & Jerry's straight from the tub for the rest of the day. The high I felt afterwards lasted weeks.

It remains the most unlikely and the most spontaneous thing I've ever done. But at the same time, I had never felt surer of a decision in my life.

We started trying for a baby straight away. I have wanted this for so long, but now I feel terrified.

It's almost too much, isn't it? To get everything you ever wanted? No one gets everything they ever wanted.

'Rob, say something!'

Why is he so quiet?

At best, he is stunned. At worst, he is devastated. Did he secretly hope it would never happen?

'I need to work out the dates,' I say, pulling my phone towards me. 'It's December now, so that means . . .'

'August,' Robin replies. 'I think. Shit. The festival. An Edinburgh baby!'

He beams.

'That's nice,' I say, stupidly. The festival. Typical that he should think of that straight away. 'A summer baby. I always wished I had a summer birthday.'

In a moment, my life has changed completely and forever. Like a train suddenly switching track. No way back. Whatever the outcome, this will define me, my life, my story.

A baby.

My face breaks into a smile; a strange gurgle of childish glee escapes.

I'm pregnant!

But then I think of Vivienne. I can picture it now: the way her lip will twist in surprise, followed by an abrupt shake of her head and look of disbelief. She will be shocked. She thought it would never happen for us.

Deep down, perhaps, she hoped it never would.

'I don't know what to say.' My voice wavers. 'I don't know how to feel. I'm just . . . I was so sure it would never . . .'

Suddenly, I am sobbing.

'Hey, Tot, it's OK,' Robin says, in a surprisingly steady voice. 'It's overwhelming, that's all. You clever girl. You did it. You did it!' He grips my hand in his, the wide smile still stretched across his face.

That's when I finally exhale. This is how our relationship works, how it has always worked. I feel guilty for my momentary lack of faith. We take it in turns. When he is feeling weak, I give him his strength. When I am feeling weak, he gives me mine. We are a team, two sides of a coin; we are perfect, but only if we're together. It makes sense that I am the one feeling overwhelmed – it's my body, after all.

'*We* did it,' I say, returning his smile.

'Yes, we did. And it's *awesome,* Tot. Imagine, a tiny boy or girl. Ours. Fuck!'

I nod, the relief all-encompassing. I throw my arms around his neck and kiss him through the mess of curly hair that hangs down almost to his chin. He smells of sleep and warmth; he feels like home.

'It's Christmas next week,' I say, my cheek pressed tightly against his. 'Are we going to tell people? What about the alcohol?'

Robin turns to me and takes my face in his hands. I can smell coffee on his breath. It would never normally bother me, but this time I feel my stomach lurch in protest.

'Don't worry about a thing,' he says, staring straight into my eyes. And then finally he leaps to his feet, his arms wide as he beams down at me and does a little dance on the spot as I sit there, staring up at him and laughing, thinking, as always, how lucky, lucky, lucky I am.

'It's going to be brilliant,' Robin says.

He will be the perfect father.

ROBIN

So this is it, she's pregnant.

After she told me, I took myself off to the bathroom and sobbed. Proper sobbed, like a baby. If she heard me, she didn't say anything. She's good like that. Understands that sometimes you need your privacy, that there are certain things you don't want to share.

Finally, it's happened.

I can hardly believe it.

I haven't known much for sure in my life, but I've always wanted to be a dad. Forget my comedy career, *this* is my destiny. Me and my little son, building the kind of relationship I could only have dreamt of with my old man.

It had always been vague talk, before. Esther knew I'd make a great dad. But when I brought it up she always used to smile at me and say, 'Yes, one day, definitely,' or 'Maybe next year?' and change the subject. She was traditional, she wanted to get married first.

So we did.

I didn't put any pressure on her, because I'm not an arsehole. And then there was the issue of her career. Head of PR at the UK's biggest diabetes charity. That was the problem with a real career. That never-ending ladder to climb. She'd worked her way up from the bottom, starting as an assistant straight out of university. When she got to the next level, she was too scared to step off, in case she couldn't get back on again.

I got it. I'd been pushed off the career ladder myself when I was right at the top, and starting again from the bottom has been a painful experience.

It was OK though. I had patience – procrastination would be top of the skills listed on my CV, if I had one. I knew she'd come round in time. And lo and behold, when her oldest friend from school, Maddie, announced she was pregnant, a switch flicked in Esther's wiring. And suddenly, it was everything she wanted too.

That was how we rolled. Whatever happened, however divergent our lives seemed, somehow they always clicked back into the same groove.

The night she told me she was ready to have a baby, we met for dinner at a steakhouse in Soho. I was about to go on as the support act for a friend at a club nearby. Esther said she'd come and meet me first. 'Save you from the inevitable kebab you'd have otherwise.' She's always been sweet like that. It didn't bother me that it was patronising, or emasculating or whatever the hell other people would think. The other comics on my circuit thought Esther was a control freak but they were idiots, thought that masculinity meant never asking for help.

Our lives back then were hectic, free-flowing and, mostly, fun, and we'd often come back to our flat to find the fridge bare and order a takeaway or head out to a restaurant. There was enough money to burn on things like that, even though we should have been more responsible. London had so much to offer; we didn't want to miss out.

It was my first gig for a while and I was experiencing that same stupid feeling of hope. The feeling that kept me going; the antidepressant of the job. Perhaps this would be the night: there'd be a booker in the audience who would love me, or maybe a decent manager. Mike had proved himself a waste of space time and time again, but he was all I could get after it all went wrong. I dreamt of telling him he was dumped. Upgrading. Who knew? It only takes one lucky break, one person to spot you, and your whole life can change. Gotta keep on keeping on.

We queued outside the restaurant, our arms entangled as always. I was waffling away about the gig, my way of taking the edge off the nerves. Talking them out. We were led to a shared table, high-level. Uncomfortable stools designed to ensure you ate quickly and moved on. Fast food with a slow price tag. I paused as I hauled myself on to the seat – was that something to work into a routine one day?

The waitress was pregnant. Esther noticed; our eyes met briefly, but I didn't say anything. She ordered a milkshake and sat there, her lips grinning as they sucked on the striped straw. We were married. We were happy. We had everything, nearly. I stroked her leg under the table. She was wearing tights and a black dress, having come straight from work.

Her work was all-consuming; I missed her. I had a vision of her, heavily pregnant, knocking off at 4pm because she was exhausted. Coming home to me. I loved the idea of us

18

spending more time together. And maternity leave – a whole year off for us to be together as a family.

'So,' she said, as she stared down at the steak in front of her. 'I've been thinking about the B-word again . . .'

'Burgers?' I said, because it wouldn't be good to look too keen. I felt like I was walking a tightrope: one false move and we would both tumble off.

My leg was restless under the table. I'd wanted this for so long, but Esther had to be ready for it. It had to be her decision.

'We're out for swanky steak and all you want is a bloody burger.'

'You know what I'm talking about, Bird,' she said, rolling her eyes at me. She has always called me that. There's some guy called Robert on my birth certificate. I got rid of him when I first started performing, changed my name officially to Robin. Everyone in my adult life has always called me Bird. 'I'm ready. Let's start trying for a baby.'

'Blimey,' I said, leaning across to squeeze her hand. 'I guess I better order something stronger then.'

She laughed. I motioned to the waitress.

'Cider, please,' I said, then looked over at my wife.

'Are you OK with it?' she said, eyes widening. 'Seriously?'

'No, I'm just going to down this cider and do a runner,' I said, and she rolled her eyes at me.

'Seriously?'

'We've just got married. Tot, it's the best news ever. My mum will be over the moon.'

She pulled a face at that, and I realised then that bringing up my parents was a poor move. She didn't want to be reminded that there would be other people involved with our baby. Her dad. My parents. My perfect brother and his perfect wife, and their perfect twins. In that moment, she wanted it to just be us.

'Let's not tell anyone yet though,' she said, her hazel eyes narrowing a little. 'I want to keep it secret. You never know, it might not happen quickly anyway. It took Maddie and Tom nearly eight months. I don't want everyone knowing we're trying and then going on about it every time we see them.'

I nodded. She's so sensible, and my heart felt swollen with love for her. Inside, a firework had been lit in my chest. I wanted to run outside and spin with uncontrollable joy, like a Catherine wheel let off by accident.

I tried to imagine my son. What would he look like? Would he have Esther's greeny-brown eyes, and my gingery hair?

We ate the rest of our steaks in an awestruck silence at the Big Decision we'd made. She kissed me goodbye outside the venue for the gig. I've never liked her watching me perform. Stand-up is a headfuck at the best of times, but having to do it in front of those who know you best, who can see through your carefully constructed artifice to the true inspiration for your comedy, is almost impossible.

At least, that's how I find it.

Maybe I've been overthinking it too much. I probably just don't like her seeing me mess up.

The gig was pretty shit, as it turned out. *Que sera*. Suddenly, it didn't matter anymore. I only stayed for one pint after, and my mood didn't drop as much as usual. At home, I found her asleep in bed, but when I climbed in beside her, she reached for me. We made love and I wondered whether this would be it, whether this one time would be all it would take.

Two years later . . .

Esther is clutching the test in her fist, staring down at the two pink lines.

'Let me work it out,' Esther says, as though she's reading my mind. She often does that. 'The night it happened.'

She picks up her phone, starts counting on her fingers.

'Shit!'

'What?'

'Remember Duncan's book launch? Oh, no, you probably don't,' she says, as she stares at her phone. 'You were paralytic . . . how . . .'

She has always put up with my drunkenness quite well, considering. It helps that I'm a lovable drunk, of course.

'Oh,' I say, remembering exactly why I got so drunk that evening. Duncan was likely the most competitive male in our group of mates – hard to say for sure though, there were a few contenders. Celebrating his success in a creative field was not something I could quite bring myself to do, even if it had taken him eight years to get published and, happily, the book wasn't great. I read it in one sitting the next day – derivative, uneven in pace. Forgettable. So I drowned it in beer instead. 'Are you sure it was that night?'

'Yep,' she says, curling herself into my lap and putting her arms around me. 'I can't believe it.'

'Let's not tell the baby that,' I say. 'Don't think they need to know their dad was pissed the night they were conceived.'

'No, they don't! Poor baby,' she says, smiling.

I pull her towards me for a kiss, but her lips twist and she turns away.

'Sorry,' she says. 'It's just . . . you . . . you smell of coffee.'

'Right,' I say, blinking at her. 'Sorry. I'll go and brush my teeth.'

In the bathroom, I feel strangely off-balance. I tried to kiss my wife, but she turned away from me. It shouldn't matter, but somehow it does. A tiny sliver of insight into what's to come.

Our beautiful life is about to change beyond all recognition.

ESTHER

I'm working my way through the updated visuals for next year's campaign, trying to ignore the fact I feel hungover, even though I haven't drunk anything since the day I found out I was pregnant, when Vivienne texts me.

Hey, just had a shit casting round the corner. Free for lunch? I need wine. X

I look at my clock. Hardly any of the others are in today, but I decided to work in between Christmas and New Year to catch up. I have a pile of things to get through, but I feel rotten and light-headed. Perhaps some fresh air will do me good.

We meet at a wine bar near Ludgate Circus and I laugh when I see Vivienne – she's pinned her mane of curly red hair back and is wearing a navy blue fitted suit.

'Wow,' I say, kissing her on the cheek. 'What was the audition for?'

'Insurance advert,' she says. 'Don't ask. There's no chance they'll cast my hair anyway. I'm so sick of these bullshit auditions.'

I grin at her and stare down at my menu. Like the other thespians she's introduced me to, moaning is her speciality.

23

But unlike the others, Viv doesn't need to audition really. Her father is a successful theatre director, her mother one of the country's best-loved actresses. Either one of them could get her a job easily. But she refuses their offers of help.

'Why are you even auditioning for adverts?' I ask, watching her unpin her hair. It cascades over her shoulders, nearly reaching her waist. Robin says her hair makes her look like an Amish girl. 'I thought you had a show starting in January?'

'I do,' she says. 'But it's fringe and the pay is shit. And ads pay loads for bugger all. But I won't get it anyway.'

I reach across the table and squeeze her hand.

'Sorry, chicken.'

I order some soup and refuse Vivienne's offer to share a bottle of wine. She doesn't take much notice of why I might be sticking to water, but that's why I like her. She's loud, attention-seeking, and always off in her own world. She's also generous and fun. She's been my best friend since the first day we met at Edinburgh University, having been placed in halls next to each other. We were both studying English Literature but she spent her whole time performing with the drama society. I spent the time that I wasn't in the library watching her in what can only be described as 'avant-garde' productions.

'So how's Rob?' she says, forking her salad and meeting me square in the eyes. 'Still resting?'

For someone who works in the same industry, Viv has remarkably little sympathy for his employment status. The ironic thing is that she introduced us. They had met through a mutual friend. We were introduced at a party I had tagged

24

along to with Viv, and he fell to his knees and thanked God when I said I wasn't an actress myself. It was totally over the top, and Vivienne pulled a face behind him, but I was hooked.

'He's weird,' she told me later that night. 'There's something about him I don't like.'

She was in the minority. Everyone I introduced him to *loved* him. He was six foot four and built like a rugby player, but with chin-length curly strawberry-blond hair and the personality of a spiritual leader. His thoughts – often unusual and always interesting – tumbled out so quickly that he left me breathless.

I am five foot five, with shoulder-length brown hair that won't grow long without thinning. He was out of my league. He was 'cool'. I decided the only reason Vivienne didn't like him was because he had never expressed any interest in her, and she wasn't used to that.

I never thought he'd like me. But apparently he did. We met at the party on a Friday evening, he called me up on the Saturday, we went for a drink that evening, and never left each other's sides after that.

'He's good,' I say, swirling my spoon around in my soup. 'He's really good in fact because . . .'

Vivienne looks up at me, one eyebrow raised in that way only she can do. I stare at her. Porcelain skin, a delicate smattering of freckles creating a butterfly pattern across her nose, blue eyes and that mane of hair. It's a wonder she isn't more famous really. I think her determination not to be seen to use her parents' influence in any way might be the very definition of cutting off your nose to spite your face.

'You're pregnant,' she says, her voice flat. For an actress, she's never been good at hiding her emotions from me.

'How did you . . .' I say, my mouth hanging open. But then I realise, what else could I have possibly meant? Viv knows we've been trying for ages and ages.

'Wow,' she says. She takes a sip of her water, rearranges her face. 'Congratulations, darling! That's amazing.'

I smile.

'After all this time!' she says. 'You must be absolutely thrilled. I'm really happy for you.'

'Are you?' I say, my heart pounding. I wish her reaction didn't matter so much to me.

'Of course,' she replies. 'No IVF! It's absolutely fantastic. You'll be a brilliant mother.'

'I was so convinced . . .' I say, putting down my spoon. Suddenly, I don't fancy my lunch. I take a sip of water. It tastes metallic, as though it's been sitting in the pipes for too long. I run my tongue over my teeth. 'I thought there was no way, after we'd been trying for so long. I'd even started thinking about adoption, you know, in case IVF didn't work.'

'Oh, Esther! You've really been through the wringer. Everything happens for a reason . . . I knew you'd get there. Like the doctor said, there was nothing physically wrong. And you're both perfectly healthy.'

She lets the silence hang. Is Rob healthy? His diet certainly isn't. He eats well with me, but when he's working he'll always have at least three pints and half a packet of cigarettes afterwards. He claims it's the only way he can 'come down' after a gig.

'Rob's giving up smoking in the new year,' I say, stretching a smile across my face.

'Again?' she says, arching an eyebrow. 'Is he going for the world record? How many times *is* that? Fifteen?'

I swallow, looking down at my lap. Time to change the subject.

'Sorry,' she says, putting down her fork. 'That was out of order. PMT, the audition . . . Sorry. I'm so stoked for you both, I really am.'

I swallow.

'It's fine. How's Sean?' I say, pushing the soup away. What little appetite I had has disappeared, but I guess that's to be expected, and I had a big breakfast anyway. 'How's living together going?'

Her eyes light up.

'He's so brilliant. Seriously, just such a talent, you know?' she says. 'I really think he might be . . . well. We'll see. He's just changed agents; the new one is really optimistic she'll be able to get him seen for films.'

'That's great,' I say, amused that, as always, my huge news – that in nine months' time I'll be holding a newborn – has managed to take up approximately thirty seconds of this catch-up, before we've moved back to talking about Viv again. Still, at least she apologised for slagging off Rob. Sometimes our friendship feels like an elastic band that's worn too thin and might snap any minute.

'I really like him,' I say.

She looks at me for a few seconds, pulling in her top lip before giving me a smile.

'Oh God, you're a much better person than me,' she says. 'I'm really happy for you. I'm sorry. I know we've never been that close but I also know that Rob'll be a good dad – he's fun, and at least he'll be around a lot, hey? Now, I know you won't be drinking but . . . I hope you're still coming to our New Year's Eve party next week? You can't miss it – not if it's the last chance you'll have to come without shelling out loads of money on a babysitter. It's our tenth year! It's going to be epic.'

I smile back at her, breathing out slowly. Rob hates Viv's New Year's Eve party, but he'll come, under duress, if I ask him.

'Of course we'll be there,' I say. 'Wouldn't miss it for the world.'

ROBIN

Big news like that and then it's back to the routine. Mad, isn't it? How everything can change and yet nothing changes.

Esther has just left for work. So I do what I always do. I go back to bed just after she leaves and wake up again at about 10am. I know, I'm a lazy arse but I've always needed more sleep than most people. We can't both be workaholics, after all.

Then I get up and eat cereal standing up in the kitchen. With a side of strong black coffee and five minutes checking Sarah's Instagram. Nothing new today. Her privacy settings are set to the max on Facebook and she doesn't use Twitter.

I can't stop the smile on my face as I leave the house. A baby. Ours. What will he look like? It's not raining today, which is a relief. I follow the towpath along the River Wandle all the way through Tooting until I get to Wandsworth. Same route, every day. It takes me just over an hour to get to Wandsworth Town, where the Wandle meets the Thames. There's a bench there. My bench. It's where I sit and watch the river, writing new material for my act.

Last year was my quietest year ever, work-wise. But everyone knows that's how it goes in this business. 2015 is coming, and it's going to be wild. New year, new chances. I can sense change in the air. After all, things will definitely be different one way or another. Because this time next year, we'll have a tiny baby.

There are tons of angles to exploit on the 'becoming a dad' thing, and I start scribbling. Jay Martin covered it at the Edinburgh Festival last year, but his show was too bitter and it tanked, as far as I know. I find myself wondering how other expectant fathers feel when they hear their partner is knocked up. It's not something that's talked about much, really, considering all the focus on gender equality these days.

Not that I have a problem with gender equality, of course. Only that it's so unrealistic. Women are clearly the superior sex.

And that's what makes it so easy to sketch out an act that will appeal to the masses. The pathetic man-child, waking in the night in fear of being usurped by a real child. It's so easy, so obvious.

I can't stop writing.

At the end of the page, I stop and watch a young teenage couple huddled in the corner by the railings that overlook the river. They've had a row; he's pleading his case while she rolls her eyes and refuses to look at him. Ouch. It's painful, his desperation. Poor sod.

My mobile phone vibrates in my pocket. Honor, my perfect sister-in-law. Married to my perfect brother Nick.

'Good morning,' I say, into the phone.

'Oh, thank God you answered,' Honor says, breathlessly. 'I'm . . . where are you?'

I look up at the teenage couple, who are now hugging, faces buried in each other's necks. She gave in, then. Women often do. But they store it all up for the future, tiny little seeds of resentment they carry with them, nurturing them with every little misdemeanour. Until before you know it you've got a triffid on your hands and it's eating you alive.

'Nowhere important,' I say to Honor. 'What's the matter?'

'I've messed up,' she says. 'Thought the dentist was tomorrow, it's today. My usual babysitter isn't free. I don't suppose . . .'

'What time do you need me?' I interrupt. Honor loves me. I'm everything that Nick isn't: present, attentive, caring. She couldn't live with me though. I'm an amusing sideshow, but she likes Nick's money and ambition too much.

'Half an hour?' she says, and I can almost hear the weight lifting from her shoulders in her voice.

Mothers have it hard. My mum was only young when we were born, but having to deal with Nick and I fighting was enough to put her off having any other children. Although that might have also had something to do with my father.

Father. The biggest joke of them all.

'I'll get some trousers on and be there right away,' I say.

Honor gives a little laugh. I like the idea that she's picturing me in my underwear. All these petty victories against Nick. Pathetic, but irresistible. It will annoy him that I stepped in to look after his kids while he was slaving away at his desk in the city, making rich men even richer.

'Oh no, were you working late last night? Sorry, hope I didn't wake you,' she says.

31

'Not a problem,' I say. Unfortunately I *wasn't* working. 'Honest.'

'You are a lifesaver,' she says. 'Thank you. What am I going to do without you when we move?'

I hang up the phone and stuff my notepad back into my bag.

It's no great hardship to babysit Nick's twins. Kids are underrated. They're three now and more entertaining than most of the adults I know. Honor is one of those typical Barnes mothers who complains that she misses working, but really doesn't know how lucky she is that the main demands on her time are lunches with friends and administrating the local mums' Facebook group.

Barnes isn't far but I've walked enough today, so I take a bus. Within twenty minutes I'm outside their deceptive terraced house, on a cul-de-sac just set back from the river. When they bought it, as bright young newlyweds, it was a wreck. Nick spent his bonus having it brought up to the same standard as all the rest of the houses in the street: adding a big white kitchen extension and poky loft bedroom. I remember Esther's face when they unveiled their transformation, the weird 'o' shape her mouth made as she complimented Honor on her choice of paint colours.

They spent over a hundred grand on the building work. I know because Nick told me. Twice.

They put it on the market a few months ago; it went under offer at £1.75 million.

Outside the bay window, Honor has planted lavender in little zinc window boxes. One has fallen off on to the perfectly arranged purple gravel in their postage-stamp-sized front garden. I stare down at it and knock the huge lion's head of a door knocker.

The front door opens.

'I love you, I love you, I love you,' Honor says, flinging her arms around me and kissing me on both cheeks. The kissing is a new thing, something she's caught from living here.

'Pleasure to be of service, ma'am,' I say, doffing a pretend cap like an idiot, and putting one foot on the step up to the entrance. 'Oh!' I say, pausing. 'Did Nick stumble home drunk last night? Something's knocked over one of your window boxes.'

Honor peers round me to look at the window box, lying side up, its contents spilling out like guts.

'Bollocks,' she says. 'It was probably the dog. Never mind, come in.'

I make my way through to the white kitchen. My nieces, Jasmine and Sienna – yes, their names sound like Disney princesses to me, too – are sitting on the sofa in the extension, eating toast and staring up at the huge television on the opposite wall. The aforementioned dog is asleep at their feet.

'I won't be too long. It's a private dentist so they don't usually run late,' Honor says, rummaging about in her handbag until she pulls out a lipstick. I watch as she carefully traces over her pale lips with it, staring at her reflection in a compact mirror. She used to be attractive but now she's too thin. Draped in floaty materials, all scrawny legs and arms that are mottled with sun damage, even in winter.

I think of Esther. Robust. Not overweight, but big-boned, with a smooth layer of fat coating every surface. Like armour to protect her from the world. Even her face. It's what makes her look young. She's flat-chested too. I quite like it; she doesn't.

As always, my mind drifts to Sarah, comparing. I don't know why, but ever since Esther got pregnant, I can't stop thinking about Sarah. Far too much thought of her today already, Bird.

'What are we watching then?' I say, turning my attention back to my nieces. 'Ahh, *Waffle the Wonder Dog*, eh? Why's he so wonderful then? Because he's named after my favourite Belgian snack? But is he covered in chocolate or strawberries, that's the question . . . let's see, let's see.'

Jasmine giggles and snuggles against me as I sit beside her. She smells like kids do: of salty skin and innocence and fabric conditioner.

I can't wait for this. I can't wait for it with my *own* kid. All of it: the inane children's television, the colouring-in, the nose-wipes and nappies, the middle-of-the-night cuddles . . . bring it on.

ESTHER

We are as late as we can possibly be without it seeming rude. I crunch up the driveway to Vivienne's flat in my block heels. I'm wearing a dark blue dress made of fabric with a velvety sheen, my leather jacket and more make-up than I have done for weeks.

We have ignored the bossy dress code on the invite. Robin doesn't do fancy dress. As he's always told me, he's 'allergic' to organised fun. And I didn't have time to get anything together. All of Viv and Sean's other mates are actors, and they have a vast array of costumes to plunder – it's easy for them. My lank hair is pinned up in a neat bun, and I'm wearing the earrings Robin bought me for Christmas.

'You look beautiful,' Robin said as we left our flat. He doesn't usually say things like that. When I once asked him why not, he replied that if he said it all the time, it would dilute its meaning. 'How are you feeling? Is the bambino giving you a hard time yet?'

'I'm OK,' I said, trying not to worry that I didn't feel *anything* really. What if this was the beginning of a miscarriage? What if the baby had stopped growing? I couldn't bear it if something went wrong. It's all too magical, and it scares me.

I've started taking pregnancy tests every morning just to make sure I didn't dream it all.

'Do you want to tell people?' Robin asks as we ring the doorbell. 'I was planning on standing on the table, y'know, megaphone in hand . . .'

I roll my eyes at him.

'No,' I say, firmly. 'I don't want them to know. If anyone notices I'm not drinking I'll just say I'm on antibiotics for a UTI.'

'As you like it.' He nods as Vivienne opens the door. She's dressed as the Bride of Chucky but somehow still manages to look amazing.

'What have you come as?' Robin says. 'Your younger self?'

Vivienne glares at him.

'Hilarious. I haven't *come* as anything anyway, I live here. Good of you two to make the effort as always,' she replies, grabbing the bottle of Prosecco Rob's holding. 'Come in, come in. Coats on the sofa in the spare room!'

In the kitchen, Vivienne thrusts a glass of Coke at me with a wink.

'Here you go, chicken,' she says.

'Thanks,' I reply.

'How are you feeling?' she says. 'Been sick yet?'

'No. I feel weirdly fine,' I say, lowering my voice. 'Listen, we're not . . . we're not telling people yet. Early days.'

'Of course!' she says, widening her eyes at me. 'I wouldn't breathe a word.'

I'm not sure I believe her, but I'm also not sure that gossip about me is considered interesting enough to be gossip at all. I look over at Rob. He's already sitting on the bench by Vivienne's expansive dining table, helping himself to a bowl of crisps and chatting to a brunette. She has a lot of make-up on.

Rob always says make-up is for dead people and clowns. I watch them for a few seconds. The girl is smiling at him, touching his shoulder as he talks, and he's rolling his eyes at her chat, as though they are old friends.

Suddenly she looks up and our eyes meet briefly. Unthinkingly I narrow mine and she frowns, looking away, before resting a hand on Rob's leg.

I have never felt jealous or insecure before. Vivienne's friends are all like this – luvvies who are really tactile. When Rob's performing, he quite often gets women coming up to him afterwards, patting his arm and telling him how talented he is. He's gracious in accepting compliments, but he's always been very mindful of how he behaves around women. You could say he's a bit obsessive about it. He once told me that reputations can be ruined by even the slightest bit of misinterpreted behaviour, that you can never be too careful.

I've never felt threatened, but tonight, something about my newly vulnerable status and the way this girl is looking at him makes my stomach churn.

Someone turns the music down and Vivienne shouts over the hubbub that it's time for us all to play Cards Against Humanity.

I sidle over to my husband, a protective hand on my stomach as I walk, and gently sit on his lap, putting my arms around his neck. I would never normally behave like this, and I feel his body stiffen in surprise.

He kisses me on the cheek. I don't look at the girl.

'Hello, wife,' he says into my ear. 'Can we leave yet?'

From the tone of his voice I can tell that he's already tipsy. He had a beer before we left, but I'm still surprised he's got drunk so quickly. Then I see the glass of whiskey in front of him. Anger floods my veins and I bite down on my lip. He says he needs alcohol to get through evenings with Vivienne and her friends, but he wouldn't normally drink neat spirits.

He shifts sideways so that I'm facing the girl.

'This is Kim. She was in that Channel 4 sitcom, do you remember? The tarty receptionist with a heart of gold,' he says. 'Kim, this is my better half, my light, my love, my one and only . . . ball and chain, Esther.'

'Hi,' she says, swallowing and flashing me a tooth-filled smile. 'Tarty indeed. Your husband is hilarious.'

'Lovely to meet you,' I say.

I give her a tight smile and turn to Vivienne who has started the game.

By 10.30pm, Rob is completely drunk. There isn't anything unusual about that, of course. But tonight he seems more drunk than normal. Or perhaps it's just that I'm more sober than normal. I've always found him an amusing drunk – funny in public, but then soppy and loving and protective in private. But as a stone-cold-sober witness, I can see that my perspective has been skewed. At the moment, he is an overbearing drunk: loud, opinionated, larger than life.

He is *annoying*.

I've drunk nothing but Coke all evening, eaten handfuls

of plain crisps. None of the party food Vivienne has served appealed to my newly sensitive stomach, and I feel bone-tired.

By 11.30pm, I haven't seen my overbearing drunk husband for nearly an hour, having left him to a heated debate about football transfers. I am trapped talking to a very serious wannabe film director in the narrow hallway of the flat. He's leaning over me, bottle of beer in one hand, too many buttons of his shirt open at the top. I've run out of small talk but it doesn't matter; he has enough for both of us.

Sean squeezes past us on his way to the bathroom, and I grab his arm.

'Have you seen Rob?' I ask.

'Uh,' Sean replies. His face is shiny with sweat, his Chucky make-up smeared against the collar of his costume. 'Yeah, he's in the garden, I think.'

'Will you excuse me?' I say to the director. My head feels as though it's made of cotton wool. I can't even remember his name, let alone anything he's been telling me.

I push past him, towards the kitchen at the back of the flat. As I pass the spare bedroom I see a couple going for it on the pile of coats on the sofa. Standard stuff for a New Year's Eve party, but something in the aggressively animal-like way they are behaving makes me feel uncomfortable, like I don't belong. Like I've wandered into a teenagers' house party or something.

Outside on the patio, the darkness of the night hits me. Twenty minutes until the new year, until the year my baby will be born arrives. Thirty minutes until it's an acceptable time to drag my drunken husband home. Where is he, anyway?

The patio is filled with huddles of people, the scent of cigarettes filling the air. No one is smoking pot, which is unusual. At the back of the garden, where Vivienne has hung tea light lanterns in the large pine tree, I see my husband's shape. Unmistakably large, his head a fuzzy, hairy silhouette against the candle behind. But something about the angle of his head alarms me. I can't see him clearly; there are too many people between us, but I know from the way his head is cocked that he is leaning down. Then someone in front of me moves, and I blink in confusion at what is suddenly too clear to deny.

Rob is kissing someone.

I feel myself retch, and suddenly the ground begins to move. I grip on to Vivienne's garden table as I stare and stare, willing myself not to be sick. And then, Rob's head moves again until his face is finally in view, his eyes rolling back slightly in his head. His hand moves to his mouth, and he has the humility to look surprised, at least.

I take a deep breath and walk towards them. He sees me before she does.

'What ... what ... what are you doing?!' I say, dumbfounded, but then my whole body is wracked with sobs and I find myself doubling over. The confusion I felt dissolves into absolute, abject misery. My husband. Bird. The love of my life.

My hands fly to my forehead. It doesn't make any sense.

'Oh fuck,' I hear the girl, Kim, say. She bends down and tries to take my arm but I push her off.

'My fault,' she says. 'Chill out ... just a bit of fun ... New Year's Eve and all that ...'

My hands dig into my knees as I look up at them.

40

'How could you?' I say, burning with humiliation. Suddenly, I feel another arm on mine. I look up and my eyes meet Robin's. He's so far gone, he's barely even there.

'Tot,' he slurs. 'Fuck. Sorry.' His head lolls and his eyes seem to roll back in their sockets. 'I'm . . . I told you she was tarty.'

He starts to laugh and it turns into a choking cough.

'For God's sake,' I say, furious with the realisation that I am going to have to be the mature one now, even though he is in the wrong. I am going to have to take charge of the situation, get us home safely, make sure he sobers up.

He stumbles backwards then sits on the ground.

'Sorry,' he says, and I see a heaviness to his eyelids that makes me worry he might fall asleep. He weighs sixteen stone. If he collapses here, there will be no moving him. I reach over to one of the patio tables and pick up an abandoned glass. It's filled with clear liquid. It's probably not water but I don't care. I throw it over him and he splutters.

'We're leaving,' I say, aware that a crowd has gathered around us. Kim has disappeared. 'Get up.'

There are gasps from the crowd, followed by sniggers. Who needs the West End when you have this kind of entertainment?

'I can't believe you've done this to me,' I hiss, as I haul Robin to his feet, but he is too drunk to even hear.

ROBIN

In case I had ever doubted myself, this proves it.

I *am* an arsehole.

I have never done anything like that before. Even when Esther and I were still what women's magazines would call 'early days' and I was out every night at a different bar or club, networking, watching shows and trialling my act, and there was a lot of alcohol and a lot of girls who made it pretty obvious they wanted to sleep with me.

I've never been that kind of man.

It doesn't help that I wake up on 1 January 2015 with very little recollection of what happened the night before. It's 7am, and I roll over in bed to see Esther, lying beside me. Staring.

She doesn't speak.

'Morning,' I say, hesitantly. My head is pounding and my stomach feels empty. It's been a while since I've had a hangover this bad. God, I'm such an idiot.

Esther doesn't say anything, she just begins to cry.

'What . . .' I say, but it all starts coming back to me in patchy pictures. The party. The Jägerbombs – who did I think I was, a fresher from Leeds? That girl with the huge eyes. What was

42

her name? The way she kept stroking my arm, telling me how funny I was.

I close my eyes. No. It isn't her fault. I won't be *that* man.

You bloody egotist, Bird.

'I'm . . . sorry,' I say. The adrenalin of the situation makes my whole body tingle. And that's when the blinding realisation hits me. I think I know why I did it.

I'm a shit. I did it because I could. Because there's no way out now. Esther's pregnant. She won't leave me over this.

I've got her, finally. After all these years. I want to cry with the relief of it, but I pull myself together and look up at her instead. Esther has always held me at arm's length. Not any-more, she won't. She can't afford to now.

But first, the apologies, because none of it is her fault and I'm in the wrong. Completely.

'I'm so sorry. I've been a total arse. God, you deserve better. I'm not even joking. You do.'

Esther continues to cry, but she doesn't get up. I tentatively reach forward to stroke her face with my hand, and she lets me.

'I just don't understand. I can't believe you did it,' she says. 'I've been lying here all night, thinking, who is this man? How could he do that to me? At a party? A party where I was just in the other room? Who even is he? What's happened to my husband? The man I love, who always looks after me and puts me first?'

'I don't know,' I say. My own eyes begin to water. My default setting is disappointment with the world; I'm always just a couple of emotional slumps away from tears. 'I'm so sorry. I

43

just . . . I was so drunk. I don't know what got into me. I've never done anything like that before. Never been that stupid. You know that.'

My stomach makes a low grumbling noise, as though trying to contradict me.

'Never,' I say, my voice firm. 'I mean, it wasn't . . . *She* kissed me. I would never cheat on you. Please, Tot, you have to believe me.'

It's true. Esther has a part of me that no other woman will ever have. Not even Sarah.

'I mean . . . I'm *pregnant*,' she whispers, her tears falling silently on to the pillow by her face. 'Who does something like that?'

'An absolute idiot, that's who. It was a moment of complete stupidity,' I say, taking her hand and squeezing it, holding her eye contact. There's a second of blind panic – what if she *does* decide to leave me? And take the baby? My stomach lurches. 'I'm so sorry. I promise you. I was just totally drunk. It was nothing. I can't even bloody remember it properly, so does it even count? Shall we just say it doesn't count?'

She frowns. A bridge too far. But I can see in her eyes that she wants me to explain it away and make everything better. She wants me to provide a reason for it, to make sense of it all, so that she can forgive me. It's a realisation that relaxes me slightly. She is still here, in our bed, in our flat. She wants to forgive me.

'You drink too much,' she says. 'You always have.'

I nod. She's right.

'I'll stop,' I say, in desperation. 'I'll give up drinking completely. While you're pregnant. How about that? We can be boring sober bastards together?'

She sniffs, turning her head away. Of course that's not enough. That's the very least.

'How are you feeling?' I ask, even though I'm not feeling too clever myself. 'Do you want me to make you toast? Tea? I can nip out and get you some freshly squeezed grapefruit juice?'

It's an in-joke – we both hate it, can't believe that some people consider grapefruit juice to be posh. But she doesn't smile.

I don't know what to do, how to make it up to her. This is uncharted territory for us. We never fight. We squabble, bicker, banter . . . we don't *fight*.

She doesn't say anything, she just closes her eyes and rolls her face into the pillow. I sit up. My stomach flops over the top of my boxer shorts, and I feel revolted by myself. I'm not overweight, but I'm heading that way. I used to play five-a-side every weekend, but that fell by the wayside over the last few years as my mates all got married and had kids. I suppose I should join a gym. Give up booze, start working out. It's January, I'd be the ultimate cliché.

I'm already a cliché. What kind of loser cheats on his pregnant wife?

I jump out of bed like a toddler, begin to pull on the t-shirt that's closest to the bed, before realising it was the one I wore last night. It's stained with something that looks like salsa. I remember that Kim girl feeding me nachos, laughing as the topping tumbled out of my mouth and fell down my chin.

Where was Esther when that was happening anyway? I should have stayed with her all night.

I throw the t-shirt into the wash basket and pull another out from the drawer. Esther is still lying in bed, her face half-buried. I pad down the hallway and switch on the thermostat. The flat is freezing, but the timer broke a few months ago and I keep forgetting to call a plumber to get it fixed. I'll do that, today. Or not today, as it's New Year's Day. Tomorrow. Penance. I'll make it up to her. I'll be the man she deserves. I'll be the father our baby deserves.

Maybe I'll even look into those cracks in the ceiling.

In the kitchen I make myself an excruciatingly strong cup of coffee and a pile of toast and take it back to Esther in the bedroom.

'Here, my angel,' I say, and she sits up as I lay it next to her on the bedside table. 'I'll just get you something to drink.'

I wonder why she's not yelling at me, then I remember that she's pregnant and exhausted and probably feeling sick.

I perch on the edge of the bed and watch her eat.

'I can honestly barely remember what happened,' I say, when Esther has finished eating her toast. 'Maybe my drink was spiked?'

Esther glares at me.

'By a girl?' she says, a hint of sneer coming through now. Good for you, I think. Come on, give it to me, I deserve it.

'I don't know,' I say. 'I honestly don't know what got into me . . .'

'Pathetic.'

'I know it sounds ridiculous, but it was only a kiss . . .' I grasp. 'I was so drunk . . . I probably just didn't want to offend her. She'd been coming on pretty strong . . . I guess . . .'

'Offend her?' Esther says, and while it's not a shout, her voice is definitely raised. I feel my blood pressure rise, but it's good. Perhaps this is what we need: a big fight, followed by a tearful reconciliation. Get it all out in the open, give me what I deserve. Let's clear the decks and move on.

'Shit, baby,' I say, rubbing my eyes. 'Honestly. I was just hammered.'

'How many other times are you just hammered? How many other times has there been "only a kiss"? We're married!'

'None! I barely ever go out anymore,' I say. 'I'm not a cheat. I can't explain it. I was just really drunk, I'm sorry. It's been an intense few weeks, you know, with the pregnancy and . . .'

'Don't you dare!' she says through her tears. 'Don't you dare blame it on me being pregnant!'

'I'm not . . . fuck . . . I'm not! Tot, I'm sorry!' I say, my voice a rush. 'I just . . . I don't know what to say.'

Our eyes meet and there's a second when I realise exactly what her reaction means. Even though it's awful. Even though what I did is indefensible.

It means she loves me. She needs me. *Really* needs me.

Finally. Pitiful validation of my worth.

But then she blinks and lies back down on the bed, turning away from me, and I lean forward and hold her awkwardly, my ageing, unfit back complaining at the position, and we both cry and I resolve never to do anything like this again.

47

ESTHER

I forgive him because I love him, but also because I don't have a choice.

Two days later, on 3 January, my nightmare begins.

It felt like Robin spent the whole of New Year's Day apologising. It became relentless by the end – my constant questioning, my brain turning over the reasons for it in my mind, wondering if he was in fact a massive cheat and I'd just never seen it before. Despite the fact we'd been together for years, that we knew each other inside out and he'd never done anything suspicious before.

He had a habit of coming home late at night, drunk, or staying out until the early hours, but I had no reason to believe it was anything more than the downside of his job. I knew he liked a drink. He certainly made the most of the social side of his work, but he always told me he loved me, that I was the only one for him, and I had never had any reason to doubt him.

But in the light of what had happened, I questioned everything. And he cried and I cried and he said sorry, and then he admitted that he thought maybe it was some kind of mini 'midlife crisis' or reaction to the news he was going to be a dad.

I could understand that, sort of.

By the end of the day, I was exhausted. And tired of it all. He promised he would never do anything like that again. There was nothing left to say. We'd said it all, picked it apart until there weren't even bones left.

I had two choices: believe him or leave him.

I'm pregnant, but even if I wasn't, I wouldn't leave him. He is my world.

Yesterday, we went for a walk at Morden Hall Park, a National Trust property just down the road. It was a bright, crisp winter's day. We talked about the future, speculated on whether the baby would be a boy or a girl.

I wondered what Viv would say about the kiss, how smug she would be, and my jaw physically ached. It wasn't OK yet, but I was assimilating it, putting his behaviour into a box and storing it under the metaphorical stairs in my mind. It was a minor transgression. Robin had always been there for me over the past five years, supporting me and taking care of me and cooking for me and cheering me up when I was down.

I could forgive him, for the sake of the baby I could already picture as part of our family.

I could forgive him, for the sake of the baby I was so desperate for us to have.

I wake up feeling weird. It's 6.30am, and still dark outside. I think back to last night – we'd ordered a pizza. I'd chosen a margherita, something bland. Pregnancy is already subtly changing my tastes.

Before I even manage to sit up in bed, I vomit all over myself and the duvet.

'Shit,' I say. The force of it takes me by surprise, making my eyes water. Robin wakes up beside me.

'Stay there,' he says, snapping from bleary sleep-state to wide awake in seconds. 'I'll clear it up. You poor thing.'

I lie back down on the pillow, reaching for a tissue to wipe my mouth. But before Robin comes back in the room, I'm sick again. This time, I try to catch it in my hands, but it drips through my fingers and on to my pyjama top.

'Oh God,' I say, my eyes filled with tears. 'I'm sorry.'

'Yeah, well, if you wouldn't mind letting me wake up properly before vomming all over the place, that would be much appreciated,' Robin says, smiling, wiping me down with kitchen roll. 'So inconsiderate.'

'The pizza?' I ask, to no one. But I know it isn't the pizza. The nausea remains, humming in my stomach and making me afraid to move my head.

'Now,' Robin says, and I can see he wants to make a joke of the situation, which is his method for coping with most things. 'Don't shoot me but ... where are the spare sheets again?'

'God,' I say, my throat burning. 'They're in the bottom drawer.' I point at the chest of drawers facing the bed.

'That's logical. Do you want to go and clean your teeth while I do this?' he asks.

I stare at him, wondering why it feels so hard to even contemplate moving to the bathroom.

'OK,' I say, slipping my legs out from under the duvet, but before I even reach the door, my stomach lurches again.

Robin brings me a bowl; I'm sick repeatedly for twenty minutes. Eventually I'm staring down at what looks like poisonous Lucozade. My stomach feels as though it has been taken out of me and shredded, then dumped back in again. Everything aches.

When the initial bout subsides, I call 111, tell them I am six weeks pregnant, that I've been sick all morning, that I can't get out of bed.

I can tell that my naivety makes the woman on the other end of the phone want to laugh.

'Is this your first pregnancy?' she asks.

'Yes.'

'I doubt it's food poisoning,' she says, briskly. 'It's probably just a touch of morning sickness.'

Morning sickness? *Morning sickness?* It isn't possible. Not this, this absolute hollowing-out of my insides.

'No,' I say, with more strength than I have mustered all morning. 'I'm definitely ill.'

'Well then,' she replies. 'Just make sure you stay hydrated. There's no risk to the baby. Just keep sipping water every ten to fifteen minutes, and call us back if you can't manage to keep it down.'

I do what she says. At noon, Robin comes back from the shops with Dioralyte, ginger biscuits and Coca-Cola.

'Here you go,' he says, glancing down at my bowl. 'Just sip the Coke, the sugar will give you strength. Mum's remedy. Quite possibly a load of bollocks but worth a try.'

I stare at the bottle, take comfort in his confidence.

My lips are dry. I reach over for my lip balm on my bedside table, smearing some over my lips. But something about the movement, the gesture, or the fact that I've sat up a little and can smell Robin's coat, the metallic tang of the cold air from outside, makes my stomach turn over, and before I know it, I am grabbing the bowl again.

My eyes are full of tears.

'I just want to sleep,' I mumble. 'I'll try the Coke later. Thanks, though.'

Robin pauses, staring down at me. I can see the feeling of uselessness flash over his forehead. He wants to help, but he can't. He has always been so concerned with cheering me up. I am suddenly so grateful for his presence, the fact he is here beside me, taking care of me, that I can barely remember how angry I was just a few days ago.

'OK,' he says, softly. He reaches a hand down and strokes my sticky hair away from my forehead. 'I'll leave you to rest, Sleeping Beauty. Just so you know, you've never looked hotter.'

'Thanks.'

'And try not to worry. I looked it up, morning sickness doesn't last very long. By twelve weeks you should be back on your feet and changing the sheets yourself again.'

Twelve weeks! He might as well have said twelve years.

'And apparently it's a sign the baby is healthy,' he says. 'Nature has it in for women, huh? But it's actually a really good thing.'

'Right,' I say. He edges nearer and the smell of his coat wafts past my nostrils again. I bury my nose in the pillow.

I am sick twenty-two times that day. By the end of it, I'm sobbing with exhaustion while Robin is on the phone to NHS Direct again, who tell him that I should keep sipping water. I go back to bed at 7pm. Lying perfectly still is the only way I don't feel nauseous.

'This can't be normal,' I say, as Robin tries to tie my hair back with a hairband. 'How can I keep being sick when I haven't eaten anything? There must be something wrong with me.'

As I lie in bed, I listen to Robin in the other room, on the phone to his mum. Making excuses for us. We're meant to be going to see them all tomorrow. He doesn't tell them I'm pregnant. I'm frightened I might lose the baby. How can a baby grow when its mother has literally nothing in her stomach? It doesn't make any sense.

I feel as helpless as a newborn myself. And I certainly can't face replying to the messages Vivienne has been sending me non-stop ever since that awful party.

How are you? I'm so sorry about Kim. I don't know what she was thinking. I'm furious with Sean for inviting her! I've never liked her much! If it's any consolation, she's a shit actress.

I don't reply, but still the messages keep coming.

You can always come and stay with us for a bit if you need to. I could kill Rob. Just look after yourself. It's not just you that you have to take care of now, remember. You're pregnant.

Melodramatically, I think, *I'm not pregnant, I'm dying.*

ROBIN

For once, I feel out of my depth.

What are you meant to do when the person you love is suffering and there's nothing you can do to stop it? I'm so used to having all the answers, to being the hero. All I've ever wanted is to make her happy. To make myself into Esther's Perfect Man.

Laid-back, but not infuriating. Constantly supportive. Funny, when appropriate. A good listener. The type to remind her that there's more to life than work, but not in a disrespectful way.

Her rock.

People gawped at us: the unlikely couple. But we've outlasted them all. I knew she was perfect for me the moment I set eyes on her. My Esther: stoic, stubborn, occasionally self-destructive in her loyalty, and in love with me for being everything she's not, for being everything she's too scared to be.

But the pregnancy has floored me. The game's moved on to the next level, and all my skills are useless. She doesn't want me to make jokes about the situation. She wants my support, but only when me being in the room doesn't make her feel nauseous. She doesn't want me to tell her that her work doesn't matter while her health is suffering. That's the hardest thing. I don't know what she *does* want. I don't know how I can help her.

I feel more useless and shitty than ever.

I want her back. The old Esther, the one I understand.

On the third day of her being bedridden, I walk to the Tesco Metro over the road on a mission to find food her stomach can keep down. My fingers are twitchy. I need to do something; some distraction. I call my mum because deep down in my messed-up wiring I still believe that it might help, even though it never does.

I've learnt a lot from my mum, but the most important skill of all is adaptability. That chameleon's skin that twists and reshapes itself to suit whoever is watching. She's had years of suffering at the hands of my father, building up layer upon layer of emotional scars, until the real her is buried so deeply beneath the crust, it's hard to believe she's still there at all.

I've learnt a lot from her without her even noticing, but this is new territory; me actually asking her for tips. I wonder what advice she gave Nick when Honor got pregnant.

He probably never asked her for any.

He knows everything, except for the fact that he doesn't.

'Esther is pregnant, Mum,' I say. The words steam up the air in front of me. 'Six weeks.'

There's a slight gasp on the other end of the line.

'Oh, congratulations,' she says. There's no hiding the nerves in her voice. Does she think I'm too hopeless to be a father?

'Thanks,' I say, swallowing. My eyes start to sting. I have a sudden, strong urge for a drink.

'How's she feeling?' Mum says, a brittleness to her tone that tells me she only cares out of curiosity. Mum likes Esther, but she finds her intimidating. Esther's career is too much – especially as Mum left school at eighteen and went to work at Dad's garage, and her life has been drudgery ever since.

'She's not good,' I say. 'I don't know . . . she's been really sick. Non-stop for three days now.'

'Oh dear,' Mum says, in a way that feels both reassuring and dismissive. 'I remember it well. Tell her it'll pass. Aren't ginger biscuits supposed to work?'

Ginger biscuits were the first thing we'd tried. I scuff at the pavement with my foot. What did I expect?

'I don't really know how to help her,' I say. 'I feel useless, Mum. I mean, we wanted this . . . but now . . . I don't know. Everything's changed. She's miserable. She's not even a little bit excited about the baby.'

'I'm sure she's just getting her head around it all,' Mum says. 'Your generation makes such a fuss about these things. Most natural thing in the world, becoming a mother. She'll be fine.'

'But she's so sick . . . she doesn't seem to want to eat much at all.'

'If she doesn't want to eat, then don't make her eat,' Mum says. 'She's got plenty of meat on her bones, she's not going to starve to death. I know it's a worry, but it'll pass before you know it.'

I thank her (for nothing) and hang up without bothering to ask how Dad is.

In Tesco, I buy the things on Esther's list: melon, rye bread, yoghurt and plain cornflakes. Weird combination, but she looked like a woman possessed when she asked for them. As I pay, I spot the cigarettes behind the counter, and ask for a packet of Marlboro Reds and a lighter too.

Smoking has always been my thing. I am sure once upon a time it was cool, but as I've got older, all I ever hear is how disgusting it is.

A year ago Esther paid a hypnotist to help me quit. I went to one session then realised it was a waste of time. I didn't need to be hypnotised, I just needed to *want* to stop. And so I did. I did it for her. I'd do anything for her.

But I'm stressed and I can't have a drink so . . . I put the cigarette to my lips and flick the lighter, the heat from the spark tingling my fingertip.

Esther's sickness isn't the only thing bugging me this morning. I sent my books to my accountant last night, who replied this morning with my figures for the year accompanied by a shitty comment about it being the eleventh hour.

The good news is, I don't have to make any payments on account.

The bad news is, I've earned so little, I don't have to make any payments on account.

And then there's the small matter of my debt.

It's never bothered me much before. Esther's always earned more than enough for us both, and I always thought one day I'd make it, and any short-term financial woes would vanish.

But the whole 'becoming a father' thing adds a new pressure. I know how disappointed in my work situation she is already, even though she'd never say it.

I can't fuck things up again. As I walk along, feeling the nicotine rush into my bloodstream, I try to picture my future a year from now. I'm a great believer in living in the present – after all, who knows if you will even still be here tomorrow? But in a year's time the baby will be four months old, or thereabouts. Esther will be on maternity leave.

Esther will be on maternity leave, and everything will change.

I push open the front door and stamp my feet up and down on the doormat.

'Another lovely day,' I call down the narrow hallway. 'How are you feeling?'

I go through to the bedroom. Esther is sitting up in bed, the ever-present bowl in her lap.

'Did you get the cornflakes?' she says, like a starving woman, which I suppose she is.

'Yes,' I say, laying out all her requests on the duvet in front of her. 'Do you want me to cut up the melon?'

She shakes her head.

'No, just give me the cornflakes.' She reaches for the packet, her hands shaking as she opens it and begins to eat them in handfuls. They scatter across the duvet.

'I've made a doctor's appointment,' she says, in between mouthfuls. 'I can't go on like this. I have to get back to work.'

Is it my paranoia or is there a dig there? She doesn't know

about the desperate emails I've given up sending to anyone and everyone I've ever worked with. I haven't done a gig since November. I can't do it anymore, can't keep begging people for support slots. The humiliation is too much, especially when I have to watch them afterwards and realise they're no better than me, they just got lucky, someone liked the look of their face, they knew someone who knew someone . . . or the worst reason of all: their dad owns the club.

I look back down at my pregnant wife, ravaging a box of cornflakes. What would my father say if he knew the months were stretching ahead of me like a vast open space, with not a single booking to fill them? Oh God, it would make his year.

I close my eyes and exhale. Gotta pull myself together.

I can't do this bit for her, but I can do the rest. Perhaps this is fate, dealing us a hand, showing us the way. After all, Esther wants to work, she loves her job. It's more than a job to her, it's a vocation. And she's as successful at hers as I am unsuccessful at mine.

Yes, perhaps this is all meant to be.

Once the baby is born, Esther can go back to work, and I can be the perfect father, the perfect husband. We'll be like all the other modern families: the breadwinning wife, the stay-at-home dad, the adorable child growing up with cool parents.

Everyone will envy us, be amazed at our set-up. They just won't admit it.

ESTHER

I haven't eaten anything substantial for over a week, and the only thing I can stomach in terms of liquids are tiny slivers of ice cubes that I push to the corners of my cheeks, keeping my head very, very still as I let them melt. I daren't even move to the loo without bringing a bowl with me, just in case, but I hardly need to go anyway. I must be really dehydrated.

It's as close to the feeling of dying as I can imagine. And it turns out, according to my GP, that this miserable condition has a name: *hyperemesis gravidarum*.

'Getting fashionable these days,' he says, one eyebrow raised, as he writes on my notes. 'Ever since Princess Kate had it.'

I feel fury boiling inside me at the indication that I am doing this as some twisted way to get attention. Thankfully, the rage turns to retching, and I throw up violently into the bag I brought with me. That shuts him up. I only wish some of it had landed on his shoes.

'I'll try you on some anti-emetics,' he says, printing out a prescription. 'I have to tell you there are some risks to the baby with any medication, especially this early on. It's up to you whether or not you want to take that risk. The likelihood is that the sickness will pass in a few weeks.'

My face crumples again at the unspoken message in his words: *if you can't deal with this for a short time, for the sake of your unborn baby, then you really don't deserve to be a mother.*

I take the prescription from him. Robin, who has sat silent throughout the appointment, finally speaks.

'What kind of risks?' he asks, and it feels like a gut-punch to my already annihilated insides. He's putting the baby first. Before me. Which of course he should, but still . . .

'I believe there may be the risk of some congenital abnormalities – cleft palate is the main one, I think. There will be information online, if you look it up.'

'Thanks,' I say, standing, keeping my breath short and shallow so as to avoid inhaling the smell of anything too deeply.

All I want is to get out of this place, and back to the cocoon of my bed.

The next day I wake to find Robin standing over me, glass of water in one hand and the pills in the other.

'Are you going to take them?' he says. My face is crusty from the night before. I feel disgusting, and cover my mouth with my hand, staring at the pills.

'I can't, can I? I can't take the risk.' My eyes fill with tears; I look up at him. 'I don't know. What do you think?'

'I think only you can answer that,' he says, but then he pauses for a few seconds before continuing. 'But of course, I'm not the one who's suffering, Tot.'

I sit up in bed gingerly, taking the pills with my shaking hand and clutching the glass of water.

'I'm not sure I'll be able to swallow them,' I say.

'Why don't you try?' he says. 'I'm here.'

I put the pills carefully on my tongue, and take the smallest sip from the glass. I can smell the washing-up liquid he must have used to wash the glass and I concentrate with all my strength on staying completely still as I sip the water.

Somehow, I manage to swallow them. The thought that these two little pills are now swirling around inside me, with the sole intention of making me feel better, lifts my spirits ever so slightly, and I find myself smiling.

'That wasn't so bad,' I say, handing the glass back to Robin. I lie back down on the bed.

'Well done,' he replies. 'Let's hope they help you.'

Help you. The guilt hits me, along with the results of my Google searches the day before. Possible heart defects. Cleft palate.

How can I do this to my baby? What kind of mother takes risks like that?

'I'm meant to be visiting Dad this weekend,' I say, feebly. 'I don't know what to do . . .'

Three hours on the train to York. It feels as impossible as swimming the Channel.

'I know,' Rob replies. 'I'll call him, tell him you're poorly.'

A single tear meanders its way down my face. My dad has emphysema. He lives alone. I'm his only child, I never miss a visit.

'Not yet,' I say. 'Let's wait . . . maybe these pills will help.'

By 11am, I am sick again, and I don't stop.

The next day, Robin calls the antenatal department at the hospital, and they agree to send someone out to see me.

'It's very rare,' the midwife says, taking my blood pressure. I can smell the grease in my own hair. The skin on my face is dry and itchy, my lips covered in flakes. 'Just bad luck, but please don't worry, the baby will be fine. He'll be taking all he needs from you, you poor love.'

She tries to take some blood from me for routine antenatal tests, but there isn't a chance of her getting any.

'You *are* dehydrated,' she says to me, and I can see in her expression something else; the flicker of concern that this won't be easily fixed. That she's been here before, and that nothing helped.

I nod weakly, hoping my eyes are imparting my desperation enough. *Help me.* I want to cry. *Please. Make it stop.*

'I think you need to be admitted,' she says. 'Stay here, I'm going to call someone.'

She finds me a place on a gynaecological ward, and they tell me I need to be hooked up to a drip, a succession of grey cardboard bowler hats on my lap. A nurse comes round periodically to take the used bowls away. She doesn't seem to understand what I am in there for.

No one seems to know much about what is wrong with me, or how long it will last. I am only eight weeks pregnant; the next thirty weeks stretch ahead like an unbearable life sentence.

I know how ill I am, because I don't care about anything. For the first time ever, I don't care about my work – my team, the board of directors, all waiting on me for answers about things that used to seem critically important but that now don't seem to matter at all. I don't care about my friends. I barely even feel bad for not going to see my dad.

But most worrying of all, I don't even think I care about the baby. The baby I so desperately wanted.

The baby I have already secretly named: Riley.

It's impossible to imagine there's a baby inside my hollow stomach anyway. How could anything be growing inside me when I am constantly throwing up every source of nourishment? Nothing makes sense.

Robin came with me when I was admitted. After sitting by my bed for hours, playing a game on his phone, he left to get some lunch. For himself, of course, not for me. When he returns, he looks paler than usual. As he leans over to kiss me on the cheek I catch the faintest scent of beer on his breath. It's 2pm.

'Have you been drinking?' I say, my throat so hoarse I can barely speak.

He frowns at me, and I wait for the lie.

'No,' he says. 'I . . .'

'Doesn't matter,' I say, turning my head away from him slightly. And it doesn't. In the state I'm in, I don't care if he's been getting drunk. He could have been snogging that Kim girl all morning for all I care.

I keep thinking about her, Kim. She appears in my fractured sleep, like some kind of witch with her long, dark hair and black-lined eyes. She sits at the corner of my bed, cackling, as I vomit rainbows. It occurs to me that she wasn't in fancy dress at the party either. She was wearing skintight jeans and a lace top that showed her bra.

Who was she? As soon as I feel better I am going to call Vivienne and find out everything.

I look back at Robin, who has sat down on his chair and is staring into the middle-distance. I'm not even sure I want him here at all.

In many ways Robin feels like another responsibility, someone else I must try to make feel better. Put on a brave face for. He's laid-back and self-sacrificing most of the time, but when things go wrong, his coping methods aren't the healthiest. He's tried to hide it from me, over the years, but I know all about his little self-medications. Smoking, to occupy his ever-twitching hands. Drinking, to block things out. Drugs, to convince himself he's happy.

Punching things, when the frustration gets too much.

'What have they said?' he says, leaning forward and taking my hand. His is cold and the sensation as it comes into contact with mine feels heightened, as though my whole body has been reprogrammed, all my senses overactive.

'Nothing, really,' I mumble. 'Except that I'm so dehydrated my veins have collapsed. They've gone to get a paediatric anaesthetist who's going to use an ultrasound machine to try to find a vein, so they can get the cannula in, and then they'll connect me to the drip.'

He nods, completely out of his depth.

'I want it to end,' I say, and a single tear escapes my dehydrated eye and runs down my cheek. I flick it away before it reaches my lip – even the thought of it landing there makes me feel nauseous again. 'I can't stand this. This isn't *me*!'

'I know,' he says.

'They weighed me. I've lost half a stone already,' I say. 'In two weeks.'

His eyes widen at that. I imagine the joke that probably flashed through his mind, unspoken: *well, you always said you wanted to lose some weight.*

He reaches up to stroke my face, and something about the rush of air that passes as he does so makes me throw up straight on to his arm.

NOW

ESTHER

'Hello, my name's Detective Sergeant Anne Tyler and this is Detective Constable Tony Williams. May we come in?' the female officer says.

There's something in her tone that reminds me of the school nurse, the time she stroked an antiseptic wipe across my knee when I fell off the slide at primary school. Matronly.

The woman is slight, her skin drawn and lined. Her eyes are round and grey, and peer at me with sympathy underneath eyelashes without any mascara. The man she's with is almost double her height, and broad.

The shock of seeing them renders me mute. I pull the door aside and let them in. It can't be . . . please don't let it be Riley. I can't even summon up the courage to ask, so I beckon them into the living room and wait for them to speak. They take a seat on the sofa in the bay window.

'We're sorry to disturb you.'

'Please . . .' I say. 'Is it . . .'

'I'm very sorry to have to tell you this,' the woman says, her face impressively calm. 'But Robin Morgan was found unconscious with a serious head injury on Downs Road in Epsom.

Currently, his injuries are unexplained. We found ID on him with this address. Are you a relation?'

I stare at her. My hands begin to tremble.

'I . . .' I reply. 'Yes, he's my . . . he's my husband.'

'I understand this must be a massive shock. He's in surgery at St Helier Hospital.'

I frown at her, rubbing the side of my forehead. I can't process what she's telling me. My brain is jelly in my skull.

'I'm sorry,' I say. 'Can you repeat that?'

She gives me a sympathetic look. I wonder how many times they rehearse this in their training, or if they never do. Maybe they expect it to come instinctively. Perhaps that's part of the calling of being a police officer.

'Of course,' she says, and her hand moves forward, as though she might pat me on the leg, but she thinks better of it. 'Your husband was found by a passer-by severely injured by the side of the road in Epsom. He's alive, but I'm afraid he's in critical condition.'

'My . . . husband,' I repeat, and I notice DS Tyler glance briefly at her colleague, the flicker of an expression that tells me she's now concerned about my mental state. 'In *Epsom*?' I don't even know where that is. Then suddenly it hits me, and I come to my senses.

'But he's got Riley . . . where is Riley?' My voice is a screech.

The policewoman glances at her colleague, looking back at me.

'Sorry, who is Riley?'

'My . . . our daughter! She's only two.'

'Your husband was with a child?' she says, and I can't read

72

her expression at all. She's not as surprised as she should be, more confused.

'Yes,' I say, my voice rising even further. 'Yes! I just got home . . . they're not here. He's a stay-at-home dad. He looks after her while I'm at work. Where was he? What happened?'

'We don't know much at this stage,' DS Tyler says, looking down briefly. 'Only that he was found unconscious with unexplained injuries, and that he's been taken to hospital. And as the situation is somewhat, um, unusual, and the location somewhat remote, we have a team investigating how he came to be there.'

'But in Epsom? Why would he be in Epsom? Why weren't they here at home? They should have been here. It's her teatime now, she should be sitting in the kitchen, ignoring her vegetables.'

DS Tyler puts her arm out. She is trying to calm me down. I don't want to calm down.

'Don't worry,' she says, 'I'll alert my colleagues straight away. Most likely she's being looked after right now, and we just didn't get the whole story.'

'Is it possible that someone has taken her?' I blurt. I shake my head at my own question. That makes no sense. The only person who might have taken her is me.

Or . . . no, it's not possible. Not her. She wouldn't. Would she?

'Do you have a recent photograph of your daughter, Mrs Morgan?' DS Tyler asks. 'That we could borrow?'

I laugh, looking around the living room. The immaculately finished alcove cupboards are topped with silver photo frames; every single one of them contains a photograph of Riley.

'Take any of them,' I say, gesturing around. 'They're all of her.'

The bile lurches into my throat. The same reaction to any stress, these days. I stand up and walk towards the fireplace, picking up the most recent photograph of Riley at her second birthday party and turning over the frame.

My whole body is shaking, and my fingers struggle to twist open the little catches on the back. Eventually, they give way and I pull the photo out, handing it to her with trembling fingers.

'I have the digital version too if you need it,' I say.

The other police officer has left the room. A shadow moves past the bay window on the pavement outside and I realise that he is out there, on his phone, telling someone to go and look for my daughter.

I want to run outside and tell them to drive me to where they found him. That I'm Riley's mother, and I will find her myself.

'Who found him?' I say, the tears streaming down my face. 'It doesn't make any sense that he'd be alone. Why wasn't she with him?'

DS Tyler stares at me. She doesn't know. She doesn't know anything. She's useless. Why did they send her? She's useless. She didn't even know he was meant to be with Riley.

'He sent me a text message earlier . . .' I start to cry even harder. 'I don't know if it means anything or not . . . it just said "Sorry". Please. Things haven't been good between us lately. But still, this is all so out of character for him . . . I'm scared. I'm scared he's done something to her.'

She is staring at me strangely now, and I can almost see the thoughts flashing through her mind. *Why has this woman left her daughter with her husband if she's at all worried about her safety?* She'll already be thinking about checking out my alibi for this afternoon. I imagine her writing it down on her notes: peculiar wife, missing child. Underlining that bit twice, her brain straining to make sense of it. She'll be wondering if Riley is hidden upstairs, safe and sound.

If only.

To explain it all would be impossible now. No one would understand my horrific, ridiculous situation. That's been the problem all along.

I have a vision of Robin, lying on the road, blood pooling from his head. I squint, trying to imagine, to feel, where Riley might be, but all I see are her big grey eyes, staring up at me, asking me not to go to work and leave her with Daddy . . .

Please, Mummy, don't go. I just want you.

'We'll take you to the hospital,' DS Tyler says. 'And keep you informed as soon as we hear anything.'

I blink the tears back and silently follow DS Tyler out of my house, climbing into the police car, looking up at the dark, empty windows of our family home as we pull away.

When Riley was a tiny baby I used to hold her and tell her I'd never leave her.

But I did. I did leave her.

I left her with him.

TWO YEARS EARLIER

ESTHER

We are on the way to visit Robin's parents. Last night, Robin and I slept together for the first time since Riley was born. I don't know if that's the reason that he seems more relaxed today, but he's definitely more cheerful than he usually is when we go to see them.

He thinks everything is back on track. He thinks I've forgiven him. Sometimes I think I have, sometimes I think I'm just playing a game because I don't have any other alternatives. I'm a mother now, and I have responsibilities that are bigger than me.

My scalp feels itchy, and I bury my fingernails in it, digging in so hard it hurts. It takes the pressure off, and I exhale slowly.

I watch him as he drives; the two-day stubble on his face that he's taken to leaving recently, the new shadows under his eyes. He's proud of these little signs that he's now a dad. And not just a *dad*, but a stay-at-home dad.

We agreed early on that he would give up his work to take care of her. Looking back to those delirious weeks before and after she was born, it feels as though I didn't have much say in the matter. I was swept along by it all, incapable of making decisions for myself. Perhaps he didn't trust me to look after her. I suppose I can understand that. But now she's older, I can see that we made the right decision for us as a family.

Our perfect daughter, Riley, is right in the middle of a sleep regression. Although Robin gets up with her every night, as agreed, my sleep is still disrupted, and I'm slowly getting used to feeling tired all the time.

It's better than feeling sick.

Vivienne said she wouldn't be surprised if I hated Riley after what I went through. But I look at her tiny curled fist, her dark, long eyelashes, and I know I never could.

It's a relief. It makes me feel like a better person.

'She's asleep,' Robin says, his voice a whisper. He presses his thumb and forefinger together in a 'perfect' sign, and I can see the relief wash over his face, suddenly painting him brighter. Poor Robin. The stress of her sleep patterns has been taking its toll on us both. At night I endlessly Google, scouring mum forums for solutions. There's a pile of baby books beside my bed, useful pages marked with Post-its.

It's all a little obsessive, but then again, what new parents aren't like this? It's such an overwhelming world to be lost in.

I crane my neck to see Riley in her reverse-facing car seat, but even if I stretch so far it hurts, I can only make out her legs and feet, sticking out in a triangle shape from the bottom of the seat. She's dressed up today, in a frilly dress and tights, with soft little silver booties that fall off whenever you pick her up. As Robin says, babies come with a lot of 'pointless cute stuff'.

Suddenly, I am taken back to my own childhood. I see my

father crouched before me, gently, patiently trying to teach me how to tie my shoelaces. My mother in the background shaking her head in bemusement as my useless, stubby fingers just tangled the laces into knots. *She can't do it. She's only five, for goodness' sake!* And my father defending me, as he always did: *So? She's smart. Smarter than the both of us put together.*

He had so much faith in me. The tears burn the back of my eyelids as they do now whenever I think of him, which is often. I never got to say goodbye. I was too ill when he died.

The regret is almost suffocating, and so I turn away from it, from any thought of my father, or what an amazing grandfather he might have been to Riley.

Riley. The present. The here and now. That's what I have to focus on.

She doesn't sleep well in the car, not like most babies. Everything has been timed with military precision in order to create optimum conditions for her to nap while we drive. She naps in single sleep cycles of fifty minutes, which is coincidentally the exact amount of time it takes us to drive to Robin's parents' house in Hampshire.

Robin lays a hand on my leg, stroking it gently. It's not suggestive, but a warmth spreads over my body. Somehow I can now see our future again, as intended. My horrific pregnancy was just a blip on the long horizon of our relationship. Marriage is tough sometimes, but nothing that was worth having was ever easy.

We are Robin and Esther, meant to be.

I am so lucky to have him. I am so lucky to have Riley.

I feel myself reach across to him, laying my hand on his leg in return. Another flashback comes to mind, of a time when we were younger, when we made love so often it hurt. I run my hand higher up his leg and he turns to me in surprise. There's no keeping the grin from his face.

'Oi,' he says. He's smiling, he's glad I still want him, even after what he did, but there's a bigger part of him that wants me to leave him alone. 'Don't want to crash the car.'

It's reasonable enough, of course, but it still makes me snatch my hand away and sit back in my seat, turning my face away to stare sulkily out of the window. It doesn't take much these days for my moods to flip, like a leaf turning over in the wind.

But he's only trying to be safe. Riley must come first, of course.

I am stunned by my love for her sometimes. Vivienne says she can't understand it. But she never understood my love for Robin either. That has never changed. He's my only family now.

He has his faults, but the main one is loving too much, which is hardly a fault at all, is it?

We are about ten minutes away from the Morgan family home – a solid, semi-detached house built in the 50s, on the outskirts of the small village that houses Mike's car dealership – when Robin speaks again. Riley is still sleeping.

'I've decided to tell my dad today,' he says, glancing across at me.

'Really?' I say, feeling my blood pressure suddenly rocket. 'I . . . Do you think that's a good idea? Riley is so fractious at

82

the moment. She's definitely teething . . . If she screams all through lunch and then you tell him that . . .'

Robin's father, Mike, is a difficult man. I have often wondered what went wrong with his wiring, what made him into the misogynist pig he is today, what trauma of his past is to blame.

He is nice on the surface, of course. A respectable businessman, with two sons and a neatly-turned-out mouse of a wife, whose bite is worse than her bark. But he's also a judgemental bully, with no space in his small mind for compassion.

He's the reason we haven't been to visit for so long.

'You don't need to tell him anything,' I protest, as we turn off the main road towards Petersham.

'Oh Tot, love the optimism. But you know my daddio. He'll ask,' Robin replies. 'He always does. He can't wait to ask. He's been looking forward to it since Christmas. He's *salivating* with glee at the thought of it.'

Rob's right, of course. Before we've even got our coats off, the question will have been dropped, loaded like a bomb, in front of us. It's the same every time.

How's work then, Rob?

'Just say it's quiet but picking up,' I say, desperately. 'And change the subject.'

'He won't buy it,' Robin replies, his jaw tensing. 'And anyway, he can go to hell. Looking after a baby is harder work than what he does. Flogging people carriers to the rich twats round here.'

I shake my head, uselessly. Sometimes I think Robin wants a fight, a huge showdown, to get out all the feelings he's bottled up for so long. Perhaps that's a good thing. Perhaps it's healthier that way.

We continue the final bit of the journey in silence, my fingers rooting around in my hair until I find a coarse strand to yank out. Slowly but surely, they're turning white, all the colour suddenly vanished.

Above the hum of the engine, if I strain my ears, I can hear Riley's rhythmic breathing in the back. In, out, in, out, the sound making me want to shut my eyes and doze as well. It's Sunday, and I have a crazy week ahead at work. Our new campaign is about to launch, and I'm so proud of it. Mum would have been so proud, too.

I've only been able to keep up the pace at work because Robin agreed to be a stay-at-home dad. Our situation is unusual, but it works for us. I can't see Mike understanding this, though, somehow. He doesn't mind the fact that I earn a decent salary, and I've overheard him boasting about his successful daughter-in-law at family parties. But I know he expected me to do the done thing and have at least a year off on maternity leave, and then maybe go back to work part-time.

Sandra never went back to work after having the boys. That was how they met: Mike employed her straight from secretarial college as his receptionist at the garage, but within six months of her starting work there, they were engaged. Once Nick was born, she gave up and never went back. Her boys are her life.

It might be an old-fashioned set-up but I admire her loyalty. She made a promise, a commitment, and she's stuck to it.

I wonder what my own mother would have made of my

situation. She died of kidney disease as a result of her diabetes when I was ten. Every day it feels as though she is further and further away from me. My work is the only way I can stay connected to her; my way of honouring her memory. It's why I'm so passionate about it.

We pull into their short driveway, and linger for a few minutes with the engine still running. If Robin turns it off, Riley will undoubtedly wake up, the change in atmosphere enough to jolt her out of sleep.

'She's had fifty minutes,' I say to Robin and he nods.

We can't stay in the car anyway. Sandra has spotted us and opened the front door. She doesn't understand our obsession with Riley's sleep.

Her advice has been unsolicited and unending. Passive-aggressive emails with links to articles about sleep training I 'might find useful'.

I have never felt my own mother's absence more acutely than since becoming a mother myself. She was good with babies and children. All my school friends loved her. She was confident with them, and they responded well to her calm and unflappable nature.

Dad told me later on that she'd desperately wanted me to have a sibling, but that she was simply too poorly. As a diabetic, being pregnant was a big risk to her health. And although Dad was always quick to say that her illness worsening so much was nothing to do with the fact that she had me, I couldn't help but wonder if he was just protecting my feelings.

Sandra is making her way towards us. I smile at her, take a

deep breath. Apparently, in her day, babies fitted around your schedule, not the other way round. She left Robin to scream himself to sleep at only six weeks old. 'He slept through the night from that night onwards.'

Sometimes I wonder if this is the cause of Robin's low self-esteem, but I don't have the courage to bring it up.

ROBIN

Bringing my daughter home. It might just be the proudest moment of my life.

Nick thought I must be disappointed we had a girl. Like he was when his twins were born, although he'd never admit it to Honor. But I wasn't. Wasn't what I had pictured, but actually, perhaps it's better this way. And she's adorable, my daughter. Everyone says so. Even Esther fell in love with her at first sight, and after what she went through, that wasn't a given.

Thankfully, Riley wakes up in a good mood. She's a cheerful little soul when she's slept well. She's pretty too, the same bright eyes as her mother.

'Oh, look what you're wearing, poppet,' my mother says, scooping Riley up and smothering her in kisses. 'What an adorable dress!'

'I think she suits that colour,' Esther says, kissing my mother on the cheek. Mum responds by holding Esther at a literal arm's length.

Dad takes the bottle of wine from Esther and examines the label. A discerning alcoholic, who knew there was such a thing?

'Not tried this one,' he says, sceptically. 'Great to see you both.'

Believe it or not, this is him making an effort. The baby has softened him. Mum must have had a word with him before we arrived.

Where did it all go wrong for me and him? Was it the whole business with Sarah, or was it before that, when he realised that I wasn't any good at rugby? I hate that I even care.

I'm about to blow his tiny mind again. Part of me can't wait. I feel a sick longing for it all: the shock and disgust on his sagging face, the angry rash that will spread from his neck to his cheeks, the shouting. Sometimes the drama is the only thing that makes me feel alive, like I matter.

I look over at Esther. Mum has handed Riley back to her, and she's rummaging in the changing bag for the bottle of formula. I watch her for a few seconds, the way she deftly tucks Riley under one arm and leans down, pulling off the lid of the bottle with her chin, while excavating a muslin cloth from the pocket of her coat. She's better at it all than I expected. I had thought she would struggle, that I'd maybe even catch her digging her fingernails into Riley's soft skin in frustration, but there's been none of that.

God, I'm tired. We go through to the dining room. The table is laid as though the bloody queen is visiting. Silver napkin rings strangle dark purple napkins; paisley placemats and coasters and large serving spoons wait for action. My father thinks it makes us look posh.

'Nick's had another promotion, you know,' he says, as he

uncorks the bottle we brought and lays it on the mahogany sideboard to rest. 'They reckon he will make vice president next year.'

I hear a short cough behind me and glance over at Esther. She's taken a seat in the bay window. Riley is glugging at the bottle happily, big eyes swivelling around, taking us all in. Her family. I wonder what she thinks of us all. Whether she would have picked us, if she had a choice in the matter.

Not a chance.

'Vice president? Is that what they call them? Jesus Christ,' I say, and Esther's eyes meet mine for a second. *Don't do it*, she is saying. *Don't rise to the bait.*

'Sit down, Rob,' my dad says, gesturing at the chair in front of me.

I don't want to upset Esther. She doesn't deserve it.

So I'm a good boy and the lunch passes without incident. My mum asks Esther about Riley's development, pointing out that the redness on her chin might mean she's about to start teething.

'Rob was an early teether,' she says. I can see her about to ask Esther if she knows what she was like as a baby but she stops herself just in time. Esther doesn't know those kind of things. Her mother died too suddenly to think to pass those memories on.

And now her father's gone too. The unfairness of life quite often floors me.

Dad sits at the end of the table, watching us as he eats. I see the way his face screws up in distaste whenever Riley lets out a yelp for attention. I press my fingers into the sides of my legs to curb the frustration. At one point, Riley begins to cry. I stand up, but Esther puts a hand across the table at me.

'It's OK,' she says, quietly. 'I'll go. Just a new nappy, I think.'

Dad flings his cutlery to his plate and makes a noise like he's been winded.

'I'm sorry, Dad, did we upset you?' I say, my voice clipped. 'Babies like to wee and poo. Shocker.'

'Rob,' Mum says, shooting me a look. 'Not at the table, please.'

'No talk of bodily functions when we're eating,' Dad barks. 'Esther, please take her to the bathroom to do that.'

'Of course,' Esther says, meek as a church mouse. This is what he does to women, he silences them with his obvious disgust.

When they leave, the tension eases. My father continues to eat, his face bright red from years of alcohol, his once thick, curly hair now patchy and grey. He's always been a big man. A big, hairy man, like me.

'They're looking into getting a place in France with his bonus,' he says, as he puts his knife and fork together, pushing his plate away. 'Somewhere in the mountains. Honor wants the children to learn to ski.'

I try not to snort in laughter at the thought of my brother on a pair of skis.

'Nick, skiing?' I say. I can't stop myself. 'Guess he's really committed to his new-found role as a total wanker.'

'Rob!' Mum cries. 'Please.'

'Well,' Dad says, draining his glass of red wine. His lip curls upwards as he sets the glass back down on the table. It seems the wine wasn't to his taste, after all. 'At least he's an employed wanker.'

'Oh Mike,' Mum says, like a strangled cat. 'Rob *is* employed.'

'Self-employed,' I correct her. I grip the edge of my seat. The moment I've been waiting for. *Fuck you, Dad*. 'Or at least I was.'

I've caught his attention now. Dad looks at me, trying to mask the curiosity in his eyes. *Busted, Dad!* I see you; you do care. Ha!

He waits for me to continue.

'I've given up work to look after Riley,' I say.

Mum inhales sharply.

'Esther's been doing really well, and there's the possibility of her being promoted in the next few months. And we all know how wonderfully useless I am at my Mickey Mouse "job". So we decided I should be a stay-at-home dad.'

'What does your brother think about this?' Dad says, his eyes ablaze.

I frown.

'No idea. I haven't told him.'

Mum gives out a small moan. I feel a brief pang of sympathy for her.

She starts to clear the plates away, stacking them on top of one another, hands trembling.

'Hopefully he'll talk some sense into you,' Dad says. 'Heaven knows we've tried. You had so much potential, coming from our family, with everything we have to offer! I know you think this is funny, Rob, but it isn't. It's not funny at all.'

I snort my wine back into the glass.

'Oh, I don't know. Your reaction is pretty amusing.'

'It didn't have to be like this. I offered you a job!' he roars, thumping his hand on the table. In the hallway beyond, I see Esther, standing by the foot of the stairs, jiggling Riley up and down. They are both staring transfixed at my father, like they're watching a car about to crash. 'A proper business! A proper man's job!'

'I know,' I say, spitting the words. 'But as I told you at the time: I think on the balance of it, I'd rather die than live my life as a car salesman.'

'It was our family's heritage,' he shouts, and with pleasure I notice that he has gone almost purple in his rage. 'But no, too good for that, aren't you? Too funny? I'll tell you what's funny – what's funny is a comedian who's so unfunny that he can't get anyone to come to his shows. A comedian so unfunny that his wife shows him up at every available opportunity. Call yourself a man!'

'If being a man means loving and caring for your child and wife, then yes, I do call myself a man,' I say. My fists are clenched.

'You're not a man,' Dad hisses, his eyes narrowing. 'Real men provide for their families. They don't give up their jobs to play nanny.'

I hear Esther give a sob and I flick my eyes back towards her. I've let her down. Again. The dining table stretches like an ocean between us and I want to reach out and take her in my arms. But she turns away from me, staring down at the floor in front of her, while Riley wriggles in her arms.

'Fuck you,' I say to my dad, under my breath.

But it's not enough to win the fight. Whatever I do, it's never enough. I throw the glass I'm holding across the room in frustration at my defeat.

ESTHER

I have never seen Robin behave like that with his parents. It's only when we climb back into the car that I feel my heart rate return to normal. Family scenes are not my thing. We never had any; it was just me and my mild-mannered, softly spoken dad. We always got on.

It was horrible to watch them fighting like that. But at the same time, I'm actually quite pleased that it all kicked off. It means we get to leave earlier than planned, and Riley falls immediately asleep as we hit the motorway. She doesn't even seem to mind Robin's ranting.

'That's it,' Robin says, gripping the steering wheel. He wouldn't let me drive, even though he's been drinking. He doesn't like me driving since Riley was born. I don't mind, really. Finding a parking space on our street is always stressful. And reverse parking has been painful ever since I cracked my rib.

'We are never going to visit them again,' he says. 'I'll see Mum if she comes up. But they can forget Christmas, birthdays, whatever. See how they like sitting there alone in their time warp of a house, passing each other the presents they both bought for themselves, because neither of them have any fucking imagination. They're dead behind the eyes, both of them. Puppets. What is the point of them? What legacy are they leaving? How exactly do they think they are changing the world? Or having any impact on it at all?'

I let him rant, and when he stops to draw breath I lean over and squeeze him on the knee. I am proud of him for standing up to his father, but at the same time I am so tired of the noise and drama. Since Riley was conceived my life has been non-stop drama. It's hard to remember a time when things were simple. When the most taxing decision Robin and I had to make was which bit of the Sunday supplements to read first.

I pull out my iPhone, opening the Facebook app. I rarely log in these days. I shared a few photos when Riley was born, but I didn't get the same reaction that other new mothers got, and I found myself burning with humiliation, imagining what they were all thinking. Even though they only knew a fraction of it.

She stayed with him, even after he snogged that girl in front of everyone when she was pregnant?

Robin is on Facebook all the time, of course, and I tap to view his page. It's flooded with images of Riley. Riley in her car seat, Riley having her first bath, Riley asleep on Robin's chest, as he sleeps on our sofa. I took that one myself. I frown. It's a private moment, not something I really wanted him to share.

'I love you,' he says, unexpectedly, and I look back at him. He looks emotional now, as though he might burst into tears. 'You know that, don't you? I love you and respect you. You're my whole world, Esther Morgan. You and Riley. You're my family now.'

'I know,' I say, swallowing. 'You're my family too.'

It's more true for me than it is for him. He really is my only family. My father died of emphysema despite the fact he never smoked a day in his life. He was only sixty-six. My mother was just thirty-seven.

Losing them at such young ages has taught me that life isn't fair. And protesting about that makes absolutely no difference. You have to make the most of what you get. There's *always* some good to be found in every situation.

My therapist, Claudia, is suspicious of my feelings. She's obsessed with the five stages of grief, says I haven't worked through them all yet. Claims that pushing away bad feelings only leads to stress. But I don't have the energy to take them on right now. Keeping busy is the best therapy.

'You're all that matters,' Robin continues. 'You and Riley. That's it. That's how small my world is now. It's a privilege to be able to look after you both. An honour.'

I feel myself tensing.

'I know,' I say, and although I know it should be lovely to hear all this, part of me wishes he would stop. Sometimes the intensity of his love is too much. It overwhelms me, his emotions flooding the room and leaving no space for mine.

When we first started dating, he used to handwrite me letters and leave them hidden around my room. They were short but sweet, and often included poems he'd written about me too. I showed my friend Catherine one of them, once.

'It's a good job you like him too,' she said, handing it back to me. 'Because if not you could do him for stalking.'

She was only joking, but her words stung a bit.

'Isn't it a bit bloody exhausting?' Vivienne used to say after Robin left our flat, having kissed me full on the lips in front of her. 'Having someone love you *that much*?'

But she was just jealous.

Viv. My stomach turns over at the thought of her. We haven't spoken for the longest time.

But I am a mother now, and that's all that matters.

I glance back down at my phone, scrolling through the album of photographs on Robin's page, entitled 'Riley Madison Morgan'.

I hated the name Madison, but it had been a concession, something Robin spent hours persuading me of, and one of the only ones I'd accepted.

My finger pauses on a photo that Robin must have uploaded before we left to go to his parents' house. It's a picture of Riley this morning. She's sitting propped up on our bed, in her Sunday best, the little silver booties still attached to her feet. The bed is made, at least, but in one corner you can see my greying bra hanging off the side. I'm not usually messy and I cringe that Robin hasn't thought to crop the photo before uploading it.

But it's not the unwelcome sight of my bra that stops me in my tracks. It's the comment below the photo. Just one little word, but it sends an icy chill through me.

Beautiful x

And just before the comment is the name of the person who left it.

Kim.

ROBIN

He's nothing if not predictable, my father. As I lean down to kiss Esther goodbye at the front door, I hear my phone start to ring in the living room.

I know it will be Nick. Dad will have told him to call me, to talk some 'sense' into me.

'Here,' I say, pulling Esther back towards me. 'Your lunch.' I hand her a Tupperware filled with salad. Quinoa, feta and beetroot. Her favourite. I'm getting good at this housewife stuff.

'Oh, thanks!' she says. 'Bye bye, you two.' She kisses Riley on the top of her head and then runs a finger across the stubble on my face.

'Maybe shave if you get time?' she says, and before I have the chance to try to kiss her again, she's hurried off down the street. Back to the other love of her life: her work. She's determined that no one else should ever have to die from diabetes. It's a noble cause, if a little naive.

I pace back to the living room and find my phone underneath the sofa. I can't remember how it got there. Riley had another bad night. I gave up at half four and took her into the

98

living room and lay on the sofa, one foot rocking her Moses basket for what felt like hours.

To kill the time I had scrolled back through Sarah's Instagram until I got to her first ever post, from three years ago. It was a blurry pair of shoes, definitely not worth the effort.

Now I look down at my phone. Shocker; the missed call is from my brother. We're not close. We're a different species, so different that it's hard to believe we came from the same gene pool. Despite everything that's happened, despite the fact he knows what an arse our father is, he's still firmly Team Dad.

The two of them have always been on the same team. When I was about eight, I put together my first ever routine of jokes. Spent ages practising it in my room, like a proper dork. Once it was ready, I summoned Mum and Nick to the living room for the grand performance. They laughed. A lot. Especially Nick. I remember that.

Then Dad came home. Mum had tears streaming down her face and she pulled him into the room.

'Go on, do it again for your dad, love,' she said. 'It was really good.'

I didn't dare look up at Dad as I performed the last few minutes of the routine. But at the end, I raised my eyes. He wasn't laughing. He wasn't even smiling.

He was frowning, staring at me like I was some kind of alien.

'I don't get it,' he said, nostrils flaring. 'It wasn't funny. He was just being stupid.'

'Oh, but . . .' Mum began.

'Yeah, Dad,' Nick said. 'I thought it was stupid too.'

And then they left the room.

'Never mind, eh, love,' Mum said, reaching out to squeeze my shoulder. 'Better get on upstairs and do your homework. Tea'll be ready soon.'

I never quite forgave Nick for that treachery.

And now I look at his life and wouldn't swap with him for all the world.

He was really good at cricket as a teenager. Wouldn't that have been so much more interesting as a career? Instead he's obsessed with making as much money as possible. Proving himself to Dad. A life chained to a desk, spent ticking off the days until your next expensive holiday. What's the point of that? Why not create a life you don't need a holiday from in the first place?

I lean in and sniff Riley's soft head, and wonder if he has any idea what he's missed.

I call him back. Partly because I'm nosy, mostly because he'll only call again if I don't.

'Bro,' he says as he picks up. I don't know where he got that from.

'Good morning,' I say, keeping my voice jovial. 'Let me guess, mein Vater rang you and gave you the whole story, and now you're calling me to try to persuade me not to throw away my life doing something as pathetic as raising another human being, so that you feel you've done your duty by him as a son and me as a brother. Well, let me save you the time: message received loud and clear; you can go now.'

'Rob,' he says, sighing. There's a load of background noise.

'Where are you?' I ask.

'On the DLR. The Jubilee line was down,' he says.

I look at the clock. It's 7.45am. He's always at his desk in Canary Wharf by 8am.

'Don't tell me you're going to be late?'

'Are you sure about this?' he says, ignoring my question. 'Forget Dad. We both know what an arsehole he is to . . .'

He is about to say 'to you' but clearly thinks better of it.

'But giving up your job, mate? Really?'

'It's not like it's much to give up,' I say, glad that no one except my accountant knows exactly how little I have given up. I try not to think of my credit card bill. I cleared the balance last year, but it's creeping back up again. 'I'm freelance, you know. It's not like I'm walking away from a steady pay packet and generous bonus scheme. I'm just turning down work for a few months so I can focus on my daughter.'

'Sure, but . . .' Nick begins, but he stops himself again. I know what he wants to ask. Whether Esther's pregnancy is the reason she doesn't want to look after Riley. Whether she's suffering with some sort of post-traumatic stress disorder from the puking that left her with internal bleeding and a cracked rib.

'I thought Honor had got you reading the *Guardian* these days,' I say, snappily. I lay Riley down on her play mat and hand her a soft book, which she immediately brings to her mouth. There's some gel I need to get for her teething, I think. Dr Google said it was the best thing. 'Isn't being a stay-at-home dad incredibly in vogue at the moment?'

'Don't be flippant,' Nick says. 'Seriously. You're only a few months down the line. We've got two kids. I know how hard it is. You really might regret this.'

I laugh loudly at this. Nick has no idea how hard it is. When the twins were born, he helpfully got seconded to a post in Singapore. Honor refused to go with him, and so he spent most of the twins' early years abroad, in a time zone that made even Skyping a challenge.

I went to visit Honor when they were five months old and found her sitting at her enormous kitchen table crying into her glass of wine, telling me she hated Nick and wanted to leave him. She said she wished he was more like me. I liked the compliment, although she doesn't really know me as well as she thinks, of course. Besides, it was just the end of her tether talking.

'Nick,' I say, keeping my voice steady. 'Do me a favour. Don't waste any more time worrying about me. Or Esther. We're happy. Go back to Dad, tell him you tried your best, but I'm not worth saving. Job's done.'

'It's not just because of Dad . . . I do care about you, mate,' he says, and the nasally twang of the last word makes me roll my eyes. Who is this *mate*, who is this *bro*, and what happened to my brother? 'After what happened, you know. I know it was tough. I know this is . . . it's a big deal for you. Riley. Esther. I mean, is she even OK? Losing her dad like that too? I just want to help.'

'I know you do,' I say, tickling Riley on the tummy. Thank the Lord I didn't end up with the brains in the family. 'But we're fine, Scout's honour. And talking of which . . . how is the very lovely, very shiny Honor? Changed her mind about what a loser you are yet?'

I get eight minutes of Nick droning on about their plans for a last-minute ski trip before the season ends, and then he arrives at Canary Wharf and has to get off the phone. At the end of the call he thanks me for the chat.

He's totally unaware that he has done all the chatting and all I have done is listen, have a piss and make Riley up a bottle (I washed my hands first, I'm not a complete animal). When I lay the phone down on the kitchen worktop after our call, the screen is illuminated, telling me I have a message from Kim.

I don't read it yet.

I shake Riley's bottle thoroughly again to mix the powder and the water. Then I go back through to the living room, where Riley is still transfixed by the animals dangling from her play gym. She's half rolled on to her side and seems a little stuck, her eyes straining to look up.

'Oh sausage,' I say, crouching down to her. 'Did you try to turn over? Such a clever girl.'

I stroke her head and gently adjust her position so that she's lying flat on her back again. She stares at me with those big eyes.

I blink, scooping her up and settling her in the crook of my arm for her feed. She's a good baby. Laid-back like her father, I used to joke to Esther, but the last time I said it she shot me a look that told me the joke was wearing thin. We've been lucky, haven't had to deal with colic or reflux or all the other things

103

the midwife warned me about. Of course, she's not breastfed, but that was a small price to pay for our unusual set-up.

As usual, I flick the television on, mindlessly scanning the channels for something of interest. But all the television programmes are aimed at women, or the unemployed.

Project Sarah beckons me. No, not today.

Riley. I have to focus on Riley. But ever since she was born, the past has felt closer than ever. Part of me is just desperate for Sarah to know that I've done it. But I don't understand why. I don't know how to make it go away.

'*Homes Under the Hammer*?' I say to Riley, but she's slurping away, and doesn't even look at me. I think about all the Marvel films that Esther falls asleep in the middle of if I ever try to watch them with her. Would it be really wrong . . . ? People take their kids to baby cinema all the time, but I don't have the cash for that.

Riley's too young to understand any of it, but what if the violence on-screen somehow seeps into her subconscious, and she turns round at six and starts trying to stab her schoolmates with scissors?

Did Dad let me watch a Western when I was six months old? Is that why I'm such a weirdo?

Nah. Dad barely even looked at me when I was six months old.

I unlock the phone's screen, and navigate to my messages, tapping on the one from Kim.

Hello!!! How's you? How's little one? Still on for this afternoon – I CAN'T WAIT XX

I look down at my daughter.

I'm not looking forward to this at all, but Kim's become increasingly pushy lately. That Facebook comment was a shot across the bow. I need to keep her sweet.

'Fancy a trip to see Auntie Kim?' I ask her. Riley stares at me.

I should feel guilt, I know, but instead I feel nothing as my thumb taps out a reply. It's self-preservation. I'm just trying to protect my family, like any good father would.

Indeed. Riley's been practising her jazz hands all morning. See you there x

ESTHER

Kim's Facebook comment about Riley feels like a grenade. A teeny tiny lethal grenade, just left there, waiting to explode.

As far as I knew, she would be away working on the cruise ship for the rest of the year. Robin told me that the internet onboard was patchy, that I didn't need to worry about her.

I didn't even know they were Facebook friends. I've never looked through his friends list; I wanted to trust him. I curse myself for taking my eye off the ball, for hardly ever using the site myself. It's not really my scene, all that endless over-sharing. Several times I've thought of deleting my account, but knowing that Robin is so active on it, I've never been quite able to.

The train I'm on pulls into London Bridge and I climb off. I have revisited Robin's Facebook page endlessly since I saw Kim's comment and there's nothing else there to make me suspicious. Just that one little word.

Beautiful.

Of course Riley is beautiful. That's all she meant. Nothing more.

It's FINE.

I think about Kim, about who she is as a person. She's not me. That's the mistake people always make – assuming that other people think like them. But she doesn't. Knowing her, she will just have seen that photo of Riley, thought how beautiful she looked, and thought to leave the comment. She won't have realised how much it might hurt me. Then she would have moved on to the next friend's photo and written something equally meaningless on theirs.

It means nothing.

Besides, she's far away, sailing somewhere round the Caribbean. Her profile photograph is her with her arms around an overly tanned, handsome man, one of her legs artfully raised across his body to reveal a toned, browned leg beneath a dress that plunges low at the front. She has cleavage, unlike me, and he's jokingly staring down at it, eyes popping in amusement.

It's impossible to tell whether they're a couple, or whether he's gay. She has a lot of male friends, I realised, as I scanned her friends list last night. She's popular. Of course she is: she's fun, gregarious, doesn't take life seriously.

I wonder how many men she has slept with. My own number is higher than I'd like to admit. Than I have admitted to anyone, least of all Robin. My teenage years were spent lost and searching for something to fill the void my mother left. All those boys . . . because they were just boys. And I was just a girl. A kid. It feels like a lifetime ago now. It was another me. The incomplete Esther. Robin fixed me. And my work did too. Doing something meaningful with my life, to ensure my mother didn't die in vain.

In those early months after Riley was born, I thought of Kim often on that cruise ship, dressed up like a Vegas showgirl, prancing around on a tiny stage in front of a load of retirees. I wondered if that's where she had seen herself ending up, when she first went off to study acting, or whether deep down she thought she'd be the next Keira Knightley.

I know a lot about Kim, now. In the month leading up to Riley's birth I researched her to a shameful extent. She graduated from a decent enough drama school, and landed a pretty big TV role when she was only twenty-two, playing a slutty receptionist in that Channel 4 sitcom. She was 'made for the part', one review said, and they weren't wrong.

But the series wasn't the success it was meant to be, and the show was dropped. After that, her career was more chequered: guest parts in soaps, appearances in music videos, some musical theatre at the Edinburgh Festival. No serious theatre. Nothing that would mark her out as anything other than a background prop, a bit of set dressing.

And that's how I have to think of her now. As a background prop in our lives.

In the office, I open the blinds to take in the view of London Bridge behind me. It's spring, and although the air is still chilly, there's that feeling of hope, that the new year is finally starting to begin, and that it will be better than the last. And for once, I have no doubt it will be.

I'm doing OK, considering. I worry about Riley, a lot. I worry about her dying suddenly, but surely that's normal for a first-time mum?

'Morning!'

I look up. My boss, Sarina, Director of Engagement, strolls up to my desk.

'Listen, I've got a meeting at ten with the team from King's College Hospital, as well as our research guys. I know you were particularly interested in the gestational diabetes screening project ... it's not technically your job, but I thought you might want to sit in and hear more about their findings? I think it's been a really successful project.'

I swallow and nod my head. It's not a research project I've been directly involved in but Sarina knows that ever since my own pregnancy, I've become even more obsessed with all gestational conditions.

She's so good to me.

'Yes, definitely,' I say, surprised but pleased. 'I would love to. Thanks.'

'Great.'

I smooth down my blouse and chew on my lip. But I can't focus. I keep thinking of Kim. Of her nerve.

I know Robin would never cheat on me again, and especially not with her, but even so. Why can't she just do the right thing?

I push the feelings away and check my calendar for the day.

I can't believe I've forgotten.

Today would have been Dad's birthday.

It feels like I've been punched in the stomach. How could I?

Our last phone conversation comes to mind. I have replayed it endlessly in my head, wishing I could go back and say something different. Tell him how much I loved him, how much I appreciated everything he did for me.

He gave up his job as an engineer after my mother died, and took a part-time job in the planning department so that he would be at home more to look after me.

Money was always tight after that. He said he didn't mind, that he enjoyed working at the council, but I could see how sad it made him inside. And it wasn't just the money. He was so depressed to have left a career he loved.

There's so much I would say to him, if only I could have another chance. But when we last spoke I was so sick, confined to hospital on a drip.

When he answered the phone he sounded breathless, as though he had raced to answer. A side effect of his condition. I felt breathless myself, could only speak quietly and softly, in case I was sick again.

'Hi Dad,' I said. 'How are you feeling?'

'Well now,' he replied. 'Happy to hear from you. And the sun's out today. Looking forward to seeing you, my love. What time does your train get in? I can book you a taxi.'

'I'm . . . I'm sorry, Dad,' I said, and a tear began to roll down my cheek. 'I'm not very well myself, I'm afraid. I'm in hospital. I won't be able to come tomorrow.'

I closed my eyes, imagining the disappointment on his face. I was always reliable. We were a team.

He gave a short breath.

'Oh love, what's happened?' he said.

'It's nothing serious. Just a bad tummy bug, but I'm a bit

dehydrated, so they put me on a drip. I'll come and see you as soon as I'm better, I promise.'

'I'm sorry, love,' he said. 'Now you don't need to be worrying about me. I'm fine. You just concentrate on getting yourself well. Some nasty bugs around at this time of year. Gastroenteritis, is it?'

'Yes. Something like that. I will. I'm really sorry.'

'What are you apologising for? Don't worry about me. I'll miss you, but Susan's coming over later, so that'll be nice.'

I was shocked by that. 'What?' I said. Susan was his consultant. 'Why didn't you say? I thought you were waiting for the results of your latest scan?'

'I think they're going to give me the nasal tubes,' he replied. 'To help me if I want to walk for a bit longer, you know.'

I sniffed. If only there was a way to will myself better.

'I'm so sorry I can't be there, Dad.'

'Oh, love, that's all right. There'll be other times,' he replied, wheezing again. I pictured him standing in his cramped living room, arthritic fingers briefly touching his forehead.

That was the last time I ever spoke to him. He collapsed the next day, and wasn't found for two days. The thought of my father, the man who had loved and nurtured me all my life, lying cold and alone on the floor of his bungalow, was too much to bear.

I pick up my phone and stare at it for several seconds.

'Happy birthday, Dad,' I whisper.

If only I could phone him now, bake him a cake, send him balloons. The photo of Riley from a couple of weeks ago blurs on my phone screen as I gaze at it. I squint to focus and I look at her, taking in those huge round eyes that always seem to be judging me silently. Asking why she's at home with Daddy, and not at home with me like most babies. Asking why she never got to meet her grandad.

How can I ever explain it all to her?

ROBIN

I stuff Riley into a fluffy white snowsuit with a hood that has ears. I think it's meant to make her look like a sheep. Or a bear. Personally I find the whole 'dressing your baby as a tiny animal' thing insane, but it's the warmest thing she owns. Esther bought it on her lunch break one day. She offered it to me, nervously, when she got home. It's upsetting that she still feels anxious about things like that.

Kim is 'of no fixed address' at the moment, as she jokingly told me when we last spoke. She gave up her place in her flat-share last year. She's staying with friends in Tooting, just up the road. She swore it was a coincidence when she told me. I don't believe her.

We arranged to meet on the common, anyway, and I push Riley in her buggy up the clogged high street, taking in the different sights and sounds. I'm never quite sure how I feel about Tooting. The open mic nights I tried when we first moved here didn't exactly go well. Since then I've got used to feeling like I don't belong.

But then, I've never belonged, anywhere. There were a few months when Sarah and I first got together that I thought perhaps finally I had found my nirvana, but it was just an illusion, like everything else.

There was a report out a few years ago, saying that stand-up comedians have high levels of psychotic personality traits. That they had to be able to see the world differently from others in order to be funny.

If that's the case, it certainly explains Sarah. Perhaps it's a good thing my comedy career hasn't taken off.

I chat to Riley as we walk, pointing out the huge rows of brightly coloured vegetables on display outside the grocery shops, the trendy new restaurant that we haven't yet had time to visit . . .

'Not since you came along, little one,' I say. 'Mummy and I used to eat out all the time. When Daddy actually had some work and some money in his account. Did you know that once upon a time the *Independent* called Daddy "the best observational comic of his generation"?'

Like everyone else, she doesn't give a shit.

After a few minutes she's asleep, the noises of the road proving a good lullaby.

I've shaved, as Esther commanded me to anyway, changed into a smart shirt and dug out my old work coat. I'm not wearing jogging bottoms for the first time in a fortnight. I've even put some aftershave on.

I'm not going to do anything. But I can't deny the cognitive dissonance thrumming in my brain. I'm a thirty-nine-year-old man, after all, and, if I'm honest, the chemistry Kim and I had reminded me of those early days with Sarah. Frantic, visceral. Nothing like the pedestrian mechanics of Esther and me.

I think of the sex Esther and I had just a few days ago. It had been a welcome relief when she initiated it, but such a surprise it only lasted seconds. Afterwards, when I came back from the bathroom, I found she was huddled in a corner of the bed, crying.

It broke my heart to see her like that. She's still taking her time to come to terms with everything. I'm trying to be patient.

I spot Kim standing by the water fountain as I enter the common. She's wearing a bobble hat, her long, dark hair spilling out from under it, all over her shoulders. She's dressed in tight jeans and a bomber jacket, and she stands up and waves at us as I push Riley towards her. I feel strange, and then I realise that it's nerves.

Unusual, for me. This is a delicate situation. I have to tread carefully, and I'm not known for my tact or diplomacy.

'Dude,' she says, ambling towards me. She flings her arms around my neck and kisses me on the cheek. Her perfume is strong, a strange musky smell that's both sickly and masculine all at once. She's more tanned than the last time I saw her, and slimmer too.

'It's freezing,' she says, laughing, her white teeth flashing as she does so. 'How's bubba?'

She leans over the pram, pulling back the cover slightly. Her face breaks into a wide smile.

'Sleeping,' I say.

Kim looks at me.

'Still beautiful like her mother?'

I shake my head. She pushes her luck. Just like me. Maybe that's why I like her.

115

Kim hooks an arm through mine and we walk together slowly, me pushing the pram gently across the wet grass.

'How are things?' I say.

'You know,' she says. 'Could be better, could be worse. Keeping on. I've . . . met someone though.'

'Anyone special?' The question is out before I have time to consider it, and it hangs there, unanswered, for several seconds.

'Why, you jealous?' she says, teasingly, and I squeeze the handles of Riley's pram so hard that my fingertips start to ache. Shit, it's all going wrong. This is not what I came here to do. But I'm on this track now, and the pathetic thing is it's a track I enjoy riding.

'Definitely,' I say, glancing sideways at her. 'Definitely maybe. Perhaps. A little bit.'

'Shush, you naughty boy,' Kim says, dramatically flapping her arms at me. 'Way too complicated. Anyway, tell me about Riley. How's Daddy Day Care working out? My mates are so impressed with you, what you've done.'

'What mates?' I say, my hand flying to my mouth in mock-shock. 'You have mates? Prove it.'

'Haha. They think you're quite the modern man. Seriously, it's amazing what you're doing, dude. You rock.'

I find myself smiling, relaxing, enjoying her company. There is something so incredibly freeing about her, the fact that she has no expectations of me whatsoever, that she just lets me be, accepts me as I am.

'It's all entirely self-serving, I assure you,' I say. 'Just doing it to scrape together material for a new show. And there's loads of it. I might try and take it to Edinburgh this year . . .'

116

We reach a bench and sit down side by side. Her leg is pressed against mine, her neat nose silhouetted against the morning sun.

'I went to this baby yoga class the other day . . .' I continue. 'Christ. I would have been stared at less if I'd turned up with a kitten instead of a baby. I know the whole "reluctant dad" trope has been done to death, but what about the non-reluctant dad? No one talks about him. It's a charitable act. I'm giving him the airtime he deserves.'

'Smarty-pants,' Kim says, clapping her hands together. 'Sounds genius. I reckon you'll make millions.'

'Do you think?' I say, suddenly shy. Her faith in me reminds me of the way Sarah believed in me. Once.

'Of course!' she replies. 'Ed Fest crowds will lap that up.'

'Thanks,' I say, smiling. I haven't even told Esther about my idea yet.

Kim turns to look at me. I stare in her eyes. They're deep and dark, framed by thick, curled eyelashes that can't be natural, but that somehow suit her so perfectly it's hard to believe she wasn't born with them.

She smiles, looks away. The air feels thick between us.

I shut my eyes and try to block out the memories.

But they pop up, over and over again: Kim, against a wall, breathless and compliant as I thrust into her unthinkingly.

Kim, lying beneath me, pulling me towards her as though I was the only man in the world.

Kim, the woman I turned to when my world fell apart for the second time.

ESTHER

I am late home from work – the meeting with Sarina and the research team was fascinating. I had so many ideas of ways we could use their findings in future campaigns that I couldn't help but stay late to empty them out of my head before they disappeared. There's so much more public awareness needed around gestational diabetes, and the risk especially to obese mothers. I don't want to pull focus from our main campaigns this year but I've decided to call a meeting with the social media team tomorrow, to see if we can push out a mini campaign based around the research team's findings.

It's incredibly exciting – to me, anyway – but it means I have missed bath time.

By the time I finally push open the front door to our flat, it's 7.30pm. Not late by the standards of some parents I know, but late enough that Riley is asleep already, in her cot that's attached to Robin's side of the bed. It's called a co-sleeping cot, and means that Robin can easily lift her up to feed her if she wakes in the night. I wanted it on my side of the bed – after all, I hardly see her in the day – but Robin said it made no sense, that I needed my sleep more than he did.

I tried not to see it as anything other than a sensible decision.

'Sorry,' I whisper, as I hang my coat on the overcrowded rack in the hallway, and climb past the buggy. Our flat is too small to house us, a baby and all the baby's paraphernalia. We want to move eventually. I just need to wait for my promotion so that we can get a bigger mortgage.

Disloyally, I have thought that Robin could still do gigs in the evenings if he wanted – we'd just need to make sure I was home from work on time. But he doesn't seem keen. We've discussed it and the decision has been made: Robin will stay at home to look after her until she turns one.

After all, if Robin was a woman no one would blink an eye at this plan – in fact, they'd *expect* it.

The television is on in the living room, of course, so I push open the wooden door and peer in.

'Hi Tot,' Robin says, shifting position on the sofa. I take a few steps over to him and kiss him on the cheek. He's wearing aftershave. I shouldn't be surprised; I asked him to shave, after all, but I stand up sharply. Certain smells can take me back to the time when I thought I might be sick just from breathing in. I still can't believe that I survived that experience. Sometimes I wonder if I really have, or if my life is just a weird dream.

'Has she been difficult?' I say, looking around at the scattered toys littering the living room rug.

He shifts on the sofa.

'Our daughter, difficult? Princess Riley of Rilesville? Let me think. Uh, yeah. Epic PMT today. Sorry about the mess. Her

Royal Highness wouldn't settle – she's literally just gone down now. I was trying to stay quiet.'

I swallow. Robin looks tired.

'Stressful day?' he says, reaching out a hand. I take it, trying not to focus on how clammy it seems, and sit next to him on the sofa.

'No, it . . .' I start. I don't find my job stressful, at all. Fast-paced, exhausting, frustrating at times, but not stressful. Stressful is trying to get a screaming baby to sleep. I know how lucky I am to be in this situation. My friends stuck at home with young babies constantly tell me. 'It was pretty exciting, actually.'

He looks up at me, and I immediately regret my words. It sounded like a boast.

'Oh?'

'Oh, exciting to me, research stuff, you know. How about you? How's Riley?'

'I think she wanted to see you,' he says, cocking his head to one side. 'She was really grumpy at bedtime. God, I wish she could speak, you know, and actually tell us what's wrong. I feel sure she would come out with something really profound. Like "more milk, Daddy".'

'I feel bad,' I say, my voice small. 'Shall I pop in and see her now?'

'Her Royal Highness requests that she not be disturbed,' he says. 'As I said, she's just stopped grumbling.'

I sniff. He's right, of course, but I miss her.

'How was your day?' I ask.

He rubs his nose with his fingers. I notice the bottle of beer on the side table, half empty. I think about his half-hearted period of abstinence last year and then shake my head. He's allowed a drink at the end of a long day. I've got to stop being so controlling.

'It was good, yeah,' he says. 'We went to the common for a bit of fresh air, then stopped at the supermarket on the way back. This afternoon we did a lot of exercise on the baby gym.'

I laugh.

'Which common?' I ask, keeping my voice light.

'Oh, Tooting,' he says. 'It was a nice day. Just fancied stretching my legs.'

I think of the words I read this evening on Kim's Facebook page. A friend had left a comment on her profile picture.

Is it true you're back in Londinium for a bit, my love?

And her reply:

YES. Staying with some mates in Tooting. DRINK PLEASE?

'There's a lot of pollution on Tooting High Street,' I say. 'I'd rather you didn't walk her up there really.'

'Yeah, fair dos,' Robin replies, but he's flicking channels on the television, not really listening. He certainly doesn't seem anxious. Not like last year. Not like he has anything to hide.

I trust him. What happened was a one-off, in exceptional circumstances.

I need to stop looking at Kim's social media. It's just so hard. I'm trying my best. I've never known anyone to have quite so many friends, to be doing quite so much stuff, to be constantly the focus of everyone's attention. Why is she so popular?

'What's for dinner?' I ask, and Robin turns to me, smiling. It's his new thing: cooking. He's been making jokes about

121

being a natural housewife ever since we agreed he would be a stay-at-home dad. He even bought a pinny – thankfully, he has yet to wear it.

'I made a pasta bake.' He laughs, as though it's a culinary masterpiece. 'I'll just serve up. Now, what would you like to drink after your long day in the office? Gin? Or we've got a new bottle of white in the fridge?'

I frown. My head is throbbing a little, the threat of a headache lingering.

'No, I'll just have some juice, please.'

'Bore.'

He disappears through to the kitchen at the back of the flat, and I chastise myself again. He's so unselfish, so good at looking after me. Yes, he cheated on me but there were extenuating circumstances. And we've made the best of it, and he's trying so hard.

As I wait for Robin to bring our meals through, I check my WhatsApp messages for the day. I'm in a group with two of my university friends; we all became parents within a few months of one another. A little red number at the side of the group tells me that I have thirty-seven messages waiting for me. I tap on the group name to read them.

Oh my God, the 6-in-1 vaccine is evil! My poor bubba.

Oh poor Seb, did he not take it well?

Been screaming the house down since we got back from the doctors. And of course Jon's away for the rest of the week for work.

Oh Lordy, you poor thing.

Different time zone too. Can't even whinge to him on FaceTime.

Has Riley had her vax yet, Esther?

Yeah, she's a couple of weeks older than Seb, isn't she? Did she get a temperature?

I continue reading, my fingers hovering over the phone keypad, trying to decide what to write. The truth is, I don't know whether Riley has had her vaccination yet. I didn't even know she needed to have one.

Robin comes back into the room, carrying my drink and a bowl filled with pasta.

'Try not to enjoy it too much,' he says. 'It's one hundred per cent pure stodge.'

'Has Riley had her jabs yet?' I say, my iPhone still in my hand. 'Zoe and Fran were just saying . . .'

'Oh shit, yes. Didn't I tell you?' Robin replies. 'They're booked in for tomorrow. 10am. It's on the calendar.'

'Oh,' I say, my voice muted. 'I would have liked to come . . . apparently it's pretty nasty.'

'Come!' Robin says, settling down on the sofa. 'I'm sure Riley would love to have you there.'

'I can't,' I say, shaking my head and pushing my fork into the mound of steaming pasta. 'I literally just called a last-minute meeting with the social media team for the morning. I was quite insistent . . .' I shake my head again. 'Maybe I should cancel.'

Robin looks at me, his mouth full of penne.

'Tot,' he says as he chews. 'It doesn't matter. She won't remember who took her. And anyway, it's bloody horrible. Last time she screamed the place down. Not surprising, given the size of the needle they use. It'd make me scream the place down, and I've got a tattoo, don't you know.'

I smile.

'Still,' I say, looking down at my phone. 'I wish I could be there.' The screen is flashing with new messages from Zoe and Fran. They're now back on their favourite topic of conversation: bemoaning the fact that their partners have no idea how hard it is to be at home with a baby all day. It feels like a dig, even though I know they're both too sleep-addled to bother taking potshots at me.

They often tell me how lucky I am though.

It's amazing what Robin does. You're so lucky to have such a forward-thinking husband! I'd give anything to be able to go back to work and know my baby was being looked after by someone who loved them as much as me.

They're right, of course.

Lucky. That's what I am. That's what I have to remember.

ROBIN

Thank God.

Kim is back in Stratford with her dad. She texted me a selfie of her waving goodbye. Nothing suggestive about it – you could only see her face and hand in the photo – but I deleted it anyway, after wishing her a safe trip.

It's easier now she's not that nearby. Although we only met up once, she had started texting me during the day, asking how we were. It was making me nervous.

I meant it when I told Esther that I would never cheat on her again. Aside from the fact that nearly losing everything last year was the real wake-up call I needed, I'm too knackered.

No one tells you how much having a baby kills your sex drive. I constantly feel light-headed, as though I'm low on oxygen. Sugar and coffee are my main cravings these days, as my even softer stomach shows.

I've also lost enthusiasm for my work. It feels so utterly unimportant. Whenever I log on to Facebook I'm confronted by hundreds of invitations to friends' gigs, and friends-of-friends' gigs. The whole thing wears me out. It all feels pointless, irrelevant. Just a load of desperate egotists trying to prove their lives have worth. Nothing they do matters. Nothing is important.

Why can't people understand that looking after my daughter isn't a second choice to my job? It's my destiny.

What's that expression?

If you want to change the world, go home and love your family.

And I couldn't love Riley more. Sometimes, when I look at her, I feel like bursting into tears. That she's mine, that I get to keep her. It's so overwhelming, the love I have for her. It's like the way I felt about Sarah when we first met, but magnified and matured to the hundredth degree. I watch her as she sleeps, the way her fingers curl up tightly around her muslin cloth, which she won't sleep without. Sometimes she puts it over her face, as though she's trying to block the world out.

She's my daughter, all right.

I wonder if my dad even has the capacity in his pickled heart, the space in his full-of-crap brain, to understand what he missed when we were growing up. Too late now. Cry me a river, Dad. We're born malleable, and slowly, as we mature, our personalities solidify like cement, fixing themselves into these twisted, ugly shapes. And that's what's happened to him. It's impossible for him to ever change back.

That's why the early years are so important; they set the shape for the clay. Last week I had a crazy idea: perhaps I could retrain as a primary school teacher? Or maybe even a childminder? But people would probably be funny about leaving their babies and toddlers with a man. Depressing.

Just another way in which the male species lets the human race down.

I lay Riley in her cot. She's fine now, after a grouchy few days post-vaccinations. The nurse smiled as she saw me come in with her.

'No Mum today?' she said. Her tone was light enough but it was still irritating.

'No,' I said shortly. The nurse looked down, as though she'd said something terrible. Probably worried Riley's mother had died in childbirth or something. That's the depressing thing; people always assume there's been some kind of tragic accident, rather than imagining that actually, we have just decided to switch the parenting roles.

'She's gone back to work. I've taken paternity leave.' The nurse had smiled, reassured. It wasn't her fault, really. It was society that was to blame. If I wasn't so lazy, I'd try to do something about it.

In the living room, I find my phone. Nothing from Kim. Relief. But a missed call from Mike, my manager. I listen to the voicemail he left.

'Rob, it's Mike. Long time . . . so, I've had a spot come up at Edinburgh. The girl I had booked in has cancelled – gone into rehab. It's free Fringe, 8pm, so not great. Good venue though. It's yours if you want it. I remember you saying you might have some new stuff? So if you're brave enough . . . give me a call.'

I push my fingers into my eye sockets and rub. It's only lunchtime, too early for a beer. I find my record bag in the hall and rummage about in it, retrieving a forgotten, unwashed baby bottle, and find my notebook.

For the first six weeks of her life, I went to the bench with Riley every day that it didn't rain, sat by the river while she napped, and wrote, but it's been a while now. There must be pages of material in there. In the living room, I slump on to the sofa. I flick my hair out of my eyes, opening the notebook and thumbing through the pages of my scrawled handwriting.

My eye falls on one page in particular, the word at the top of it drawing my eye like a firework.

Esther.

My wife has been diagnosed with post-traumatic stress disorder. She had a complicated pregnancy, with severe morning sickness. So bad that she couldn't turn her head without vomiting. She pulled a muscle in her back, and it still bothers her today. Her skin peeled off in flakes, her eyeballs turned yellow. One vomiting session left her with a cracked rib. Every day of her pregnancy she thought she was going to die. At some points, I thought I might kill her to put her out of the pain she was in. I genuinely thought that might be the right thing to do.

Pause for sad reaction

But hey, what with all the puking, at least I finally defeated my arch-enemy: the washing machine. That thing is finally under my control.

HA FUCKING HA.

No wonder I never made it.

Comedy is truth, that's what they say. You have to make them laugh, but you also have to make them think. But Esther has been very secretive about her PTSD, and what happened with Riley. I know she wouldn't want me to talk about any of it. Private's her middle name.

I turn the page.

Kim.

Five foot nine. Hair that smells of coconut. Skin that smells of sweet vanilla, like a boiled lollipop that leaves a film stuck to your teeth, the kind that you regret before you even lick it. Lines under her breasts – silver, like slug trails. Perfectly symmetrical. Too firm, silicone. She's amazed you're surprised. Teeth that have been whitened, skin that's been darkened. The ability to find everything funny. Doesn't give a shit. But does she? Deep down?

Loved her mum. Finds her dad frustrating. But who else is in her life?

Nothing like Esther. Uniquely Kim. Rootless. Floats through life without getting attached. Drinks too much. What does she really want? What is she afraid of? What's she hiding?

As summaries go, it's not a bad one. But there's nothing funny about it, is there? I can't laugh at Kim. She's too much of an enigma.

After our walk on the common earlier in the week, we went to a cafe. Riley woke up, desperate for milk, her mouth opening and closing like a fish gulping at the surface. I fed her, and Kim shifted about in her seat as she watched us. My coffee got cold.

'Let me hold her while you drink that,' Kim said, looking down at it.

I felt myself holding Riley a little bit tighter. I had thought she would act differently . . . I had hoped she wouldn't be interested in Riley at all.

'Um,' I replied.

'Come on, hand her over,' she said. 'I haven't had a cuddle yet. I'm not going to drop her.'

I passed Riley over the top of the table and watched as Kim nestled her into her lap. There was an awkward silence that Kim filled with baby talk, tickling Riley under the chin and making her smile.

She was better at it than I expected. A natural, almost. I swallowed.

I'd never much believed in the power of genes, given my shitty relationship with my own parents, but there it was, right in front of me, slapping me around the face.

I sat back and watched them. Kim looked up at me and I saw it then, the unmistakable likeness between the two of them, caught in her expression. Those shared saucer-eyes. The neatness of their noses.

It would always be there. No matter what Esther told people. No matter how strong she thought she was being, taking on another woman's child. And not just any other woman's offspring, but a baby that was the product of her husband's infidelity.

It would always be there. Even if Kim had lost interest, as I'd assumed she would. Even if she did stay away and let us live as a family.

It would always be there: a bond no one could break.

Kim and Riley.

Mother and child.

NOW

ESTHER

Should I tell the police Riley is not my biological daughter? Would it make any difference?

As we drive away, I notice another police car pull up outside my house.

I look out of the window at the cold streets as they flash past in a blur. Again, I desperately want to tell DC Williams to drive me to where Robin was found in case Riley is somewhere nearby, rather than to the hospital. But DS Tyler seemed sure that I would want to go and see him, my poor injured husband, who's fighting for his life in A&E, and told me to leave searching for Riley to them.

Why would he have been in Epsom? I rack my brains, trying to think of something – anything, any connection he might have to that part of the country.

'Please,' I say, leaning forward from my seat in the back of the car. 'Please let me know as soon as you hear anything about Riley.'

DS Tyler turns and stares at me.

'Can you think of anywhere your husband might have taken

your daughter? Anyone he might have left her with? A friend or relation? Next-door neighbour?'

I shake my head.

'No,' I say, 'he . . . his family lives miles away. His brother and his wife moved out of London a few years ago. My neighbour Amanda had been watching her for a few hours earlier on, over lunchtime, but she said she dropped her off just before three.' I try to breathe slowly to combat the nausea but it doesn't help much, as I learnt during those life-changing weeks when I was pregnant. 'She's the only one he'd ever leave her with – we have daughters the same age. But Robin . . . he doesn't have any proper friends.'

She widens her eyes.

'Really,' I say. 'Riley is his whole life. He's been a stay-at-home dad since she was born.' I tail off. I can't start explaining the whole sorry situation to her. It's just a mess, a story that feels as though it has no beginning and no end. A catastrophe.

'A babysitter?'

I shake my head.

'He wouldn't . . . Look, he just wouldn't leave her alone. It doesn't make any sense. She's only two. He'd never leave her.'

There are so many thoughts ramming my brain, and I suddenly feel utterly exhausted. The stress of the last few weeks – the secret talks with my solicitor, Jeremy; the endless paperwork; the legal dead ends; the thought of it going to court; and, finally, the deadening realisation that there was probably only one way to remain in Riley's life, and it might as well have been a life sentence.

But what will happen now? And Riley. Where is she?

I find myself sobbing hysterically in the back seat, the fat tears hurtling out of me, making me choke on my own breath. I bury my face in my hands. *Riley, please God, whatever happens, please let her be OK.*

'Is there no one else you can think of?' DS Tyler says, her voice loud enough to cut through my crying.

I need Jeremy here, with me. Someone to make sense of it all, to unpick all the threads and lay them straight, and make sure I don't tie myself up in them.

I'm selfish, thinking of myself. But it's only because of her. My baby girl.

'No one he might have left her with?' DS Tyler repeats.

I shake my head at the policewoman.

I check my phone. Nothing. No messages. Nothing from anyone. If only Riley was old enough to have a phone of her own, some way I could track her whereabouts.

'Can you think of anyone who might want to harm your husband?' DS Tyler asks, and I look back at her in surprise. Surprise that she hasn't asked this before.

'I . . .' I say.

I begin to cry again.

Kim?

Could she . . .

'I don't know,' I say, shaking my head. Words are fighting in my mind, desperate to escape. I want to scream that I don't give a shit about Robin, that I was planning on leaving him anyway. That it's worse than that – that I hate him. That I'll be glad if he dies.

'I'm so sorry, I wish I could be more helpful. But I just don't know.'

ONE YEAR EARLIER

ESTHER

Jo, the photographer, takes another burst of shots then smiles up at me from above her camera.

'Brilliant,' she says. 'I think we have all we need.'

'Can I see some of the pictures?' I ask, tentatively. Jo motions for me to come over to her laptop, set up on a stool near the tripod, and flicks through a few on the screen.

'Wow,' I say. 'You've made me look like a totally different person.'

'Hope not,' says Jo. 'That would rather defeat the point.'

I smile at her.

'Sorry, you know what I mean. I look like me, but better. Me when I've had eight hours' sleep.'

'Then I've done my job,' Jo says, beaming. 'It's a big promotion, right? Communications Director. You need to look the part.'

'You can't even see my eye bags.'

'Good lighting, eh? Works miracles. But anyway, you don't have eye bags.'

I snort.

'Thanks, you're very kind, but my daughter has taken to waking up at 5am recently . . .'

'How old is she?' Jo asks, closing the lid of her laptop.

'Sixteen months,' I reply. 'It's exhausting. My husband's looking after her today . . . I feel terrible for him, we're both shattered.'

'No childcare?' she asks.

'No,' I reply. 'Rob's a stay-at-home dad.'

Her eyes widen. It's always the same when I tell people – one of two reactions. Surprise tinged with interest or badly concealed disapproval. I wonder if this is what my dad always had to deal with. But it was probably different for him – people would have been more sympathetic because my mother was dead. He didn't have a choice.

I launch into my usual speech.

'His own father wasn't around much when he was a kid, and I think he's trying to make up for it . . .' I feel a stab of disloyalty. 'But he's brilliant with her. Much better than me.'

'That's amazing,' Jo says, but I'm not sure she means it. 'I've got two kids – my husband barely changed a nappy when they were younger. Not that he wasn't a good dad, it's just with me being freelance, having the more flexible job, it made sense for me to look after them.'

'Yes,' I reply. 'My husband's self-employed too.'

'Oh interesting,' she says, and she pauses, computer cable in hand, to look at me. 'What does he do?'

'He's . . . a writer,' I reply, swallowing. I wish I hadn't brought Robin up now.

'Journalist?'

'No, creative . . . he's . . . he writes comedy . . .'

She smiles.

'Oh wow, anything I might have heard of?'

I shake my head, burning with humiliation on Robin's behalf. Remembering all the work he did for the Edinburgh Festival last year, the way his so-called manager replaced him with someone more famous two weeks before he was due to go up.

'It's a competitive world,' I say, lamely. 'He's working on a sitcom at the moment. But still trying to break out, I suppose.'

'Guess it's a good job you're so successful then. Well done you.'

She's joking, making small talk, entirely oblivious to the fact she has identified my sorest spot and ground the toe of her shoe into it. It has started to become a problem. My success; his lack of it. A little crack in our relationship that's slowly turning into a chasm.

I think of Rob's reaction when I told him I'd been promoted.

The smile he slapped across his unshaven face, the way it didn't reach his eyes. The bottle of champagne he bought me with money from the joint account, that he left on the kitchen table instead of putting in the fridge, so it was too warm to drink.

I leave work after the shoot, wondering whether to text Robin to tell him I'm on my way or not. I try to keep him informed of my whereabouts, but he never seems to check his phone, and sometimes I wonder why I bother. When I get home it's as though he takes perverse pleasure in telling me how busy

141

he is, and how little time he has to read his messages or send me a reply.

Too busy to chase Kim too, apparently. Sixteen months on and the adoption still isn't finalised, despite her promises.

On the Northern line, I look at my personal emails. I've got one from Dad's solicitor. The sale of his bungalow went through last month, and finally the probate is sorted. It's taken over a year, and I can't quite believe it's all done. Nothing more for me to sort out, no more trips up north to arrange house clearances and speak to estate agents and investigate auction houses. Soon I will be a rich woman, the sole benefactor of my dad's estate, worth just under half a million pounds.

I haven't told Robin exactly how much money I'm going to inherit. I don't know why. We're married, and we used to share everything. But he hasn't asked, and there's an uncomfortable lump in my throat whenever we have to discuss money these days. As I'm the only one with an income, almost all my money goes straight into our joint account to pay the bills, which Robin uses too. He's pretty frugal, but he still smokes from time to time, which annoys me.

It's a relief to know that I won't have to worry about money for a while. With my dad's money, and my promotion, we'll be able to relax a bit.

Things have been so tight ever since last year. All of my savings, gone in an instant. But of course I didn't think anything of it at the time. I was so desperate.

Perhaps we could even afford some childcare, give Robin some real time to get back to his writing. He says he can do bits when Riley naps, but it's not the same. It's not a commitment to his work, and I'm worried he'll get so left behind that he can never get back to it.

I walk slowly to the flat, passing the petrol station opposite. I've missed Riley's bedtime again, and I feel a strange, sudden melancholy. It catches me at the most unexpected moments and I wonder if all mothers are this sentimental, or if there's something wrong with me?

But there was no getting out of the photoshoot. My photo and new job title will be up on the website next week; the firm might even put out a press release about me. Communications Director for the UK's largest diabetes charity. Finally, I'm on the executive board. I can't quite believe it.

I push the key into the lock and open our front door. The flat feels dark and cramped, and the usual mess greets me as I enter. But something is different; Riley is awake. Not just awake, but crying. I dump my handbag on the floor and rush through to her tiny bedroom.

Robin is holding her tightly, but she's wailing in his ear.

'What's happened?' I say, checking her for any visible sign of injury.

'Nothing,' he replies, shortly. 'Overtired, I think. She just wanted you . . . I explained that you were working but . . .'

'Mama, Mama!' Riley screams and flings herself towards me. Robin hands her over awkwardly and she buries her face in my neck. Far from lessening, her cries seem to be increasing.

'Shh, shh, it's OK,' I say, stroking her messy blonde hair. 'Oh sweetie, it's OK, Mummy's here.'

Is it my imagination, or does Robin give a snort? He turns to leave the room.

'The dinner's burning,' he mutters as he retreats.

I manage to calm Riley by reading her two stories while she's sitting on my lap. I'm still wearing my coat, but she won't let me put her down. Eventually, she settles in her cot as I lie down on the floor beside her. I'm desperate for the toilet, but I stay next to her, our eyes locked together, wishing I could get a message to Robin to go ahead and eat his dinner. It must be nearly 9pm by the time she falls into a deep enough sleep for me to tiptoe out of the room. I leave the door ajar, and join Robin in the kitchen.

He's standing by the hob stirring something, a dark frown on his face.

'It's ruined now,' he says. 'Shit. Why did I think it would be a good idea to do risotto? Typical. It's like she knew!'

I glance down into the saucepan. The rice has congealed into a single lump that looks like dough.

'Is that fennel?' I say, impressed.

'Yes,' he replies. 'Ottolenghi recipe. I know how you like his stuff. I was trying to do something nice for you.'

It's unlike him not to make a joke out of the situation – it must mean he's really upset. I put my arms around him, leaning in. It's been a while since we've been physical like this.

I'm trying, I really am. I made a commitment, a promise that I am determined to stick to. I know he's been pestering Kim, that it's not his fault that she's so evasive. He wraps an arm around my waist and pulls me in closer.

'What was up with Riley?' I say.

Robin pushes the wooden spoon into the lump of congealed rice and lets go. It stands up straight, as though positioned in Play Doh.

'I don't know,' he says. 'Just separation anxiety, I guess. She misses you.'

I miss her too.

I feel my body stiffen and I pull away, reaching above Robin's shoulder for a glass. Wine will help.

'Things will calm down again soon. Perhaps she doesn't get enough stimulation? Just being here at home with you?'

'What?' Robin says, and any warm intimacy between us immediately cools.

'I mean . . . I just mean, if she was at nursery, maybe even one or two mornings a week, it'd . . .'

'She's too young! And anyway,' he replies, 'we can't afford it.'

I pause, thinking of my father's money, that could pay for her to go to the most exclusive nursery in Wimbledon, plus private school beyond. But for some reason I don't want to tell Robin about it. Not when he's in this mood. He's already emasculated enough by our situation; this would push him over the edge.

'I suppose,' I say.

I am a coward. It's my newest favourite position – head in the sand. There are so many things niggling at the back of my mind, not least of all the adoption.

'Anyway, she's not alone with me all day,' he says. 'We do go out, you know. I don't cage her up the second you leave for the office and spend the day sitting in my pyjamas in front of the television.'

I flinch at his words.

'Yes,' I say, feeling my temper rise. 'I know. And it's great. I just thought, maybe a more formal setting, where she might learn . . .'

'She's too young,' he snaps. 'It's best for children up to the age of two to be looked after by a single primary carer.'

I hold his gaze as he stares at me. His eyes are bloodshot, and I can't tell if it's from the large glass of red that sits by the hob, the cigarettes he half-heartedly leans out of the window for, the long-term tiredness that permeates our very bones, or whether he's actually been crying.

A single primary carer.

That's all he thinks Riley needs. His way of telling me what I already know, that I'm superfluous in this relationship. That he can do it all without me.

I narrow my eyes. That's what he proved to me when he got Kim pregnant, and whether he means to or not, in a million tiny ways he's been reminding me of it ever since.

ROBIN

I thought the risotto would work. Glass of wine, nice dinner, get her to open up. I'm tired of her hiding things, of us slipping back to the way we were. But I messed up the dinner. Typical. And as usual, she's clammed up inside herself.

Why won't she let me in? Why does she *still* push me away when she needs me most?

Sometimes I wonder if I chose the wrong woman. But it's an idle thought. Ridiculous. Of course, I didn't have a choice at all.

When Kim told me about her pregnancy, she was a wreck. Even though she never actually said it, I genuinely thought she might have an abortion. Surely fate couldn't be that cruel twice over? She was torn; I was terrified. It took some persuading – and I'll admit, some intense emotional blackmail on my part – to convince her to let us take the baby on.

I haven't seen Kim since that day on the common, more than a year ago, when I looked into her eyes and realised that, as long as she was alive, she could never truly hand her baby over. It made me uncomfortable. Like the air in the room was suddenly too hot.

Nothing has worked out as I'd hoped. And now, she won't

leave me alone. She's far too involved with Riley. The messages aren't daily, but at least weekly. Little check-ups, seeing how we're doing, requests for pictures.

It won't be long before she asks for Riley back, and then what do I do?

Why can't she just leave us alone?

I swallow, push the sleeves of my jumper up my arms. Even my wrists are sweaty.

Esther's eyeing me, a perfect poker face. We're like boxers in the ring, trying to work out who will make the first move.

I stare at her, covered in thick make-up from the photo-shoot she did earlier. It doesn't suit her. Make-up suits Kim, it suits her persona, the character she always plays. But Esther is just Esther, and the make-up makes it look like she's trying on someone else's face.

'I'm tired,' she says. 'Long day. Long week.'

Same old excuse every time.

'Sure,' I say, flicking my eyes towards the pan of burnt risotto. Still hiding things. Still doesn't trust me. 'Domino's?'

She sniffs. 'Fine. I'll go and wash this off.' She points to her face and heads towards the bathroom, pausing with her hand on the door handle.

'You know I'll always be there for you, don't you?' I say. It's not exactly a reassurance. 'If there's anything . . . anything on your mind.'

She gives a half-hearted smile. Nope, she's still not going to do it.

'Yes, Bird. I know.'

*

Later, after we've eaten our pizzas, we sit on the sofa together in front of the television, watching the comedy roadshow programme as usual. Esther at one end, laptop on her lap, me at the other. I am trying to ignore the anger that's bubbling away inside. I wish she'd put the computer down and just talk to me. Or even look at me.

'Work busy?' I say, turning off the television just as Jay Martin is about to make his biggest gag. I've heard his set a hundred times before, analysed it to death. His popularity and success astound me. So MOR, so pedestrian, but the brainless idiots in the audience lap it up. I press the button on the remote control so hard that my fingertip hurts: perverse, pathetic satisfaction in cutting him off just before his big delivery.

Esther looks up.

'What?' she says. 'Oh. No, I was . . . nothing. Doesn't matter.' She shuts the lid of the laptop. 'Sorry.'

'It's fine,' I say magnanimously, although my hands are twitching. 'If you have to work, you have to work.'

The edge to my voice gets her attention.

'No, it was nothing,' she says, looking at the television. 'Sorry, was it funny? He was getting rather hysterical.'

'No,' I say. 'It was crap. I'm much funnier. Talk to me instead.'

She looks nervous as I reach out and stroke her on the leg. I swallow.

Talk to me!

'I'm sorry,' she replies. 'It's just . . .'

'Yeah, I know,' I reply. 'Too important to talk to your

149

husband. Work, work, work. You know, you could spend a bit more time with us. With . . . me.'

'Jesus, Rob!' she shouts, suddenly springing up off the sofa. 'What do you expect me to do? We can't both be out of work! You know it's important to me, that we're not struggling. You know how hard it was for me growing up, my dad not earning enough. We need the money!'

I frown at her. Her explosion has come out of nowhere, and I don't like it. So we've both been sitting here, simmering away, have we? My own anger rises. She's left me with no choice.

'But that's not true, is it, Esther?' I say, and my heart is pounding.

Fuck you, Esther. Fuck you and your lies and your deceit and your pretending to love me when you're just like all the others, you're just like her. What a disappointment you are, you treacherous wage slave.

'Because your dad's money has come through . . .' I stand up and walk to the bookcase, picking up the letter that arrived that morning and handing it to her.

'Before you say anything, Riley opened it. From your solicitor. Five hundred thousand pounds of your dad's money, coming our way. Further to your email correspondence . . . so when exactly, when exactly, were you going to tell me about it?'

ESTHER

I stare at my husband, hunting for a memory, a time when things felt right. How can things between us have changed so quickly and so completely? And now we're trapped in this situation. Like we've climbed on a rollercoaster and want to change our minds and get off, but we can't. We're strapped in until the end. Hold on tight for the ride of your life!

I want to shout but as usual I don't have the energy for the fight. I don't have the confidence you need, the utter belief that my side of things is right.

I can't trust myself. I lost that trust the day I sent that email, and I can't get it back, no matter what I do.

I miss Viv. I think about what she said when I told her our plan to take on Kim's baby: 'Jesus, there's making lemonade out of lemons and then there's you two. Are you serious? Is it even legal?'

But what could I do? Kim was going to get rid of the baby. *Robin's* baby. He was the father, after all. And I was so desperate, after everything I went through. What choice did I have?

'I . . .' I say.

'Come on.' His voice is almost a snarl. 'I can't wait to hear it. The excuse . . . sorry, I mean "reasons", to explain why you decided to hide this from me. I'm your *husband*.'

He never used to be like this. Not this . . . nasty.

I try to hold his gaze but the intensity in his eyes is too much for me. He exhausts me. He asks too much of me. He needs too much of me. I still love him, or at least I love the water-stain memory of how he used to be, but I can't cope with the reality, of our life as it is today.

'I just . . .' I say, looking away. One of Riley's socks is lying on the floor beside me and I reach down and pick it up, smoothing it flat between my hands. 'I haven't *hidden* it from you.'

'You didn't even tell me you'd found a buyer for the bungalow!'

'I know . . . I just . . . I just didn't want to think about it. The money. What it meant. My dad . . .'

I start to cry.

'My dad's money . . .' I say, letting the tears fall. If only he could accept what the tears really mean, without being offended. Leave me alone, give me some space. 'I only have it because he's dead. He's gone. I still can't . . . I can't believe I never got to say goodbye. I'm so angry. I'm so furious! If only you'd let me . . .'

I stop. That's not fair.

'The house . . . where they found him . . . everything it means . . . I find it hard to talk to you, because I know you don't see eye to eye with your dad, and I didn't want to rub it in . . . that I loved him, I loved him so much but . . .'

Rob walks towards me and wraps me in his arms. I try to

152

relax, but my body won't do as it's told and I'm as stiff as a board.

'I'm sorry, Esther,' he says, smoothing his hands over my hair. 'Why didn't you tell me? For God's sake, I'm your husband, I love you more than anyone. I'm here for you. You don't need to put me first; you don't need to protect me from . . . from my feelings about my own bloody father! For fuck's sake. I'm here for you. Why didn't you tell me you were so upset? I just want to help you.'

He pulls away and cups my face in his hands, lifting it up so that I'm staring straight at him. He used to do this a lot, this possessive gesture, right before he kissed me. It made me feel chosen, special, cared for. It turned me on, how small and delicate he made me feel. But this time his hands feel thick and heavy around my jawline. He's so much bigger than me. He could wrench my head clean off.

I hold his gaze. He's never been violent. I'm just tired. I'm so tired and sad and fed up of my own mind. My own self-flagellation, the streams of nonsense that rampage around my brain on endless loops.

I have everything I ever wanted. Why can't I just be happy?

'You need to trust me again, Tot,' he says. I am grateful, briefly, that he hasn't kissed me, that for once we haven't fallen back into our old ways, covered up the cracks. The lust I used to feel for him in this situation seems to have dissipated completely. Instead I feel uncomfortable, like his behaviour is inappropriate. 'Look what happened last time you tried to hide how you were feeling. Look where that got us.'

'I'm sorry,' I say, and with difficulty I reach my arm up

to tuck his thick curly hair behind his ears. 'It's just the money . . . it's difficult.'

I swallow. He's still staring at me, pinning me with his eyes.

'What about the money?' he says. His voice is gentle. He's not angry now. He's sad.

'It's . . . emasculating,' I say, the word almost a whisper.

Rob gazes at me, his eyes popping, and then he clutches my face harder, jerking my head upwards so that it hurts. Then he laughs.

'Oh my God,' he says, throwing back his head. 'Oh, my darling girl. Oh that's good . . . that's really good.'

I frown and he lets go of my face. My fingers find my jawline, rubbing it where it aches.

'It's not funny.'

He's still laughing.

'Oh, Tot . . . Oh, I love you.'

He shakes his head from side to side, gazing at me as though I'm some kind of alien creature.

'Rob,' I say. 'It's not funny.'

'You're right,' he says, pursing his lips together. 'It's not funny at all.'

I can't say anything. I can't point out that I know how much his lack of income is affecting his self-esteem. Despite this . . . show. Despite everything he says.

Time and time again I tell myself that if Robin was a woman, no one would bat an eyelid at his decision to give up work and look after Riley. But without his career, I find it hard to see the shape of him.

When we first met, his work was everything to him. He

was brilliant on stage, transforming into something else, larger than life, a firework of energy fizzing and popping and lighting up the whole room. I understood why he had to drink so much after a show, why his comedown involved staying up late and smoking until all the adrenalin had left his body. People constantly told me how hilarious he was, how surely his own roadshow was just around the corner? Even Vivienne admitted he was good at what he did.

'Your work,' I say. 'It was everything to you. What about your sitcom? You haven't done anything on it for ages.'

I look down. I'm a coward. I've left the important things unsaid. The real reason I miss him working: because it gave me space. It allowed me to breathe. It meant I didn't have to be everything to him, all the time.

His jaw hardens.

'My work isn't going anywhere,' he says. 'There are other things at the moment that are more important. Like being your husband. Like being Riley's father. The real stuff. The important stuff.'

'I know,' I say. 'But . . . you can't . . . you need something for yourself, too. Something . . . else.'

He frowns at me.

'I'm fine,' he says. 'Let me worry about what I need.'

I look away. It feels like he's closed the door on this conversation. And I still haven't brought up Kim.

ROBIN

I lie in our bed, staring at the ceiling. There are three cracks that run across it. They've been there since we bought the place; I have stared at them nightly. I suppose a more responsible man would have investigated by now – some problem with the ceiling itself, or the joists above? Or just the inevitable movement of an old building? Who knows?

Esther is taking ages in the bathroom. It's gone 11pm, and Riley will be awake at 5.30am for the day, if we're lucky. How could I have continued my career on that timetable anyway? I would have been going to bed when Riley was waking up. We would all have been absolutely exhausted.

Where is she?

I roll over on to my side, staring at the alarm clock. Thinking about what Esther said. *Emasculating.* Is that how she sees me? As some poor pathetic bloke who's had his balls cut off just because his wife brings home all the money? I thought she was more intelligent than that. I thought she understood me.

I feel my fists tighten with anger that the world still sees fathers who look after their kids as failing somehow. I read a report in the paper last week that said take-up of shared parental leave had been as low as two per cent. All those men out there, still measuring their success by the size of their pay packets, not the size of their hearts.

I'm ashamed of my gender.

I'm ashamed of her too. Esther.

I'm doing a good job! I'm a good dad. I might have failed at everything else, but I'm not going to fail at fatherhood.

At least now it's out in the open. Her father's money means we can move house, get somewhere bigger. I've never been particularly interested in interior design, but this place has started to feel claustrophobic. Riley's bedroom is little more than a cupboard, really, and she accumulates more stuff by the day.

I roll over again. The pillow feels too hot, so I flip it, but it's just as hot on the other side too.

Where is she?

I know what she's really angry about, of course. It's Kim. The adoption. Esther won't admit it, but that's what's causing all this; the secrecy, the increasing sense of distance between us. It's like a festering sore, eating away at our relationship, growing bigger every day.

But I don't know how to fix it. It's not something I can fix. Not easily.

I sit up, pushing the duvet away and swinging my legs out of bed. Then I pace through the hall barefoot, my toe catching on one of the nails we missed when we pulled up the old carpet, sending a spike of pain through the skin of my foot. That's another thing. These floorboards. Not exactly child-friendly.

It's not hard to work out where Esther's gone. Riley's

bedroom door is ajar, the pink warmth of her rabbit night-light throwing a shadow on the floor outside.

I creep slowly up to it, carefully avoiding the floorboards that squeak. A ninja move, much perfected ever since Riley came home with us and the horror of waking her up consumed our every moment.

I peer round the door, but all I can see are Esther's socked feet, drawn up against her legs. She's sitting beside Riley's cot, arms wrapped round herself.

I strain to listen.

At first, I think she's praying and my eyes widen. But then I realise she's singing, ever so softly.

No need to run and hide

It's a wonderful, wonderful life . . .

I struggle at first to place the song, but then I remember it. Eighties jazz-pop. Obscure.

I linger for a few seconds, listening, wondering whether or not to interrupt. But I know she won't appreciate it, that this is a private moment between her and Riley.

That she's trying to convince herself, and Riley, that everything's fine.

Signature Esther. Her only way of coping; push the bad feelings away.

ESTHER

Thankfully, considering I have only had about two hours' sleep, I have no meetings this morning. Instead, I am seeing my therapist, Claudia.

I like Claudia, even though she's intimidatingly posh and I find it hard to believe she could ever empathise with the unconventional mess that is my life. She's softly spoken, with short, dark hair and sharp eyes.

I have been seeing her every week since before Riley was born. Sometimes I have dreams that she's killed by another of her clients, and I have no one to turn to. I haven't told her about that though. I don't want her to realise quite how dependent I am.

Robin knows nothing about her. He'd be offended that I need someone else to talk to and take it as another sign of me not trusting him enough, not sharing enough with him.

Her practice is in Battersea, a few streets back from the river. I arrive with time to spare and pace the street outside, trying to work out what I will say to her today. Whether today will be 'the' day. When I finally let it all out. I know it's what she wants, what she's been working towards. She thinks afterwards that I'll feel stronger. That I'll be able to tackle Kim myself.

Up until now I've been completely unable to talk about what happened to me. But last night has made me realise I can't go on like this. My mind is like a pressure cooker: waiting to explode.

As I stride up and down the tree-lined street, I pass a man smoking a cigarette. A real one, not a vape. The smell hangs in the morning air, and takes me back to the time I cracked my rib. Just outside the hospital. Someone was leaning against a lamppost, several metres away, chatting on their phone and sucking away on their cigarette. It was usually food that made me retch, but the strength of the smoke seemed so overwhelming that it turned my stomach over anyway, and I leant across the pavement and was sick in the road.

The pain when I tried to breathe afterwards was unlike anything I had ever experienced. I fell to my knees, the tears streaming down my face, and briefly caught the smoker's eye. Her lips curled in disgust, and it took the little strength I had left not to throw myself in front of the next bus that came by.

My side still aches at the memory. No matter how many times I explain it to him, Robin will never understand what it was like for me. How desperate I felt, how I got to that place.

Inside the clinic, Claudia smiles and offers me a glass of water as she always does. I take my seat opposite her in the bay window that overlooks the busy residential street. She coughs.

'Excuse me,' she says, and I realise she's sucking on a sweet. 'I've got a bit of a tickle. Nothing serious.'

'I want to talk about the day it happened,' I say, abruptly.

'I just think . . . maybe if I get it all out . . . it will help. Sorry, I interrupted you.'

She smiles.

'Not at all,' she says. Her voice is mesmeric, a little croak at the end. 'Please.'

'The night before I lost my baby, I slept well for the first time in weeks,' I say. My own voice is hesitant, so I continue speaking. I'm desperate to empty all the thoughts from my head. 'I wonder if it was because I had done something – sent that email to the clinic. Given myself something to cling on to. A sense of hope. A sense of an ending.' I sniff, reach for a tissue. 'It's all ironic, isn't it? Maybe I already knew? Maybe my body was trying to tell me something.'

Claudia nods.

'I woke up and I still felt sick – of course. I had no energy at all. But I managed to keep an ice cube down. I managed to get to the bathroom, to wash my face and brush my teeth. I had to do it all really slowly; every movement was like a tiny test and if I pushed it too far, then I'd be sick again. I pulled my pants down, sat on the toilet . . . I never expected to see the blood.'

'Robin was out. He'd left about half an hour before. He was helping his brother move house . . . they'd escaped to the country, got a big place in Hampshire near Robin's parents. Before he left I told him it was fine – that I was fine. And it was easier without him there, most of the time. I couldn't stand having him see me in that state. It was humiliating. And most of all . . .'

I take a deep breath.

'Most of all I worried that he'd go off me. I felt so revolting . . .

and then there had been the incident on New Year's Eve, when he had kissed . . . her. I was so scared he'd leave me.'

I rub away the tears with the tissue, pushing forcefully against my skin.

'Which makes no sense, because he's always telling me he'll never leave me, how much he loves me. But if that were true, how could he have cheated on me? Sometimes, I think he's in love with the idea of me, or the me he wants me to be. I should have rung him,' I say. 'I know that now . . . if I had . . . then who knows. But I didn't. I phoned the midwife instead, and she told me to go to the early pregnancy unit for a scan. I should have rung him then. That's what . . . that's why he's still so angry with me, I think. He can't stand the fact that I didn't let him know what was happening.'

'No one knows how they will react in these situations,' Claudia says, her words like balm. 'You did what you had to do.'

'I was a coward. I knew I couldn't cope with his feelings as well as my own. I knew if I told him I was bleeding, there'd be all kinds of . . . I don't know. His *emotions*, to deal with. We'd fought the night before, when I mentioned that I couldn't go on, that the pregnancy was killing me . . . Sometimes, his emotions are so big it feels like they swallow me up. And I was confused myself, because I'd been praying for it to end, and now there was a chance it might be . . .'

Claudia's head is tilted. I watch her swallow, wonder briefly if she's fighting the urge to cough.

'At the unit they saw me straight away. I'll never forget the way the sonographer looked at me.'

I pause, take another deep breath.

'She asked me if there was any possibility I had got my dates wrong. I remember staring at her, confused, wondering why that mattered. Then she said it. She couldn't find a heartbeat. That they'd expect one by ten weeks but that there was nothing there. *Just an empty sac. No fetal pole. I'm sorry to tell you that you are having a miscarriage.* And then – I remember this bit most of all – I realised that I hadn't been sick since I left home. I was still queasy, of course, but I hadn't actually been sick since I got to the hospital. I had made it to the hospital – we only live ten minutes' walk away – got into the lift, sat in the waiting room with all the various smells, plastic bags at the ready . . . and none of it had made me sick. And that's when I realised that I'd done it. It was my fault. I had wished my own baby away. I'd . . .' I gasp, letting out a huge sob. 'Killed her. By wishing she wasn't there.'

'It's natural that you should blame yourself, but you know that it's not possible that your feelings about your pregnancy and your suffering are in any way related to what happened.'

'But how do you know that for sure?' I say, staring at her. I'm suddenly angry, with everyone, and everything. 'Everyone told me that hyperemesis in pregnancy is a sure sign that the baby, at least, is developing well. That it meant the baby was strong, healthy. So how come I beat the odds? How come I got HG and then had a miscarriage – what are the chances of that? One in a million. Mind over matter. Of course it was my fault. Our brains control everything . . . all of us.'

'But with something like this . . .' Claudia says, her gentle voice back, her arm reaching forward to comfort me, to make me feel better, to try to assuage my pain.

I am furious.

'No! No, no, no! You don't understand! The night before . . . I sent an email to an *abortion* clinic. Just an enquiry. I told them I was desperate, that the HG was killing me, that I wanted to die. I wanted to know if other . . . if other women in my situation had considered it. I don't know if I would have been able to go through with it, but the thought was there. And that was enough. I put my intentions out there into the world, and the world answered me. I got what I wanted. I got what I deserved. I took that medication, despite the doctor's warning that there were side effects, that it might harm the baby. I did it because I was weak and selfish, because the sickness felt never-ending, because I felt like I wanted to die. This is why I didn't want to talk about it before. I don't want you to talk me out of my guilt, or persuade me that it's not my fault. It *is* my fault. I deserve what happened to me, what Robin did. I failed my baby on the most basic level. It's the most fundamental part of motherhood – to protect your children – and I was too weak, too . . . pathetic to do it.'

I stare at her, my face burning.

'The night before, when I reached rock bottom, for the five minutes it took me to send that email, I thought I wanted to get rid of my baby. And instead my baby got rid of me.'

ROBIN

I haven't seen Stu for more than three years, but needs must. I'm not going to have Esther pity me. She's right, I *have* taken my focus off my work, ever since Mike messed me around with the Edinburgh Festival slot. But my sitcom is in pretty good shape, so perhaps there's still hope.

Stu has upgraded since I last saw him. Shiny new girlfriend who works in development, shiny new flat on Chiswick High Road, overlooking a bus stop, right in the middle of the action, just a few short strolls to Turnham Green station.

'This place must cost a fortune,' I say, staring round at the huge open-plan kitchen-living area.

'Verity's parents bought it for her,' he says, leaning back on the battered leather sofa in front of the window, without a hint of shame.

I take a swig of my beer.

'I'll have to meet her one day,' I say.

Stu nods.

'Yeah, maybe. She's tight with Sarah,' he says, eventually. 'They worked together on the Sky Atlantic show last year.'

'Right,' I say, squeezing the beer bottle between my fingers.

165

'Anyway . . . did you have a chance to read my pilot episode? I know it's been ages, man, but . . . as you can see, I've been a bit busy . . .'

I gesture towards Riley, who's sitting on the rug by the glass coffee table, pulling everything off it.

'Yeah, sure,' Stu says, leaning forward. He doesn't smile at Riley and I feel my insides tighten. 'It's a great piece. Really. Funny, chaotic, charming . . . all your signature moves.'

I bite my lip. It's been so long since anyone said anything kind about my writing, and I allow myself a few seconds to enjoy the feeling of appreciation.

'Well,' I say. 'Written from the heart, you know.' I suddenly feel embarrassed, shy. 'So do you think you'd know anyone who might be interested? It's just, man, it's fucking hard to get back in . . . as you know. It's hard enough when you're starting out, but at my age, and after I've . . .'

'Yeah,' Stu says, not meeting my eye. 'Listen, I think it's great. I really do. But . . .'

I stare at him. He gives me a patronising smile.

'I know it's water under the bridge, mate, but . . .' Stu says. 'It's just . . . she's put in a few favours for me over the years, you know? I don't want to piss her off.'

'But I thought you said it was great?'

'It is!' he says, hands in the air as though in defence. 'I'm sure someone will snap it up. Seriously. Just go the normal route – submit to agents, that kind of thing. You don't need me.'

He knows I need him. I need someone. I need some kind of leg-up.

166

This fucking industry. Everyone sucking up to the people they think will get them the furthest.

I stay just long enough to finish my beer and then make my excuses and leave. People and their long memories! And as if Sarah would really care about me and my measly sitcom anyway. She's far too busy being rich and famous to worry about what her inadequate ex-boyfriend is doing.

Esther doesn't see this. Doesn't see all the times I've tried to get back in. Doesn't realise it's not like a normal career, where you send your CV off and if you're good enough, with the right experience, you get the job.

My phone vibrates in my pocket. I pull it out, expecting it to be Esther. But it's not. It's Kim.

That's all I need.

'Hello?' I say, pushing Riley's buggy back towards the station with my free hand.

'Mate!' Her voice rings out, overly enthusiastic and loud. I find myself frowning. 'You picked up! Miracle. I'm back! How are you? How's the little lady?'

'Generally, she's still pretty angry with the world and with not being able to coherently articulate her feelings about life,' I reply. 'How are you?'

'Yeah, I'm . . . all right,' she replies. She sounds slightly out of breath, as though she's been running shortly before phoning me. 'As well as can be expected. What you up to? Want to meet for a drink?'

'I . . .' I say, looking down at Riley. 'When?'

'Now? Where are you? I'm in town. Just by Victoria. I can come and meet you?'

'Um,' I say. I've avoided her for more than a year now. Maybe it's for the best if I see her again. Perhaps she's changed her mind. Perhaps she has news.

'OK. I can be in Victoria in half an hour,' I say. 'I'll see you there.'

We meet in a cafe just behind the station. Riley has woken up by the time we get there, and happily destroys a cheese sandwich as I drink a strong coffee. Kim looks tired, as though someone has taken her Instagram filter off. Her eyes are wide, as usual, but they're bloodshot. And something else. She seems slightly manic, telling me all about her latest unsuitable suitor.

It hasn't worked out with him. I was hoping it might have done, that she'd be too distracted to keep bothering us.

'He was an arsehole,' she is saying, seemingly oblivious to Riley's presence. 'It's the oldest story in the book, you know. Told me he loved me, told me he'd do anything for me, but as soon as I told him about . . . you know – this, my situation – he was off. But honestly, I thought we had a connection, that he really understood me.'

I swallow. Riley squirms in my arms and the jacket potato in front of me begins to congeal.

'Give her to me,' she says.

I pass Riley over to her, remembering how awful it felt last time this happened. Everything is unravelling. Nothing is working out as it was meant to.

'Does it feel strange?' I say, suddenly, the words seemingly making their way out of my mouth of their own accord. 'Holding her?'

Kim sniffs, glancing up at me. It's not like me to be serious; she's confused. Her eyes are sharp, like pins prickling my face.

'Of course not,' she replies, but I know she's lying. 'That's DNA, I guess. Nothing more powerful than biology. Even if you are the ones doing the parenting at the moment, while I sort my life out. Which I do appreciate. I really do. I'm getting there.' She turns and addresses Riley in a baby voice that curdles my stomach. 'I'm sorry. Sorry it's taking longer than I thought . . . But she knows. You know I'm your real mummy, don't you? You do, of course you do, you clever little sprout.'

She turns to me.

'Listen, mate,' she says, and her eyes are wide now, imploring. 'Can we get something sorted? Something regular? Monthly, at least? I know I'm a state but it would make such a difference if I had something to look forward to. Some time with her. She's growing up so fast. And it might help . . . it might help me get better. What do you think?'

This conversation has gone far enough.

I can't do this. I need her out of our lives, once and for all.

My head is a mess. I leave the coffee shop, making my way to the Tube and wondering when Esther will get home.

I managed to fob Kim off, told her I'd discuss it with Esther. But the idea of her wanting a permanent role in Riley's life quite frankly terrifies me.

Of course, I should tell Esther that Kim has been in touch. It would make her day – she's desperate to get the adoption sorted, finally. If only she knew how unlikely that was now. We had promised no more secrets, but she's not exactly stuck to that, has she? All her dad's money . . . She's more secretive than ever.

I never used to feel this angry with her. I never used to get angry with her at all.

But, despite everything, I still find it hard to forgive Esther for what happened.

What I did that night was a direct consequence of her refusal to let me in. It was the day before Valentine's Day – ironic indeed. She had been off sick since before Christmas, was in and out of hospital on a drip. I could see she was in agony, but she wouldn't let me help. I didn't know what to do.

One freezing January evening, shortly after the hospital had discharged her, saying her levels were finally stable enough for her to go home, I sat at the end of the bed, holding her hand. She was in her usual half-upright position, the only one she said didn't make her feel sick.

I wasn't allowed to move. So I sat there as still as I could, but then I felt it in my nose. A tickle at first, that grew into the inevitable: a sneeze. A simple, everyday sneeze, but one with such force behind it that I dropped her hand and the bed shook. I looked up at Esther, but it was too late, she was retching again. I grabbed the bowl, but the puke from the meagre portion of porridge she had managed to eat when we first got home hit me full in the face, soaking the clean bedding.

I wiped my eyes and looked over at Esther. Tears streamed down her face. Her body was shaking, perspiration springing to her forehead as though on a timer.

'I've wet myself,' she sobbed. 'I've pissed myself!'

As I watched her cry, I felt as though I was watching her breaking in front of me.

Once we'd cleaned her up, and I'd changed the bed, and she was resettled, I told her to try to get some sleep. It was only 8pm, and I had wanted to stay with her, but she had told me to leave her alone.

'OK, I'll just be in the other room,' I said softly, about to turn out the light.

'I'm not doing this anymore,' she said, her voice low. Different. 'I can't. This . . . baby. It's going to kill me.'

I paused. I didn't know what to say. I had nothing, no tools left to handle this. I'd never had any tools in the first place.

'Try to get some sleep, Tot,' I said. I wanted to get out of that room as quickly as possible. I just couldn't face seeing her like this. Where was her strength? Where was her defiance? I was angry with her. No, worse – disappointed. It was a tinge of my father, threaded through me: that disgust at the weak and feeble.

'I can't do it anymore,' she cried, and then she turned and spat into the plastic bowl beside her. She was producing excess saliva – another side effect of the condition. 'Some women in my situation . . . feel they have no choice but to terminate . . .'

'You're tired,' I said. 'You don't know what you're saying. Get some sleep. You'll feel differently tomorrow.'

'I won't,' she said. Her voice was quieter now.

'Do you know what you're saying?' I said. 'You're saying you're thinking about *killing* our baby.'

'I can't cope any longer. Please! You need to help me. If you love me . . . please, make it stop,' she begged, looking up at

171

me. Her eyes suddenly seemed dark. I didn't recognise her. 'Please, it's me or the baby. Bird. I can't . . .'

She reached up, scrawny fingers clasping my arm, but I shook her off.

'You're being irrational because you're tired. Get some sleep. I can't talk to you when you're like this,' I said. 'And think about what you're saying, Esther. Really think about it. It's my baby too.'

And then I turned and left the room. I shouldn't have done, but I slammed the door behind me.

ESTHER

I leave Claudia's feeling emotionally spent, but lighter somehow too. And as the adrenalin wears off, I feel ashamed of how angry I got. I hope she isn't cross with me for losing my temper like that. I never wanted to upset her. I just wanted her to understand what it's like to be in my head. Even though I don't suppose anyone ever can.

I hail a black cab and, on the way to the office, check Facebook. Kim has an open profile. Privacy doesn't seem to be a concern to her. It's become a habit now, a way of keeping an eye on her, and, though I hate to admit it, Robin. I have gone through so many different emotions with Kim – from revulsion and envy to hatred and admiration, and everything in between. Sometimes, I even felt I loved her. After all, she gave me the best thing in my life: my daughter.

The number of times I've wanted to send her a message, asking her what the hell she's playing at delaying the adoption for so long . . . but Robin has said we have to be careful, that we can't risk upsetting her.

But what about me? I'm upset. She's completely out of order, treating us like this.

Facebook helpfully reminds me that it's Vivienne's birthday today. I haven't spoken to her in months. She's the only one of my friends who knows the truth, that Kim is Riley's biological mother. Everyone else thinks we chose to use a surrogate after the trauma of my own pregnancy – even Robin's parents. Viv said if Sean ever cheated on her, that'd be it, game over. Tried to convince me I was in no fit state after my miscarriage to make major decisions.

But I never told her about the email I sent to that clinic, and so she doesn't understand the depth of my guilt. Or that taking on Riley felt like a gift. A way of atoning. Something I could do *right*.

'You know I've never liked Robin,' she said, as we sat in a bar the night I told her that Kim was pregnant. 'I'm sorry but he's too controlling. Possessive. All this *I love you so much, I'd die for you* crap. But then he does this. Esther, seriously. You don't have to do this. Taking on someone else's baby! You're still grieving your miscarriage – you shouldn't make decisions like this!'

'You're the one who told me you always have a choice in the way you think about things,' I said, trotting out the words I'd been using to convince myself ever since Robin suggested the plan to me. 'That you can reframe any situation positively, if you just try. That's all I'm doing.'

'For fuck's sake, Esther! There's reframing things positively, and there's staying in an abusive relationship because you're too weak to leave it!'

I walked out then. Chose Robin and the baby I was so desperate for over my best friend.

People never understand other people's relationships. You simply can't, from the outside. No one knows what's going on under the surface.

Claudia always tells me I need to stop worrying what other people think. If the situation works for us, then that's all that matters.

But does it? Does it work for us? I'm not sure anymore.

I start to type a generic *Happy Birthday* message on Vivienne's page, but something stirs in me. I miss her. I call her. She picks up on the third ring.

'Hello, stranger!' she says, and I feel the breath I've been holding escape. She's not cross with me. And then I remember: she never was. It's me who's been avoiding her all this time. I'm the one that's put the distance in our relationship, because she held a mirror up to my life that I didn't want to look into.

'Happy birthday,' I say, and I suddenly feel a spark of happiness burst in my chest. My friend. She still cares. Before I know what I'm saying, the words are out. 'What are you up to today? Got time for a drink tonight?'

'I'm meeting Sean after work for dinner, but hell yes, let's meet for a drink! It's been forever. Crystal Bar? For old times' sake?'

I laugh at her suggestion, but find myself agreeing to meet her there at 7pm. I can work late in the office and go straight there. It means I'll miss Riley's bedtime again, but I can't face Robin at the moment anyway.

I'm early to meet Vivienne, and so I take a seat in the window of the bar and order myself a martini. I don't drink often

175

these days – hangovers with 5am starts aren't the best combination – but I feel like letting my hair down for a change. Dad's money means one thing: we can definitely move house. Finally. Perhaps this is what we need: a fresh start.

I just need to look forward. This storm will pass, like all the other storms, and the sun will be brighter for it tomorrow.

I am browsing Rightmove on my phone, wondering what kind of place we could get with a bigger mortgage and using Dad's money as a deposit, when Vivienne appears in front of me. She's dressed in a tight, shiny dress under a giant pink furry coat. She looks like a marshmallow.

'Hello!' she says, almost squealing as she leans down to kiss me on the cheek, falling on to the sofa beside me. 'Oh golly, these seats are a bit low.'

She pulls her dress down over her thighs and shrugs off her coat, snatching up the drinks menu.

'What are you having? Martini? Very nice. Hmm . . .' She looks up, winking at one of the barmen, who immediately ambles over as though summoned by the queen. 'Porn Star for me, and another for her, please. Oh, and some crisps. Salt and vinegar, two packets.'

The waiter gives a nod and walks away.

'Happy birthday,' I say, raising my glass and draining the rest of its contents.

'How are you?'

'I'm . . .' I begin, but then stop myself from trotting out the obvious line. 'OK. It's been a rough time, what with my dad . . .'

'I bloody loved your dad,' Vivienne says, staring at me. 'He was great. I'm sorry, Est. Life's absolute shit sometimes.'

I nod and fiddle with the cocktail stick in my glass.

'How are you doing?' I say.

Now that she's sitting still, I see that she's looking a lot older than she used to.

'How's work?'

She screws her face up.

'Sean's doing well,' she says. 'They're touring the show after the West End run is up, so he'll be away for a year. Nothing much going on with me at the moment. I've had some voice-over work lately, but nothing else. I'm getting to that age. Too old to play the piece of fluff, too young to play the mum. Although I am definitely getting put up for more of those parts. Last week I had an audition and I was meant to be a mum of a fifteen-year-old! As if!'

She rolls her eyes, gives a brittle laugh. I do the maths in my head. It's more than possible, but I don't expect she'll want to be reminded of that.

'Ugh,' I say. 'It's a hard business. I don't know how you cope with it.'

'Wouldn't want to do anything else though,' she says. 'My dad keeps offering to help but . . . between you and me, I think he's lost his touch. His last two productions were absolutely mauled by the press. And anyway, I just can't bear to be *that* person, you know? Only where I am because my dad helped me.'

I think of the flat he bought her, and then realise I'm about to do the exact same thing – use Dad's money to buy myself somewhere to live. That's what parenting is too, after all. Putting food on the table, a roof over heads. In which case, I am just as much of a mother as Robin is a father.

'And how's Sean?'

'Yeah, he's good,' she says, but there's a sadness in her eyes. 'The reason I'm not so worried about work at the moment is, well . . . We've been . . . trying. You know. For a baby. But nothing's happening yet. How did you cope with it? I know it took you ages too.'

I swallow.

'Yes. It was dreadful. And then . . .' I say.

'I know, I know,' she says. 'Seems that everyone has a story. I can't believe what you had to go through.' She pauses, gives me a beatific smile. 'How's Riley?'

'She's amazing,' I say, and I feel my face flush with joy. Because she is. She is what makes everything bearable. My little sixteen-month-old walker and talker. I pull my phone out and start flicking through the latest pictures of her. 'She's super ahead on all her gross motor milestones, amazed us all.'

But of course it's not surprising. Her mother's a trained dancer. I swallow again. These are the thoughts that Claudia says I must accept and wave away.

'She's beautiful,' Vivienne says, flicking through my phone. 'Her eyes! And that hair – such an unusual combination.'

She hands the phone back, smiling, but embarrassed that she's said the wrong thing.

'Do you ever see her?' I say, unthinking. 'Are you still in touch?'

She knows who I am talking about. Kim.

'Not really,' she says. 'I think I saw her a few months ago. At a party. She was back for a bit. But she's doing back-to-back cruise contracts now, isn't she?'

'That's what I've heard,' I say. I frown. 'When was she back?'

'Oh, I can't remember. February?'

I swallow. Robin never mentioned she'd come home earlier this year, just like he didn't mention when she was back a year ago. Did he know?

'I guess you're not in touch with her?'

'No,' I say. 'Robin's been handling it all. I'm pissed off with her, actually. There's still some legal stuff to finalise with the adoption but . . . well, she's been really evasive. Not replying to Robin's calls or messages. Let's just say it's my priority to get it sorted.'

I look down, ashamed.

'You know what, Est?' Vivienne says, sighing and leaning back into the leather sofa. 'I used to think you were crazy, agreeing to that situation. But now I know . . . we've been trying for months and months now, and nothing. Had all the tests; there's no reason that I'm not pregnant yet. Unexplained infertility. And now I get it. I'm sorry I was so harsh and judgemental of you at the time. I thought, how can you put up with this? Robin cheats on you, and then gets some other woman pregnant, and you just accept it and agree to adopt the baby? But now I get it. I know how devastated you were when you had your miscarriage . . . how tough your pregnancy had been, how long it had taken you to get there. And I know how much you wanted a baby. So I get it. What you did . . . taking on Riley; it was selfless. And look how it's all worked out! You've done so well. You've proved me wrong. Both of you.'

I lean back and smile, taking a sip of my drink. It all sounds so neat, so perfect, when you put it like that. It's ironic really, isn't it? That I've finally convinced Vivienne just as my own faith has started to desert me.

ROBIN

Esther sent me a text at 5pm saying she was meeting Vivienne for a drink and ever since, I've been pacing the flat. I preferred it when they weren't talking. Vivienne will know that Kim's been back in London. And who knows what will happen if the two of them start talking about her.

Once Riley is in bed, I tidy up the living room and throw together a casserole, which I leave to slow-cook. I'm getting better at cooking – something else my dad would see as a failure not an achievement. Then, in a fit of something, I decide to clean the kitchen thoroughly, and then I do the bathroom too. It's well overdue.

Satisfying, but nope, I still don't enjoy cleaning. It doesn't help.

When everything's sorted, I go back into the living room and open my laptop, logging on to Facebook. Stu hasn't mentioned his catch-up with me – of course he hasn't, I'm not popular or successful, and he's still friends with Sarah on there. I wonder if he'll tell her we met up today. I wonder what she'll say.

I lean back, bottle of beer in hand. Then I type her name into Google.

I haven't done this for a while now. The page flickers before my eyes as it loads.

So much stuff about her. Years and years' worth of press articles, hundreds of photos from shoots with glossy magazines, interviews and appearances on daytime television.

One of the headlines reads: '*Sarah Harrison: Queen of Comedy*'. I click on it.

Her face fills the screen. She looks the same as she did back then. Just softened slightly, her jawline a little lower, her eyes a little smaller behind her trendy glasses. She's wearing lipstick too – a jaunty shade of pink. Her hair has never changed, not since I met her. Shoulder-length, mud-brown and thick, with a fringe that practically obscures her eyes.

The lipstick doesn't suit her.

It's a recent article, waxing lyrical about her BAFTA for best female comedy performance. Her writing partner/husband gets a brief mention. Dean. He's American, his teeth an ungodly shade of white, his hair thick but grey. But the focus of the article is her career, how she has risen through the ranks and is now the UK's most 'in demand' female comedy writer. The misogynist in me wants to shout out loud that she doesn't have much competition.

At the end of the article there's a brief mention of her desire to get back into theatre, since the birth of her two children. She wants to do something they can watch, apparently.

I swig the beer, staring at her face, then slam the laptop lid down so hard I almost break it.

*

I'm watching my usual mind-numbing television, third bottle of beer in hand, when I hear the key turn in the lock. There's a thump, followed by a giggle, from the hallway. It's 10.05pm. Not late by my standards, but late for Esther.

'Oops!' she says, giggling some more. There's another thump, and then I realise: she's trying to take her boots off.

I don't say anything. The three bottles of beer have somewhat dulled the feelings of fury towards Sarah – that she has everything she wants, even after what she did, that she can still sabotage my career even though we haven't spoken for ten years – but I'm not sure how I feel about Esther at the moment.

'Hello!'

I look up. My wife's face is peering round the door to the living room, grinning.

'Stone-cold sober, I see,' I say, choosing sarcasm, my favourite disguise. 'How much have you had?'

She pads her way over to me, collapsing next to me on the sofa.

'Not gonna throw up all over me, I hope?' I say, but the dig goes over her head this time.

'Sorry,' she says, muffled. 'I had a pizza in the bar. Vivienne . . .'

'. . . made you do it?' I joke, but I feel relaxed finally.

'She wants a baby,' Esther says. 'They've been trying for ages. Nothing's working. The doctors are baffled.'

I feel my muscles tensing, but I don't say anything. Esther sits up, twisting her neck to face me.

'You're drunk.'

'I thought you liked me best drunk,' she says. 'Vivienne said . . . we used to be so much fun. And then I thought, no, I was never fun, but Robin was. Do you? Do you miss being fun?'

I am frozen, thinking of Kim.

There's a strange second of tension, before she leans forward and begins to kiss me. She tastes of something sweet – a schnapps, or maybe ice cream – and the effect is so surprising that I find myself kissing her back hungrily, thinking of Sarah and her stupid writing partner and all the accolades she's taken that should have been mine, and before I know it, Esther's tugging off my trousers, and it's as though we've only just met.

Later, we lie together on the sofa, pretending that it's not uncomfortable being squashed together on it. I stroke her hair and tell her I love her, and when she's silent for a long time, I ask her if she's all right.

'We are really lucky,' she says, and I realise she's crying. 'We have so much.'

'We deserve it,' I say. 'You're working too hard. You need a break, that's all.'

She sniffs a little, then sits up, wrapping a blanket around her shoulders. It's nearly 11pm now, and the tiredness is permeating my every pore. It's been an exhausting day: Stu, then Kim, then Sarah, and now this.

'I've been thinking about my dad's money,' she says.

'I haven't,' I say, disingenuously. 'Fuck it, fuck the money. Let's blow it all on a round-the-world holiday. Or donate it to a cat charity. Did your dad like cats?'

'Listen,' she says, ignoring me. Her eyes are clearer now, she's sobered up. 'I was . . . talking to Vivienne got me thinking how lucky I am. How lucky we are. Despite what we went through . . . I know she would kill to be in our shoes. Sean still won't even marry her. She thinks he's waiting to see if she's fertile first. Can you imagine? I've never liked him.'

Bonding over our dislike of others. It's funny the things that bring you together.

'You know what I think of him,' I say, wondering if I've actually ever really told her. She's got the general impression though.

'I know, I know,' she says. 'But they've been together for so long. It can't just be because of who her parents are . . .' She pauses, shakes her head. 'Anyway. It just made me think, what we have . . . it's amazing. But the flat is too small, and I don't like that Riley lives so near the main road . . . all that pollution. So let's spend the money on a new house. A bigger house. A family house. It can be a fresh start for us. Away from . . . all the stuff that happened here.'

I smile, nod gently.

'It's your money. If that's what you want, then that's what we'll do,' I say.

'It's *our* money. We're married. You do such a good job taking care of Riley, you deserve the money just as much as I do. And it is. It is what I want,' she says.

She pauses.

'Is there a "but" coming?' I joke.

'This stuff with Kim,' she says, her voice wavering slightly. 'I want it sorted. Once and for all. She needs to sign those adoption papers, Robin. No more tiptoeing around her. I mean it.'

'Of course,' I say, swallowing.

Shit.

Time to get creative.

ESTHER

No one said relationships were meant to be easy. Look at Sean and Vivienne. All those years messing around, pretending they were too cool for commitment, and now that they've finally realised what they really want – a family – they can't have it.

You're not meant to compare your life with others', but knowing that even people like Viv have problems has made me hopeful about the future. I've got to be grateful for what I have. After all, I'm so lucky. So, so lucky. I just need to look forward. No more looking back. I feel positive that finding a new, bigger home will bring us closer together again.

We are walking down the road to our first house viewing of the day. There are seven booked in, but thankfully Robin's mum is looking after Riley. She's at that age now where she doesn't want to sit still for a minute. She's feisty too, and fond of screaming if things don't go exactly how she wants them to. It's a little intimidating. Robin probably spoils her, but I can't blame him for that.

He's a wonderful father. So loving. Who wouldn't want that for their child?

The sun is out, and I take off my denim jacket and fold it over my arm as we walk along, enjoying the late-spring warmth.

'I'm optimistic about this one,' I say, as we round the corner into the pretty, tree-lined street. We're just north of Wimbledon, near Southfields. It's an area I don't know that well, but as soon as we left the Tube station I thought it was somewhere I could see us living. Still near enough to public transport and shops but with a slightly more suburban atmosphere that feels more mature, like the next step in life we should be taking.

'Cherry trees – tick,' Robin says, but he's closed off and I can't tell why. From the listing online, it looks as though this house is finished – been done up to the nines by its previous owners. I know he would rather we bought a project. Project managing a renovation would be the perfect way of keeping himself busy. I think it would be brilliant for him; something to help bolster his self-esteem.

The estate agent is waiting for us outside, a dark-haired chap who looks about nineteen. He shakes both of our hands rather vigorously, then leads us in.

The house is nice enough, but Robin's right, it's not for us. It would feel like borrowing someone's coat if we bought it. It'd never quite fit.

Five houses later, and I'm exhausted. We stop off for some lunch at a cafe near the Tube to 'regroup', as Robin suggests with a wink that takes me back, suddenly, to a time when our lives were simple and we spent most of our days laughing.

As we sit at the table, I remember with a pang of shock that we have left Riley with Sandra. I feel dark with guilt. Is it possible I had actually forgotten that we had a daughter?

When things like this happen it's impossible to shake the feeling that it's because I didn't give birth to her.

'Hey!' Robin says, looking over at me. My eyes have filled with tears. It's been a while since I've been caught out like this, and I grab a napkin and start frantically dabbing at my eyes. 'What's the matter?'

I try to speak but instead I just cry even more. Perhaps it will do me good, to get these feelings out of my system.

'We'll find a house,' he says, placing his hand over mine across the table. 'It's a good problem, right?'

I nod.

'How is Riley?' I say, eventually. 'Has your mum sent an update?'

Robin pulls his phone out of his pocket and shows me a picture his mum has sent. Riley is on the swing at the local playground, laughing with glee. She loves the swings.

'Apparently she's had a two-hour nap today. Git!' Robin says, looking at the photo. 'She never sleeps that long for me.'

For me.

It's constant, the reminder that I don't play much of a role in Riley's life. I'm like a 1950s father, bringing home the bacon but barely around enough to make an impact on her in any other way. Will she even remember me being part of her life, when she's older?

'She always plays up for us,' I say. 'We're her parents.'

Robin holds my gaze.

189

'Of course,' he replies.

There's a silence that lasts too long. I feel the tears pricking the backs of my eyes again and stare down at the sandwich in front of me.

'Why didn't you tell me your mum had texted?' I say.

'God,' Robin replies. 'What's the matter? I don't know. I didn't think.'

I sniff.

'What's wrong?' Robin says.

'It's . . . the adoption,' I say. 'You haven't . . . have you even spoken to her? After our conversation the other night? I don't understand what she's playing at . . . Riley's nearly eighteen months now! We need security, safety. I want to know she's mine.'

'She *is* yours,' he says, softly. His hands are twitching. 'Tot, seriously. She adores you. You're her mum. She loves you to death.'

'I can do it if you like?' I say. 'Why don't I speak to her? Maybe it would be easier coming from me?'

'No,' he snaps. 'I told you before, she's mental. We can't risk upsetting her. She needs careful handling.'

'But . . .' I say, angrily. 'It's upsetting *me*.'

Robin sighs and puts down his drink. He won't meet my eyes.

'I know, I know,' he says. 'I'm sorry, Tot. I'll chase Kim again about getting it sorted, I promise. You know what she's like – her life is a mess. It won't mean anything; she's probably just too chaotic to get around to it. I'll set her a deadline – Riley's second birthday.'

I frown. Where has the optimism of this morning gone? I can't tell him I'm crying because him saying Riley is mine is somehow not good enough. That I want proof. A piece of paper that makes it legal.

I can't tell him I feel overwhelmed most of the time, because whenever I think about what I went through with my pregnancy I feel as though I'm drowning in the contradiction of feelings.

I can't tell him that I think he's pushing me out, when all he's doing is being the perfect husband and father, taking care of our daughter with such love and precision that I can never repay my gratitude.

I can't tell him that even though I know I am the lucky one, that millions of mothers who've had to kiss their careers goodbye would kill to be in my position, all I want is some time alone with Riley, so that I can really feel like her mum.

So I tell him the only thing I can. My get-out-of-jail-free card.

'It's just . . .' I say, trying to push away the surfacing guilt. 'Everything. My dad. You know. The money. Thinking about the fact I didn't visit him. At the end. But even before I got sick, I was so busy with work . . . and . . .' I tail off. 'Everything feels so unstable, so . . . fragile.'

He sits back in his chair, his whole body relaxing.

'I know, darling,' he says, and the word sounds strange coming from his lips. Has he ever called me darling before? I don't think so. 'You're doing your best, and that's all anyone can do.'

I know the words are meant to be comforting, but somehow they feel like a criticism, an unnatural response to my words. My anger rises.

What he's left unsaid sounds louder than the rest. *You're doing your best, but we all know that's not good enough.*

By the time we get to the seventh house on the list, I'm feeling thoroughly despondent. The houses we have seen already have ranged from bland to awful, with not much in between, and certainly nothing that has excited me.

'It's the project,' Robin says, suddenly taking my hand as we walk up to the gate of the final house. A typical Edwardian terrace. It had been lived in by the same woman for her entire life.

'I've got to warn you,' the estate agent says as she pushes open the door. 'It needs everything doing.'

'We don't mind,' I find myself saying as I step inside. She thinks we're a blissfully happy couple.

'The lady who lived here was born here, inherited it from her parents, married and raised her four children here. A real generational home.'

I see past the peeling wallpaper, the ominous damp patch above the living room bay window, the threadbare carpets and lethal wiring. The house has an atmosphere I can't explain. It calms me, it soothes me, it says *life is hard, but you will be all right*. The light that floods into the bay window fills me with a strange sense of optimism.

I think about Robin's promise to me earlier. He won't mess it up this time, I know it.

And this house is the hope I have been searching for – the bright spark on the horizon.

I love it straight away.

NOW

ESTHER

I have been to this hospital before, I think, as the police car pulls up outside it. It is where I first met Riley.

Riley, who, once I met her, looked so much like the pictures of Robin as a baby that I stopped breathing for a second. Riley, who had come to wash away all our sorrows. The ray of light. The bringer of sunshine.

Kim had a Caesarean section. She told us that it was her choice, but she didn't share why. The night before the birth, I imagined the scalpel slicing into her stomach, like puncturing a balloon. She was older than me, but twice as lithe and her tummy muscles had held the baby in a tight embrace. I had barely had the chance to develop a baby bump before my pregnancy ended. Kim's pregnant stomach looked as hard as nails, taut and somehow unbearably sexy.

She hadn't let us come to any of the antenatal appointments, but we were there for the birth. Over and over I repeated the words Robin had said to me when we settled on the plan. *It's a surrogacy.* The same as so many others. She will be our child, not Kim's.

We had paid her twenty thousand pounds for the

197

'inconvenience'. Robin told me not to mention it, that it might upset her.

That was always his line. His excuse.

We were so desperate not to upset her.

I had had five months to get used to the idea, but it was still taking time to sink in. But my arms had felt empty ever since I'd lost my baby, and I couldn't wait to fill them with a real-life baby. What did it matter if she came to us through unconventional means? Plenty of babies are adopted.

It was only in the night that I remembered it wasn't a normal adoption. That Kim wasn't a surrogate, in the traditional sense. That my husband, who had sworn to stay faithful to me until death, had been inside this woman, had slept with her for reasons that had nothing to do with getting her pregnant, and everything to do with getting revenge on me.

I climb out of the police car and make my way through the hospital. The policewoman is talking to me but I'm not listening. Instead I'm remembering it all. The toxicity of the situation, how we tried to repaint it as something else, when in truth it was rotten to the core.

No. That's not right. Riley isn't rotten. Riley is my daughter, and I love her. Blood isn't thicker than water. Robin's relationship with his father is more than proof of that.

I have loved that child since the first second I held her. It was as though all the grief and guilt vanished and a little voice whispered in my ear, 'This is who you were meant to love. This one.'

Kim was laughing as we came in the room, all gowned up. It was the first time I'd seen her since the New Year's Eve party. I found it hard to believe that the woman in this situation was me. But there I was, nervously laughing along with them. My heart was thumping with desperation for this child, and with something else too: a shame I couldn't push away, a fear that the carefully stacked cards could fall at any time.

What if she changed her mind? Took one look at her little girl – because she told Robin it was a girl after the twenty-week scan – and decided there was no way she could hand her over?

But Kim wasn't me. We were so different. Robin said she'd already had two abortions, in her early twenties. He said she spoke about them with a strange kind of detachment, as though she had had no choice in the matter, with no sense of regret. She seemed to be very good at accidentally getting pregnant. I never probed that too deeply. I didn't want to know.

Everything about Kim is casual. Her motto is 'live for today' – she has it tattooed just below her tummy button. I looked at the letters as she lay there on the delivery table, stretched to accommodate our baby, trying not to think about the number of men who must have buried their heads against the scrawly writing. Trying not to think about the fact my husband had probably done so too.

Vivienne said I was mad. To forgive Robin for betraying me like that. For taking on another woman's child. But what I had done to Robin had broken him. I knew that. Kim was his way of punishing me. It had seemed like the best solution all round. And it had worked out, for a little while at least.

Until I found out what Robin had been hiding.

*

The policewoman ushers me into a small room and tells me to take a seat. The Bad News Room, as it so clearly is, has had a recent makeover, and I can smell the faint scent of paint in the air. There's a sofa that I vaguely recognise as being from IKEA, a coffee table, and a water cooler set up next to a table with coffee, tea and a kettle. Sachets of long-life milk crammed into a paper cup.

'The doctor is going to come and give us an update shortly,' DS Tyler says, smiling at me. 'But I believe they have stabilised his condition. For now.'

For now.

'Have the police found out how he got there yet?' I don't know what I'm even doing here. I should be out there, looking for my daughter. But I can't tell them I don't give a shit about Robin. They wouldn't understand, and I can't risk them asking questions.

'As soon as we have any news, you'll be the first to know,' DS Tyler says. 'Would you like a drink? Cup of tea?'

I shake my head. I wonder if she has a family at home waiting for her. There are rings around her eyes, but no ring on her finger. That doesn't mean anything though, these days.

When I took my marriage vows, I took them seriously. Perhaps it was the fact that I'd seen my father nurse my mother through her illness. Looking back on this time as an adult, I'm in awe of his complete lack of selfishness, something I had always thought was reserved for your children.

'For better or worse,' he whispered to me once as he gently cleaned her face as she slept. He wouldn't let her go into a hospice, saying he wanted her to die at home, surrounded by her things. He was off work for six months to care for her and then he had me to look after, so he chose never to go back. I remember seeing him in a completely different light after the experience. He was my hero.

I thought Robin was like my father, once. Unselfish, caring, always putting others first. But his behaviour was for completely different reasons. He was a people-pleaser, constantly seeking praise and admiration, whereas Dad was the definition of humble.

I sit on my hands and stare down at my boots. I was freezing cold on the way here, but now I feel suddenly sweaty. But I can't bring myself to remove my scarf. Because I want to be leaving soon, to go and pick up my daughter from wherever Robin has left her.

She will be safe. It will be OK.

He would never hurt her.

DS Tyler's phone rings, a shrill sound in the stuffy space. I sit up in my seat as she answers it, turning away from me.

'Yes, OK, great. Yes, I'm with her now . . . of course. I'll tell her . . .'

I want to grab the phone from her hand.

'Yes, that's a relief. Thank you. I'll let her know.'

She taps to end the call and turns to look at me.

'A little girl matching her description has been brought in,' she says, and I see the humanity in her eyes that shows she was almost as worried as I was about Riley. 'She was in a car, a little further along from where your husband was found. It looks as though he was involved in an accident, but he left the vehicle – probably in order to get help – before collapsing.

The car was more than a mile away. I'll find out where she is so you can go and see her.'

'The car!' I say. 'Oh my God!'

I can't believe I've been so stupid. How could I not have thought of it?

'I forgot, I forgot all about the fucking car! We hardly ever use it! It's so hard to get a parking space on our road, it's usually halfway down the street, so I didn't even notice it wasn't there. Is she OK?'

'She's in a stable condition. I don't know any more details I'm afraid,' she says, squeezing my hand, but the look in her eyes tells me that she's trying not to panic me. 'I'll get more information when I find out where she is.'

I think back to all the signs that have been mounting over the recent weeks. All the little hints, all the things that have unsettled me, that I've tried to fight away with logic.

I should have listened. I should have trusted my instincts. And now it's too late.

After everything I've found out about him recently. Now it all makes sense.

The car. Of course.

Of course he was in the car. Driving through Epsom.

There's only one reason he would have been doing that.

He was kidnapping her.

ONE MONTH EARLIER

ROBIN

I have to blink three times for my stupid brain to fully process what it's seeing.

Sorry, mate, I really tried. But no go. You know they loved it but . . . your reputation precedes you. You know what it's like at the Beeb. Any whiff of a scandal and they run scared. Stupid, really, the publicity wouldn't have hurt. We can try some of the networks, but it's probably too British. As you know, we haven't had much positive feedback with it elsewhere. Keep writing, and all that. Nothing's ever wasted, etc.

Could always rework it for the festival? One-man show?

Pint soon?

I slam the lid of my laptop down. It's becoming a habit. I'll probably break the fucking thing soon, and then I'll have to go begging my rich, successful wife for a handout so I can buy a new one.

This was the closest I've come since Stu basically told me to fuck off. Eight months of endless, humiliating submissions to agents who didn't even get back to me; the decision out of desperation to let Mike, my stand-up manager and general waste-of-space human, try to place it instead; one promising email from one junior exec at BBC3, one agonising wait for a commissioning meeting – during which time, like an idiot, I went and wrote the whole bloody series – and now Mike wants me to shelve the whole thing. Six perfectly crafted episodes of my sitcom, *Manchild*. Two years of my life. The development executive said it was the funniest thing he'd read in years. But none of that matters; none of that counts. I have to bin the thing. All that work. Just because ten years ago my ex broke my heart and I didn't handle it very well.

Fuck you, Sarah Harrison. Fuck you and your BAFTA and your rich American husband with his ridiculous teeth and your house in Maida Vale and your red-carpet appearances and your constant sucking up to every single successful comedy writer and actor on Twitter like some kind of pathetic arse-licking, social-climbing sycophantic embarrassment who's too blind with ambition to even acknowledge the shame you know you should be feeling.

Fuck you that you broke my stupid naive heart into a million pieces, and never even looked back.

From somewhere deep inside, I feel the rumblings of an eruption, and before long I am heaving with sobs, my entire body convulsing and shaking with the absolute, abject failure of my life, my talent, my purpose, my everything. I am nothing. I am less than nothing. I am invisible.

And it's all because of her. All because I fell in love. All because I was tricked into thinking for one tiny second that I might matter to someone, that I might be important, that I might have some value.

My sobs are interrupted by the sound of my phone ringing. I pull it out of my pocket, wiping the stupid tears away with the sleeve of my hoodie.

Kim.

Of course it's her. The only woman who ever calls me. The only person I don't want to hear from. Now threatening me with legal action. Why can't she just fuck off and die?

How did I get myself into this mess?

I think back to the night that started all this, the last time I felt this wretched. The day that everything went wrong. I had got back from helping Nick move house to find Esther sobbing on the bathroom floor.

'The baby's heart has stopped beating,' she said, in a voice devoid of emotion. 'I'm already bleeding a little bit. There's nothing we can do but wait.'

She wouldn't meet my eye.

'Why didn't you call me?' I shouted at her crumpled figure. 'Why the hell didn't you call me?'

But she didn't explain. She just shook her head and pushed me away, locking the bathroom door.

'Just leave me alone. Please.' She was begging through her sobs. 'Just leave me alone. For once, just let me be.'

It made no sense. I hammered and hammered on the door but she wouldn't let me in; didn't want me near her. It was the first time she truly rejected me. It felt like part of her had fallen out of love with me. Did she blame me? I couldn't tell. I was so upset myself, but she didn't seem to acknowledge it. She didn't seem to realise how devastating it was for me as well.

It wasn't fair. I was losing my baby too.

I sat outside the bathroom door begging for over an hour. Eventually she unlocked it and came out. I tried to hold her, but she pushed me off.

'I need to go for a lie-down,' she said. She was still crying, but there was no energy in her tears. 'Please, please, just let me sleep. I'll . . . I'll be better if I sleep.'

What choice did I have? She went to bed. Worn out from the bleeding, malnourished and dehydrated from weeks of not eating.

She left her phone on the kitchen table. When it rang twenty minutes later, I answered it. The helpful caller ID function told me that it 'might be' the Miller Clinic ringing, and I had no idea who they were or why they were calling her.

I told them I was her husband, that she was asleep. They told me they would call back later. No, they didn't want to leave a message. I hung up. And then I sat down and Googled the Miller Clinic.

She hadn't mentioned a clinic, or anything about any follow-up appointments. I was so stupid that when I Googled the name of the clinic I expected it to be something to do with her miscarriage.

But no, it was clear as day on the website in front of me. Private abortion clinic. There was no doubt about what she'd done.

The rage was immense. My wife was a stranger to me. The Esther I had picked specifically because I thought she would never hurt me had done something so unthinkably not-Esther. The only explanation seemed to be that all women were witches, that none of them could be trusted.

She didn't love me.

I left the flat, without thinking. She was still asleep. I walked for ages trying to make sense of the shouting in my head – all the way to Wimbledon. And then I went into the nearest pub and began to drink. There was so much noise in my head. I had to drown it. We knew the baby was a girl. Esther had had a private blood test when she was only a few months pregnant, to find out whether or not there were any chromosomal issues with the baby. Through that test we were able to find out the gender.

But without even consulting me, Esther had killed her. My child. The one I was put on earth to protect. The woman I had taken care of for all those years had murdered her, without even thinking to ask me. In fact she had done it specifically, *deliberately*, without asking me. Six pints in, it felt like my stomach had been hollowed out with a shovel, before someone set fire to my heart.

I found out later that this wasn't the case, of course. That it was one of life's cruellest coincidences – she really had had a miscarriage. But it wasn't my fault. How could I have done anything but jumped to those conclusions?

If she had only talked to me, if she'd only let me in . . .

I don't remember much more about that evening. At some point, I was asked to leave the pub. I sat outside on a bench, in the freezing February wind, and thought of Sarah, as I always did when I was drunk, and I found myself so consumed with anger that I thought I might kill the next person who looked at me. Esther had called me by then – clearly she'd seen the answered call on her phone history, and was desperate to explain. Perhaps I should have answered, but it was too little, too late. She'd had her chance to confide in me earlier, and she'd refused.

A tragic misunderstanding, but an entirely preventable one.

I needed somewhere to go, somewhere to take my anger.

Eventually, I got on the District Line and stumbled towards Vivienne and Sean's. I felt sure that Vivienne would have had something to do with it. She would have been Esther's co-conspirator. The two of them shared everything. It had always bugged the hell out of me, that she trusted Vivienne just that little bit more than she trusted me.

I must have been a right state when I rang her doorbell. Even though I'd stopped drinking more than an hour earlier, I was still so drunk I could barely speak. I relieved myself in the bushes outside the entrance to Vivienne's flat. It wasn't even a childish idea of revenge, I was just drunk and needed a piss.

But when the door opened it wasn't Vivienne behind it. It was someone else. House-sitting for them while they were on holiday, as it turned out. Kim.

Kim didn't care that I was drunk. I don't think she even noticed.

'Blimey, you're blue,' she said, pulling me off the doorstep into the house. 'What the hell happened to you?'

I grunted at her, I think.

'Vivienne . . . Where is she?'

'Not here, I'm afraid. You're stuck with me, instead. Soz.'

She dragged me to the open-plan kitchen at the back of the flat. The garden was lit up with fairy lights, even though the bifold doors that ran across the back were closed. I collapsed on to the leather chesterfield in one corner of the kitchen and let Kim make me a cup of coffee. My head was ringing, and then I remembered that I'd deliberately banged it on the brick wall when I'd left the pub. Hard.

My phone kept vibrating in my pocket. I barely noticed it now, but Kim did.

'Why don't you get that?' she said, pointing at my crotch. I pulled the phone out. Esther's face filled the screen. I pushed my thumb down on the glass so hard that it went white.

'What happened to your head?' she said, sitting cross-legged next to me on the sofa.

I touched it, the crusts of dried blood flaking away against my fingertips.

'Nothing.'

'Let me guess, you've had a row? Did she throw something at you? Little Miss Buttoned-Up?'

'I don't want to talk about it,' I grunted, still staring at my phone as it eventually switched itself off, the battery dead. To my addled brain, it felt like the universe's way of telling me that I was right to be here. I looked back over at Kim. I had barely noticed her up until now, but suddenly I could smell her perfume – something coconutty and cheap – and I took in what she was wearing.

'I was literally just about to have a bath,' she said, as she noticed me looking. She was in a dark grey silk nightdress, with a long woollen cardigan wrapped around her. Her thighs, tanned and smooth, seemed to go on forever. As she leant forward her nightdress gaped, giving me a clear view. I closed my eyes, turned my head away.

There were voices in my head that I didn't recognise. Had Esther been laughing at me all this time?

Kim unwound her legs and lay them across my lap. There was nothing that sexual about the gesture, I supposed. This was the way Vivienne's friends all behaved. Tactile. Luvvies.

Fucking luvvies.

I placed my hands on her legs. I don't know if she noticed, if it was all deliberate. Probably. It was all a game to her. All she wanted was the attention.

I pulled off her socks. Her toenails were a deep ruby red, with a little diamond buried in each big toe.

'Some pedicure,' I said.

Kim squirmed a little, smiling, flexing her toes. Even they were tanned.

'Thanks,' she replied. 'My mate's training to be a nail technician; I'm her grateful guinea pig.'

'You're good at that, aren't you?' I said, aggressively. 'Borrowing things from other people. Flats . . . pedicures . . .'

'Husbands?' she said, winking.

'I don't think I should be here,' I said, and then she laughed. She was ridiculously attractive, more attractive than any girl I had ever slept with before.

'Probably not,' she said.

'I'm breaking all my promises.' I reached across and took her hand, turning it over, running my fingers over her palm. 'This is definitely not allowed, is it?'

'Oh, chill your boots,' she said, shifting her weight on the sofa beside me.

'Don't you think I should go?' I asked, leaning towards her. She smelt of coconuts and vodka. 'Do you want me to go?'

'Up to you,' she said, shrugging, but she wouldn't meet my eye.

I pictured Esther's treacherous face in my mind, and before I knew it, it was game over.

ESTHER

Kim's back. I saw it on her Facebook page. 'Prosecco o'clock with my ladeez' as she captioned the picture of her with two of her friends. She's wearing a skin-tight purple dress in the photo, her arms and legs bare but bronzed, her long black hair curling suggestively across her shoulders. She looks amazing.

I can't tell where they are in the picture – she has unhelpfully forgotten to tag their location – but it looks like the sort of place in Soho I might have gone to with Rob when we first met, before he went on stage at some run-down club nearby.

The picture has eighty-seven likes. She's so popular. I scroll to look at her friends list. More than a thousand people on there – how is it possible to have a thousand friends? It isn't. I remember reading an article about it once – how it was only possible for the human brain to manage 150 true friendships, at most.

A thousand friends. What was the point of them all? These acolytes?

I scroll down to see the comments left by the handful of her 'friends' who've taken time to actually look at her picture. Someone called Jae Worth is first up.

Hey beautiful! Looking stunning, hun! Hope all is well? When can we catch up? XOXO

I imagine her uploading the photo then staring at her phone waiting for someone to reply and tell her how fantastic she looked.

What about us, Kim? What about the promise you made us?

I sit back in my office chair, and realise my heart is racing. I am furious. I can't remember another time I felt this angry.

How can she just carry on like this? How *dare she*?

I shouldn't be looking at her Facebook page at all, I know that. Claudia told me that it was borderline masochistic behaviour, but I had a five-minute break in a day of back-to-back meetings and I couldn't resist.

I hate Facebook. I hate the voyeurism and the narcissism and the pointlessness of it all. I rarely upload anything to my own page. But perhaps that's because I have nothing much to say. After all, what do I do? I go to work, I come home and I see my daughter for maybe an hour before bed and then I go to sleep.

Not so with Kim. She's always so *busy*. Her life is non-stop action – just following it all exhausts me. And she does always look incredible, if dressing like a lap dancer is your aspiration in life.

She's a show-woman, I suppose. Just like Viv. They've both created their characters, the fronts they display to the rest of the world, keeping their real selves safely hidden. We all do it to some degree, but their personas are so much more interesting, so beautifully detailed and realised. Viv's is boho thespian child, with her crazy curly hair, freckles and youthfully clear skin. Kim's is glamour puss, someone who would never be seen without 'her face on'. Easy, but charming with it, and won't take any of your nonsense.

Then what am I?

I'm Esther, what you see is what you get. I'm not trying to hide anything. Or am I? I'm a hard-working woman who loves her daughter but has no confidence in her mothering skills. And Robin doesn't make it easy for me. They have so many little inside jokes and ways, the two of them. Mummy is always the outsider. 'Poor Mummy,' he will often say. 'She does want to play with you, Riles, she's just had a very busy day at work.'

I can never tell whether he's being patronising or trying to let me off the hook. Or if there's something more sinister going on. His chance at a little power, after years of emasculation.

I push my tongue to my teeth and try to ignore the doubts in my mind. I look back at Kim's picture.

She's replied to her friend Jae Worth.

Helllllloooo gorgeous. All good, hunny, just got some life admin to sort through . . . NOT FUN. How are you? XX

Life admin. What does that mean?

My anger dissipates. Could it be finalising the adoption, finally? Robin's 'deadline' of Riley's second birthday has been and gone. The same old excuses. Perhaps this is it.

My heart lifts, then plummets again.

Or could it be the worst thing of all? My greatest fear, ever since we came to the agreement: that she would change her mind, and try to take Riley back.

I was amazed that she was able to hand her over to us in the first place – it felt unnatural.

But then I remembered I had considered having an abortion – for a few minutes actually thought about terminating the baby I was so desperate to have – without ever being able to successfully explain it to anyone who mattered to me.

And then of course, I beat all the odds by waking up one morning to find myself bleeding.

Was it all my fault? The pills I'd taken, despite the doctor's warning? My inability to hold down liquid? But the night before my miscarriage, I had reached a point so low that it seemed impossible I would ever stand again. It was just an email to a clinic, but it was worse than that, because it was an *intention*.

To this day, I still have no idea if I would have gone through with it. But that didn't matter. At 9.24pm that evening, the thought was there. Recorded forever in the Sent Items folder of my email.

I had wanted to get rid of the feeling that I was dying, and if that meant getting rid of my baby, then at that exact moment, I just didn't care.

So how could I ever judge Kim for giving up her daughter? Riley Madison Morgan.

Her middle name had been the only thing Kim had asked of us. It was her mother's name, apparently. She was American.

I wrack my brains, trying to remember those early days with Riley. I only saw Kim once, the day Riley was born, but there was nothing that day – which surely must have been the hardest of days – no sign that she was doubting her decision, or that we had coerced her into it. She was strangely detached during the whole process.

I suppose the money we gave her helped too.

Robin said Kim simply wanted the best for the child, that we would be much better parents than her. And she was right, of course, on the face of it. If you were ticking boxes, counting the things that people thought *mattered*. We were married, I had a good job, we owned our own home. We actively wanted a child. We were meant to have had one.

I was desperate to fill my empty, guilty arms.

And most importantly and devastatingly of all, Robin was Riley's biological father.

I think of the house we're about to move into tomorrow. We promised ourselves that it would be a fresh start. The fresh start we so sorely need.

But how can it be, when nothing has changed? When I have no security whatsoever, and Robin doesn't even seem to care?

Life admin. What does she mean?

Despite everything, all the times I have nagged Robin, nothing has changed. Kim is still Riley's legal mother. I still only have parental responsibility for her. I'm still *just* her stepmother. Our relationship is even more inadequate than mine and my own mother's. I had just ten years before my mother was taken from me. Is Riley only going to get two years before she loses me? She won't even remember that I ever loved her.

But I'm powerless. I can't force Robin or Kim to do anything.

My thoughts begin to race and I struggle to pull them into order. I ping the elastic band on my wrist that Claudia recommended. But I know it's too late to stop it, the same rollercoaster of symptoms that attacked me from time to time after Riley's birth, and led to my eventual diagnosis of PTSD.

Robin thought it was ridiculous.

'Post-traumatic stress disorder? I thought that was just for soldiers?'

But thankfully the psychologist shot him a look that shut him up, before recommending a course of CBT.

'Flashbacks and re-experiencing are very common after you've undergone a traumatic event,' she said. 'The nausea, vomiting and feelings of panic you're experiencing are completely normal, I'm afraid. But the good news is that they can be managed effectively with the right treatment.'

She was right about one thing. They are still common today.

Before I know it, I have scrabbled about under my desk for my small wastepaper basket, and I am throwing up the salad I ate an hour ago, the burning in my throat so familiar that it's almost a brutal kind of comfort, a reminder that I survived.

I stare down into the bin as I finish, wiping the tears from my eyes with the back of my hand.

That's it. I'm not going to go on like this. I refuse. It's been too long, too many unkept promises.

I'm going to find Kim, and I'm going to have it out with her once and for all.

ROBIN

I'd forgotten just how knackering moving house is. Even more so when you have a young child.

'Takeaway?' I say to Esther as she takes a seat on the sofa beside me. The bay window area of the living room is still stacked high with boxes, but at least we have somewhere to sit now.

'OK,' she replies. 'There's that fish and chip shop on the corner?'

'Sounds perfect,' I say, standing up and grabbing my wallet from the table. 'Cod?'

She nods, pushing her dishevelled hair from her eyes. It's nearly 9pm. Riley is finally asleep – she was far too excited by her huge new bedroom to settle earlier. I went in four times, read her eight stories, Esther went in twice. But, finally, she seems to have worn herself out.

'Won't be long,' I say.

Esther smiles at me, but the smile doesn't reach her eyes. She looks tired, not just from the exertions of moving house after six months of renovations, but tired of me. It reminds me of the look in her eyes as she lay on the bathroom floor. She wants me out of her way.

I don't like it.

I should never have told her about the sitcom meeting, that there was potential. She's excited – too excited, more excited than me. For someone who always said she doesn't like change, she suddenly seems to want everything to change. And I haven't. I've fallen back into my black hole of failure, and I'm about to disappoint her again.

It's a cold evening and I button up my coat as I stroll along the streets of our new neighbourhood. I can't quite believe that we live here. In *Wimbledon*. How nauseatingly provincial. Nick would be proud.

I find the chippy – a quaintly done-up building on the corner of one of the residential roads – and perch on a stool in the window as I wait for them to make my order. I take out my phone and upload the photograph of Esther and Riley outside the house, taken earlier today, to my Facebook page.

Esther is grinning. Riley is holding the keys aloft. I know Sarah probably won't see it – but she might. I've got an open profile and who knows what browsing she does when she's sitting there waiting to go on stage?

After last week's pathetic meltdown, I Googled her again. She's just about to go into the West End – her first theatre show in years – to star in the acclaimed kids' musical *Dragons and Dinosaurs*, based on the popular book. Apparently, it's her daughter's favourite and when the opportunity came up to star in it for a short run it was 'too good to miss'.

Funnily enough, it's Riley's favourite too.

*

The television is yet to be plugged in or set up, so after we eat on our laps, the fish and chips still in their cardboard trays, we sit together on the sofa in silence. Is this the right moment to tell her about the script?

On the one hand, I want to. On the other . . . there's so much that I'd have to explain if I did. She'll ask questions, I know she will. And she doesn't know anything about Sarah. How could I explain that situation to her? How could any man explain that in a way a woman could understand? I know how bad it sounds. I've been told enough times.

'Happy, Mrs Morgan?' I say.

She looks at me hesitantly.

'Yes,' she replies. 'I love it.'

She's thinking about something. She's not here. Not really. Not here with me.

Is it Kim that's on her mind? She hasn't brought her up in a while – the stress of the move has pushed Kim nicely to the back of her mind. I was hopeful I was off the hook there, but perhaps I was being a fool.

I consider suggesting we go to bed, but experience has taught me that that doesn't work very well for Esther. So instead I lean over and kiss her forehead, and I stare at her face.

'What are you doing?' she says, after a few minutes.

'Just looking at you,' I say, smiling. 'Just looking.'

She squirms, frowning slightly, then closes her eyes again. 'Don't.'

Her best feature has always been her mouth – full lips lining immaculate white teeth that fill her face when she smiles. Her

222

straight brown hair used to be long and neglected. But last year she cut it to the shoulder, and added a fringe.

'To hide the wrinkles,' she said at the time. I called her Chewbacca for a week afterwards. I thought it was pretty funny.

I brush the hair away from her forehead. The roots feel tacky under my fingertips.

Sarah has a fringe. It's her trademark, almost.

'I prefer you without a fringe,' I say.

'Really?' she replies, frowning, her hands touching it. 'It's just greasy, I need to wash it.'

'No, it's all right,' I say, and her eyes tighten a little. 'I just think it's too heavy, covers too much of your face.'

'Oh,' she replies, staring at me. 'I thought it made me look more grown up.'

'If you like it, that's all that matters,' I reply, and I move my face back a little from hers.

Her nose is shiny with sweat, her eyes so wide they could almost be Kim's. We stare at each other for what feels like ages before she swallows, then leans forward slightly, shifting away from me.

ESTHER

'Well, it was lovely to meet you,' I say, shaking hands with the tall, slim-built man in front of me. Pete Sewell, our newest head of marketing. I notice with surprise that he's slightly intimidated by me.

Sometimes it amazes me that I'm quite so senior. Imposter syndrome looms large on my shoulder.

'And you, Esther,' he says. His palm is warm and dry, the skin strangely soft. 'Looking forward to working together.'

I smile, look down and pick up my handbag.

'I'm leaving early tonight,' I call to my assistant, Anna. 'But I'm on my phone if you need me. Don't work too hard!'

She grins.

'It's 5.30 – you're not leaving early! I'm just finishing up myself. Have a nice evening, boss.'

I smile back at her. It's only once I'm outside on the street I notice that my underarms are damp.

I hail a cab to take me to Sean's party. Sean is back from his tour and so instead of something low-key, Vivienne decided to hold an enormous party for all his friends as well as hers.

I have no idea if Kim'll be there or not, but it's worth a try. It's the only way I can think of to confront her head-on. She could easily ignore a Facebook message, and I don't want to give her any more chances to wriggle out of this.

I turn up at the bar, a well-known haunt of theatre types underneath some railway arches near the Thames. It's only 6pm. The party isn't due to start until 7pm, but the place is already pulsating with people. I push past the smokers huddled around outside, and make my way in.

I remember there was a theme – 'still bright young things', or something ironic like that. A nod to the name of the show Sean has just left, and a nod to Vivienne getting older. Everyone is wearing rainbow colours, like I've walked into a gay pride march. I stare down at my black shift dress, tights and boots in horror.

A girl who looks ridiculously young tugs on my arm.

''Scuse me, where are the loos?'

She thinks I work here.

'What . . . ?' I say. 'I don't know. I don't work here, I'm here for Vivienne's party?'

'Oh God, sorry, haven't got changed yet? She's over there, by the bar.'

She points me in the right direction and I follow the line of her finger. Viv is standing at the end of the bar, surrounded by a group of people. She's wearing a dress covered in rainbow stripes.

I walk over to her, squeezing my way through the throngs of people, who apparently don't notice me at all. I pause for a second, wondering where the ridiculous feelings of inadequacy come from, and I acknowledge them, as Claudia always tells me to do, and then tell them to fuck off, which is a technique I developed on my own.

I'm an executive board member of one of the biggest charities in the country, a mother and a grown-up. Just because I don't have mermaid hair doesn't mean I don't belong here.

'Hello!' I say, pushing rather rudely through Vivienne's entourage until I am standing right in front of her.

Her face splits into a smile and she draws me towards her in a hug.

'Hello, chicken,' she says. 'Thank you for coming. Glad to see you've made an effort with your outfit, as always.'

She winks at me but her eyes aren't sparkling as they usually are.

'Sorry, I came straight from work . . .' I tail off. I can't bring up Kim yet. 'Didn't want to upstage you. Amazing dress. How are things?'

She pulls on my arm and gestures for me to come and sit down in the corner with her.

'I'm six weeks gone,' she says, so quietly that at first I'm not sure I've heard her right. 'Don't tell anyone.'

A strange feeling of shock washes over me. Viv has been trying to get pregnant for what feels like years and for some reason, in my head, I had decided that she never would.

'Wow!' I say, swallowing. I'm so surprised, I don't really know how to react. 'That's brilliant! Congratulations!' The words come out on autopilot, shortly followed by that crashing wave of shame that I feel whenever I so much as see a pregnant woman in the street. That little voice that haunts me: *look, there's someone stronger than you. Someone who could cope with the most natural thing in the world.*

'Thank you so much!' This time, her whole face lights up as she throws her arms around my neck. I respond by holding her tightly, breathing in the thick scent of her perfume. I feel my stomach turn over.

What the hell is happening to me? Not here, please, God, not now.

'I . . .' I say, but my hand flies to my mouth and I feel that familiar cramping in my stomach muscles.

No, no, no, I tell my brain. You do not feel sick. You are not going to be sick. You are not pregnant.

Vivienne notices.

'Are you OK?' she says. 'What's the matter?'

I shake my head, hand still covering my mouth, eyes wide. Then I gesture towards the toilets at the back of the bar, and stand up.

'Let me come with you,' Vivienne says. 'God, you poor thing. Must be something you ate?'

I don't trust myself to speak, so even though I want to tell her that I'm fine, I let her follow me to the loos. She rubs my back the whole way, clearly concerned that I'm ill, but thankfully lets me go into the cubicle on my own. I shut the door behind me, giving her concerned face as much of a half smile as I can muster, and then lean over the toilet, my hair hanging in my face.

I'm not going to be sick, of course. I haven't eaten anything

227

since lunchtime, and there's nothing wrong with me. It's all psychosomatic, in my head, although Claudia says this doesn't make it any less real.

I allow the nausea to subside, and then I straighten up, put the lid of the toilet seat down and sit on it, blowing my nose and wiping my eyes on some toilet paper. I'm crying and I hadn't even realised it.

For God's sake! I need to get a grip.

There's a gentle tapping on the door.

'Do you need me to call someone?' Vivienne says. 'Are you OK, darling?'

I stand up and open the door, pulling myself together.

'Sorry,' I say, smiling at her. 'Funny turn. Must have been something I ate earlier . . .'

'Ugh, food poisoning is the worst,' she says, taking my arm. 'I'm lucky, I haven't had any morning sickness yet – just trying to gear myself up for it.'

I smile weakly, grateful that the initial rush of nausea has gone. It was just the shock. As Claudia always says, *to be expected*.

'I'm so sorry. I totally rained on your parade there.'

'Don't be daft.'

We go back through to the bar and take our seats at the same table.

'Tell me everything,' I say, swallowing. All the while my eyes are scanning the room for any sign of Kim. 'I'm so excited for you.'

'Well,' she says, leaning forward and taking my hands. 'It was kind of crazy. I had just persuaded Sean to book an appointment for a fertility assessment, and then I realised my period was a day late. I didn't think much of it at all, given how often it had happened and it had been nothing, but I thought, just maybe . . . so I took a test, really expecting it to be negative, but there it was. Two lines. No doubt!'

'That's amazing,' I say, squeezing her hands. 'It really is. I'm so happy for you.'

'That's why we're doing this ridiculous party,' Viv says, glancing around at the crowds of multicoloured outfits. 'A kind of last big celebration before our lives change forever and all that. Although it's shit for me to be honest because I can't drink, and Sean seems to be on a mission to get as drunk as possible for some reason.'

The tone of her voice changes as she talks about him. I think about Robin, at her New Year's Eve party, how completely paralytic he was. The beginning of everything.

I want to tell her to keep an eye on him, but I doubt she'd appreciate the advice, and anyway, Sean is not Robin.

'How did Sean take the news?'

She pauses, picks up her drink and takes a long sip.

'I think he was a bit surprised,' she says. 'If I'm honest, I'm not sure it's totally sunk in.'

'It's a massive life change,' I say. 'It takes time to adjust, but you will be fine. You will be the most fun mum of anyone I know. I take it your parents are pleased?'

'Oh God, yes, my dad's embarrassingly excited. Really. It's quite ridiculous.'

We chat for a few more minutes before being interrupted by another of Vivienne's friends.

I hug her again and slink off into the crowd, looking all around me. No sign of her, but it's still early, so I decide to order a glass of wine instead and sit at the bar alone.

I don't understand why the news was such a surprise. Over the past three years plenty of friends and acquaintances have announced their pregnancies. Even when the news has been expected, I have always felt the same mix of shock and inexplicable devastation. Claudia thinks it's just the guilt, but also that I'm worried all my friends are joining a club and I feel left behind. A club I was kicked out of.

I sigh, draining the last of my wine. The situation is what it is. Friends will get pregnant, friends will not get HG, friends will have lovely, trouble-free pregnancies and beautiful, easy labours that result in healthy babies.

I have to set this fact aside, and concentrate on getting things sorted with Kim, and then everything will be OK.

I look back over at Vivienne, plagued with guilt that I spoilt her big moment. I should have jumped up and down and squealed and hugged her tightly.

I can't do that now, though. It would look too weird.

I stand up, pushing the empty wine glass back towards the barman with a smile, and turn around. The bar is even busier now, and I squeeze my way through the people, searching as I go. And then, suddenly, I see her. My heart seems to stop. But there's no doubt it's her. That long, curly hair, swishing as her head moves from side to side, as though she's looking for someone too.

I take a deep breath, and march towards her. She turns

just before I reach her and our eyes meet. I open my mouth to speak, but she beats me to it.

'Hello,' she says. 'I hoped you'd come tonight. I need to talk to you.'

ESTHER

Suddenly, I am terrified. This is all back to front.

She wasn't meant to want to talk to me.

She's going to say it, isn't she? She's going to say she wants Riley back.

I stare at her. And then I notice how terrible she looks.

The last time I saw her she was perma-tanned, her hair long and so shiny that it looked as though it was spun from glass. Now, underneath the make-up that's caked across her features, I can see that her tan has gone, her eyes are rimmed with purple, and she's lost weight. She looks ill. Her hair is still long, but it's a mess, the once-immaculate curls turned to dark candy floss, as though she's been caught in the rain.

But there's still energy in the hard, defiant line of her jaw as she juts her chin out at me.

'I . . . I wanted to speak to you too,' I say, irritated that she's stolen my thunder.

Her hand shoots out and she grips my arm tightly.

'Let's go over here where we can talk.'

I'm so surprised by the force of her grip and the hard look

in her eyes that I find myself following her to a corner of the bar that's unoccupied. She gestures for me to sit down.

I frown at her and she begins to cough; a loud, hacking cough that shakes her entire body, her face turning almost purple with the force of it.

'Do you want a drink?' I say. Listening to people cough is sometimes a trigger for me, and I feel my stomach do its usual rollercoaster thing. This bar. Something about the darkness, the heat, the smell of sweet, sickly cocktails and even sweeter, sicklier perfume . . .

Kim stares at me, her huge eyes now impossibly wide as she continues to cough. For a second I see Riley's face flash in front of me as I look at her, and I squeeze my eyes shut, the vision unbearably painful. This is the face Riley pulls when she's ill, I think. Angry, impatient for it to be over. Never sorry for herself, just irritated.

They are one and the same.

I walk to the bar and push in front of the people waiting to be served.

'I need some water,' I shout, ignoring the irritated cries of the people around me, 'my . . . friend's not well.'

The barman hears me and fills a plastic cup with water, handing it over. When I look over at Kim, I see she's wiping her mouth with a tissue. The tissue is streaked with blood.

I walk back to the table and hand her the water.

'Your lip's bleeding,' I say. 'Are you OK?'

'It's nothing,' she says, her voice croaky and unsteady. She stares at the glass of water as though it might be toxic.

'Just drink it,' I say, and she takes a sip, scrunching up the tissue in her hand.

I sit back down, staring at her fingernails. They're still long, talon-like, but the nail varnish that always used to be perfect is chipped and faded, as though it's weeks old. I want to feel some kind of satisfaction at seeing her like this, but it's all too weird. Has she suddenly got a drug problem? Is she going to ask for more money?

'Listen,' I say, taking a deep breath. I have to take charge of the situation. I came here tonight for one reason, and I'm not going to let myself down now. 'I wanted to talk to you. We need to get the adoption sorted. I . . . I can't . . . I can't wait anymore.'

'There's something I need to tell you,' she says, and suddenly her eyes look watery.

I have never seen Kim cry. She didn't even cry when she first saw Riley. She just stared down at her, gave a brief smile and touched her lightly on the head, before looking away.

'Looks like I made a good one,' she said, before lying back down in the hospital bed. And that was it, the most interest she had ever shown. Or so I thought. It suited me, made the whole thing so much easier than if she'd burst into tears as we took Riley away.

Hard as nails, that's what I thought.

'What?' I say, losing my patience. 'What is it?'

She swallows, taking a sip of her drink.

'What do you know about Sarah?' she says, slowly. It's the first time I've heard her talk like this, as though she's considering the weight of each word.

Alarm rushes through me. I want to raise my hands to my ears and shout 'No, no, no'. I don't want to hear it.

Sarah.

The name I've heard whispered so many times. Between Robin and Nick, between his parents. But worst of all, by Robin, in his sleep. For some reason I have never confronted him, never had the guts to ask him who she was, or what she did. I assumed she was an ex, that it was nothing to worry about.

It's so easy to avoid things that scare you. It's what I have been doing all my life. The only coping mechanism I ever developed. Push them away, don't confront the danger. Hold on to what you have.

I stare at Kim. I can't bear it.

I swallow.

'Whatever it is,' I say. 'I don't want to know. I want to talk about the adoption. About Riley.'

Her face contorts, one side of her nose rising as though pulled up by an invisible thread. She is angry with me, but because she cares, and my brain aches with confusion.

'Have you never once thought you deserve better than Rob?' she says. 'Seriously? What is it you see in him? Why do you put up with everything?'

'I don't put up with anything!' I snap. 'I don't know what you're talking about. He's good to me, he takes care of me, our daughter . . .'

She looks away.

'He's a liar,' she says. 'Doesn't it ever bother you? He cheated on you while you were having a miscarriage.'

'Why are you being like this? He was confused,' I say, but my voice is so quiet, I doubt she can hear me. I don't understand this conversation, it's like we're speaking different languages. 'He thought I had . . .' I think about the email to the abortion clinic, the proof of my guilt. 'It was a misunderstanding. I deserved it.'

She snorts, and suddenly the colour is back in her face.

'Is that what he told you? I'm going to get a real drink,' she says, putting the glass of water back down. 'Want one?'

I shake my head, but I stay sitting on the bar stool, staring at the drops of liquid that coat the top of the table, spilt by its previous occupant.

A few minutes later Kim returns, placing a glass with a small amount of clear liquid in front of me.

'Vodka shot,' she says.

I pick it up and down it in one, looking up at her as she does the same.

'Should you be drinking?' I say. I think of my dad, the agony of his condition in those final weeks. 'Your cough . . .'

She shakes her head.

'It's nothing,' she says, but her eyes don't meet mine.

'I need to talk to you about the adoption,' I say again. I have to get this conversation back on track. I don't care about Sarah, whoever she is. 'Robin's been trying to get hold of you for months now. It's not fair. You need to sign the forms, we need to make it all official . . .'

'He's been trying to get hold of me for months?' she says, frowning.

'I know you've been away . . . But anyway, you're here now.

We need to get this done and dusted, once and for all. Then we'll get out of your life and leave you alone. You've got to understand how stressful this is for me . . . for us. We just want security for Riley. She's two now, she . . .'

'I know how old she is!' Kim says. 'For fuck's sake, I gave birth to her. You don't forget things like that, you know.'

I sniff, the tears springing immediately to my eyes.

'I know,' I say. Briefly, I wonder how she can be so horrible. But then how could I ever understand a woman who would sell their baby for twenty thousand pounds?

'I'm sorry,' I say. I have to placate her. The last thing I want is to make her angry. 'I don't want to get into an argument with you. But please. You have to see that this is what's best for Riley . . . You have to sign the paperwork.'

'I don't have to do anything,' she says, staring me straight in the eye.

'We gave you twenty thousand pounds!' I hiss, flinging my arms in the air. The gesture reminds me briefly of my mother, when she used to get flustered. She was such a calm, unflappable woman usually. Dad would laugh at her if she ever used hand gestures. 'You can't . . . you can't just take the money and not stick to your side of the bargain!'

'What . . . what did you say?' Kim says, her eyes widening. 'Twenty thousand pounds?'

I frown at her. I'm speechless. I find myself burning with humiliation. This woman. This woman, who infiltrated my life and took what was mine. Like a parasite. I hate her.

'The money,' I say, eventually. 'You know what the money was for. You made a promise.'

'I don't know what you're talking about,' she says, and there's something in the look of confusion on her face that makes me catch my breath. 'What money?'

'The money we paid you,' I say. My brain fumbles for the way Robin put it, the way he framed it, so it didn't sound so horrendous. 'The money we paid you as . . . compensation for the fact that you couldn't work while you were pregnant. The money we paid you for . . . for Riley.'

'Jesus Christ Almighty,' Kim says, and she runs her talons through her hair. 'Jesus. Your husband. Now it all makes sense. Fuck me. He's a piece of work . . . he's a piece of work, all right.'

'What? What are you talking about?'

'He never paid me a penny,' she says, fiercely. 'Nothing. Not a cent. I don't know what he's told you. I don't know what fucked-up game he's playing. But I can tell you this: I didn't sell my baby to you. He didn't give me twenty thousand pounds. I never made any promises. I never agreed to anything.'

'You're a liar!' I say, gripping the edges of the table so hard my fingertips hurt. 'You have to be . . . you have to be lying. I gave him the money . . . it was my money . . . I transferred it . . .'

'Where did you transfer it?' she says, staring straight at me.

'To his account, but that's because . . . that's because . . .'

I think back to the state I was in when it was all agreed, the way Robin pressured me, told me we only had a day to decide or Kim was going to go ahead with the abortion. I transferred the money straight away to his account. He said he would deal with it. He didn't want me to have to speak to Kim, didn't want me to be upset.

I'll take care of it, Tot.

It was my savings, all my life savings.

'He said you were going to have an abortion. He was desperate, said this was the only way you would be persuaded to keep the baby . . .'

Kim leans forward.

'He's the liar,' she says. 'Not me.'

'No. I don't believe you. You've made a mistake. It's not possible. Something . . . I need to talk to Robin. I need to . . .'

I stand up, grabbing my handbag from the floor.

She takes my arm again, but this time I wrench her off me, pushing her backwards so that she nearly falls off the bar stool. Then I push my way through the rainbow-coloured partygoers until I'm back on the street, the sudden drop in temperature like a slap to the face.

NOW

ESTHER

At some point, as I pace the tiny room at the hospital waiting for news of Riley, Viv arrives. She doesn't speak, she just pulls me towards her in a tight hug. DS Tyler pretends not to watch. I still have no idea what she thinks about me, about the situation.

'My God, Esty,' Viv says. 'I'm just . . . it's . . . such a shock.'

I nod and we sit together on the uncomfortable sofa. My legs are shaking, I can't keep them still. She rummages in her handbag, pulls out a packet of Percy Pigs.

'I always have them with me to stop the morning sickness,' she says. 'Maybe it'd be good for you to keep your blood sugar up?'

I nod and take one, turning it around in my mouth, tasting nothing.

'Is there really no update on where Esther's daughter is yet?' Viv says, her arm around me as she stares up at DS Tyler. 'Why is it taking so long?'

'I'm not sure,' she says. 'But it's a good sign, that it's not serious.'

My head snaps up.

'Really? Is that what you think?'

'I'm sorry,' DS Tyler says. 'I promise as soon as I have something definitive to share with you . . .'

But her mobile phone begins to ring, interrupting her useless excuse. She stands and leaves the room. Through the slatted blinds at the window I watch her talking, her face a myriad of different expressions. Confusion, irritation, anger. She starts to talk animatedly down the phone.

I stand up.

'I want to hear what she's saying . . .' I say, but Viv pulls me back.

'Best not,' she says. 'Let them do their job.'

'For God's sake!' I say, suddenly releasing anger I didn't even realise I was harbouring. 'What the hell is going on? Where's Riley? Why aren't they telling me anything?'

Viv squeezes her lips together and shakes her head.

'I don't know, chicken,' she says. 'I'm so sorry. Have they . . . are there any updates on Rob?'

'I don't give a shit about Rob!' I say, and it's such a relief to be honest about it that I almost laugh. 'I couldn't care less about him! I just want to see my daughter.'

Viv doesn't say anything, but she hugs me again. My whole body is vibrating with adrenalin. Seconds later, the door opens and DS Tyler comes back in.

'She's absolutely fine,' she says, a smile spreading across her face. 'She's actually in this hospital, in a ward on the eighth floor. I can take you to her right away.'

'Really?' I say, and Viv rubs my back.

'Thank God,' she says, closing her eyes.

'Yes, I'm so sorry,' DS Tyler says, picking up her bag. 'There was some confusion about which hospital she'd been taken to. As it was logged as a separate incident.'

I don't care about the police and their mistakes. I care only that my daughter is OK.

'But then why is she still on a ward?' I say, the film of the Percy Pig sticking to my back teeth. I wish I could spit it out. 'If she's totally fine?'

DS Tyler swallows.

'The doctors will tell you more. Let's go.'

ONE MONTH EARLIER

ROBIN

'Where Mummy?'

'No Mummy again tonight, sweetie,' I say, as I pull on Riley's pyjamas. 'She's at work.'

Riley starts her mock-crying, a new trick.

'I know, I know,' I say, smiling at her. 'Naughty Mummy and silly work. But you'll see her in the morning. Now, here's your milk.'

She still has milk from a bottle before bedtime – Esther thinks it's a failing, that by now she should be fully weaned off bottles, and doesn't like that she has it after she's cleaned her teeth, but there are more important things to worry about in my opinion. They're only her milk teeth, after all, and she's not likely to still be sucking on one when she turns eighteen, so why pressure her to give up something she loves before she's ready?

There's enough of that nonsense when you're an adult.

I tuck her in and kiss her on the head and we sing three versions of 'Old MacDonald' together. Her speaking is getting so good now, I can understand every word.

I didn't tell Riley the truth. Esther isn't at work. She's gone to Vivienne and Sean's party. I was invited too, half-heartedly at 3pm this afternoon, but Esther knew we weren't going to go to the effort of getting a babysitter so that I could go as well. It was weird, her not telling me about it beforehand.

After I tuck Riley in, I do something I've been meaning to do for ages. I go up to the loft and dig out a box of my old DVDs. Esther had told the removal men to put them up there. Annoying, but she either thought she was protecting my feelings, or she didn't think I would care. Not sure which is worse.

She's never even asked to watch them.

I don't have as many as I thought. Just eight. My own scribbled handwriting on the covers.

Halls Club June 2001

French House March – Support 2001

The Comedy Cellar August 2002

Best of Edinburgh Shows (Compilation) 2002

Robin Morgan Showreel 2002

Etc., etc.

Not much for a lifetime's work.

I sit back.

I take out the *Best of Edinburgh* DVD and push it into the slot on the small portable television we've had for years that's been sitting on the floor in the corner of the loft conversion, waiting to be found a home. It takes a few seconds to sort itself out, but eventually the screen fills with the image of me, standing in front of a dark purple curtain someone has clearly masking-taped to the back of the titchy stage.

God, what a dive.

But my eyes are drawn to her, of course. Sarah.

She is standing next to me. We begin our old routine – sparring off one another, riffing and laughing and loving it. It was original, back then. Our whole thing was her outwitting me as I struggled to argue my case for being a belligerent, self-indulgent waste of space. *My Better Half*, that was the name of our first show. At the end we got the audience to vote for who they thought was the better half – a show of hands, not particularly accurate, but even so. Sarah always won, but that's only because the blokes in the audience wanted to fuck her.

I watch a few minutes, but that's all I can stand. I press the pause button, freezing myself mid ridiculous leap across the stage. The audience are laughing along with me, but it's obvious it's just because they're all pissed out of their heads.

I've got the energy and enthusiasm all right. I'm young, sweaty and hairy, bouncing about like some demented Tigger. They're swept up in it – my unshakeable self-belief. That's what always got me through. But there's no point in denying it: watching now, in 2018, I'm not funny.

Just like the drugs, the jokes don't work anymore. I just look like a tosser.

I sit back, staring at the image of a much younger me. A much younger me who still believed he was going to do something with his life. Still believed he had the talent to stand out. Still believed he would be famous one day.

And then I look at Sarah. She was always funnier than me. That's what hurt.

Sarah, the love of my life. The one I thought I'd keep forever. But no, of course I didn't. Set myself right up for that one, didn't I? We spent two years touring this show until Sarah herself also realised that she truly was the better half, and upgraded.

What's not fair is that I know my sitcom is better than the shit we used to perform. Much, much better. I've matured as a writer; I've got nuance and subtlety and the wisdom and humour which come with age. And yet, because of *her*, there's no chance of it ever seeing the light of day.

There are only two choices available to me now. One is to cry.

I don't cry.

Instead, I do something more 'in character'. I kick the television screen. I'm wearing the old-man slippers Esther bought me for Christmas. I like the irony. The TV screen shatters against the force, makes a strange fizzing noise.

Blood pools inside my slipper, soaking through the material. I shake it off and grab my foot right before the blood drips on to our new oatmeal carpet. Seconds later the throbbing starts.

There's a small – also oatmeal – towel in the en-suite bathroom that adjoins the loft bedroom, and I yank it from its rail and wrap it around my smashed foot. Then I go back to the bedroom, where the television is still hissing and buzzing, and turn it off at the socket.

I'll deal with it later.

As I limp downstairs, I hear someone scratching at the front door lock. I am standing in the middle of the bottom staircase as Esther comes in.

Her hair is a mess, her cheeks flushed. I thought she would be out for hours.

She stares at me for a few seconds.

'What have you done to your foot?' she says, as a spot of blood escapes from my towel-bandage, and drips on to the floor.

'How was the party?' I say, in the kitchen, my foot wrapped in a bag of ice.

'It was . . .' Esther says, looking away. She is panting slightly. 'I don't know. Loud. Fine. Whatever. How was Riley?'

'Still coughing a bit but the rivers of green slime have stopped cascading from her micro nostrils at least. I did really hate that towel,' I say, looking over at it, offering a grin. Esther has left it soaking in cold water in the sink, but it'll never be the same again. Blood is one of the trickiest stains to shift. 'I mean, it's *beige*. But sorry.'

'It doesn't matter,' she says. 'What happened?'

She hasn't been upstairs yet. I consider my options.

'I tripped,' I say, my head down. 'I . . . was watching some of my old stuff back. And I tripped, and my foot went through the television screen.'

'You tripped,' she repeats, and I look up at her.

'Your hands are trembling,' I say, taking one of hers with my free hand and rubbing it.

'Just low blood sugar,' she says, pushing her fringe out of her eyes and pulling her hand back. 'I haven't had anything to eat.'

'There's some leftover pasta in the fridge if you're starving,' I say. 'From Riley's lunch. But I was going to order a takeaway when you got in.'

253

'We're always getting takeaways,' Esther says, pulling the Tupperware of pasta out of the fridge. 'Expensive habit.'

I don't say anything.

'Guess who I saw at the party?' she says, inhaling deeply.

'No idea.'

'Kim,' she says, glancing at my foot.

'What?' My throat is suddenly dry. I reach for the glass of water in front of me, taking a deep glug.

'Back from her cruise ship,' Esther says, and then she turns away, to reach into the drawer for a fork.

'Good for her,' I reply, swallowing. This is what happens when you take your eye off the ball, Bird. Why the fuck did I let her go to the party?

'Back from her cruise ship,' Esther repeats, staring coolly at me in a way I don't recognise. It's as though she's borrowed someone else's mannerism. 'And denying any knowledge of the twenty thousand pounds we paid her when Riley was born.'

She takes the lid off the Tupperware.

'So,' she says, but her hand is still shaking. 'Tell me, Rob, why do you think that might be?'

ESTHER

My hand grips the lid of the Tupperware. I realise my whole arm is shaking, that my stomach is turning over like a washing machine. I should have eaten something first. Before I tackled him. I should have thought this through. Had a game plan.

That's what he must have done.

Planned it.

The thought makes me shiver.

I look up at him.

His face is impressively impassive. He turns away and hauls himself up on to the bar stool, still clutching his stupid foot.

The silence stretches. I find myself itching to fill it, as I always end up doing. That's the dynamic of our relationship these days: he sulks, I rush to console. But no, not tonight.

I swallow.

He takes a breath.

'I thought she might do something like this,' he says, sighing.

'Something like what?' My voice is almost a screech. 'What has she done?'

'Try to come between us,' he replies. 'She's been

255

threatening . . .' He tails off, a beat of consideration. 'What exactly did she say?'

'She said you never paid her a penny. She said . . . she said . . .' What did she say? I can't remember. I didn't give her a chance to speak. I was so flustered I just ran off. 'She said she never got any money, that she would never sign away the rights to her daughter!'

'And you believed her?' Robin looks up at me, his face breaking into a smile.

I swallow. It's that same face he always pulls. The condescending one. The one that says 'oh silly Esther, what a gullible twit you are'.

I hate him.

'Yes, I believed her,' I spit. 'Why would she make something like that up?'

'Because she wants more money, of course!' he shouts. 'For God's sake, Esther. What did you say to her?' He stands up, his voice a roar.

'I didn't say anything!' I shout back. 'I said I had to talk to you.'

'Well, that's something,' he says, calmer again. Shifting tone as always, trying to keep me on the back foot. 'I guess. I knew she couldn't be trusted. I should never . . . I should never . . .'

'Have slept with her?' I reply bitterly. The tears begin to stream, and I'm filled with fury at myself, my own weakness. Why do I always cry when I'm angry? It's so unfair.

'I can't regret that,' Robin says, his voice suddenly soft, staring straight at me. 'You know I can't. Because I love our daughter. *Our* daughter, Esther. She's yours and mine.

Remember that. We've raised her. Not *her*. Not that . . . woman.'

I don't say anything.

'Of course, I regret the situation that led to it. Of course I do. But we've gone over that enough.'

I narrow my eyes, try to clear the muddled thinking in my head.

'Let me get this straight, then,' I say, speaking calmly and slowly, like I would to a belligerent colleague. 'You're saying that Kim sat there opposite me this evening and looked me straight in the eyes and denied ever having taken any money from us, and that she is lying? You're saying she lied to my face?'

'Are you surprised?' Robin says. He scoffs. 'Think about what you're saying for a second. This is a woman who snogs other people's husbands in front of them. Sleeps with them when they're in no fit state to make that kind of . . . decision. And then happily sells her unwanted baby. And you're surprised that she might be capable of lying to you?'

'But . . .' I frown, trying to straighten the tangled pieces in my head. She didn't seem like she was lying, but then again, I don't know this woman at all.

'But no,' he continues, his voice rising again. 'No, you'd prefer to believe that I'm the one who's lying. Even though I've never lied to you! Even though I'm your husband. Even though I told you as soon as she got pregnant. I told you what I'd done, that I was sorry, that I'd only consider keeping the baby if that was what you wanted too. Only if you felt you could cope with that situation. I have *never* lied to you! I've been honest with you throughout this whole . . . mess, Esther. Unlike you. But no, you prefer to believe her – a woman who basically sold her baby – over me!'

'But why would she do that? Why deny the money? It doesn't make any sense.'

'God knows. But more importantly, why would I do it?' he says, ignoring me. 'Think about that for a second. And where exactly do you think this money went? To pay off my drug dealer? To my secret family? Where exactly did this twenty thousand pounds that you put into my account go? Did it vaporise into thin air?'

'I . . .' I say. 'Don't shout at me. Please. I don't know. I've never gone through your bank account.'

'For fuck's sake,' he shouts. 'We're *married*! Jesus, Esther! Think about what you're saying. Why would I steal money from you? You're my wife!'

'I . . . I don't know,' I say, shaking. 'I just don't understand why she would lie to me, either . . .'

'There's one thing I didn't tell you,' Robin begins, and I look back up again in fright. 'It's not a lie. I just decided not to bother you with it. Because I didn't want you to worry. But she's been pressurising me for weeks. Asking for more money. Saying that if we don't give it to her, she'll make a claim for custody of Riley. She's been hassling me non-stop – endless phone calls and threats. I've been ignoring her. Never give in to blackmailers, that's what they say, isn't it? I was going to tell you but then . . . well, she went quiet. But I suspected she might be planning something like this . . . trying to get to you . . .'

He pauses. I am back in the washing machine, but instead of it being just my stomach that's turning over, I feel like my whole body is being flung this way and that. I don't know what to believe. I don't know who to believe. I don't know anything anymore.

'Why was she even at the party?' he says. I stare at him and then out of the corner of my eye I notice something. His fingers, twitching, his forefinger rubbing over the nail of his thumb, moving round and around as though he's trying to work loose a knot. 'She must have gone deliberately to track you down. Did she say anything else? Anything about trying to take Riley back? Did she threaten you?'

His words have come out in a rush. Unlike the furious denial of a few seconds ago, he sounds nervous suddenly.

'She didn't say anything,' I say. His nerves have calmed me. 'Just that she never received any money from us. I was so shocked, I just left . . .'

I pause. His fingers have stopped twitching, his shoulders visibly drop. His face opens, all the tension in it suddenly vanished. He's relaxed now. Now he knows that's all Kim has said to me.

And that's it. That little gesture I know so well. That's what gives him away.

And that's when I know for sure. He's lying.

ESTHER

'Wakey-wakey,' Robin says, handing me a mug of tea. 'You're going to be late for work.'

I'm sitting at the kitchen island, watching Robin make Riley breakfast. Neither of us slept well last night. I could hardly bear to lie next to him in the same bed.

'I . . .' I begin. 'I'm not feeling great. I'm going to call in sick.'

Robin raises one eyebrow.

'More Shreddies! More Shreddies!' Riley calls, giggling as she pours almost the entire carton into her bowl. They reach the rim and begin to spill over the top, but I don't snap at her as I usually would. Instead I find myself transfixed, watching and waiting to see if Robin will be the bad guy and tell her that enough is enough.

I have only just realised how often I have had to be the bad cop – how often Robin has let me take the lead on discipline and boundaries. He has sat back and watched me be strict, knowing that it would make him the popular parent. The fun one.

'I don't think Mummy will be very happy with you for doing that, Riles,' Robin says, taking the carton away from her. 'You'll make Mummy cross.'

I lift the edges of my mouth but I don't speak. He notices, sees I am not rising to the bait.

'What's the matter?' he says, as he tips Shreddies back into the box. I am perched on a stool at our perfect island unit. Part of me feels as though I've been reformed in the same stone as our shiny new work surface.

He raises his eyebrows at me, the gesture asking if I'm still upset about last night.

'I've got an upset stomach,' I reply, and bile rushes to my throat. I swallow it, breathing in sharply, trying to ignore the acidic burn. 'It's . . . it's fine. I just didn't get much sleep. I've got a lot on my mind.'

'Not the nonsense we discussed yesterday, I hope.'

'No,' I lie. 'Work stuff.'

He smiles; a fixed, insincere grin.

'Tell me. I'm all ears!' he says, pouring milk into Riley's bowl, and facing her. 'That's what you always say, isn't it, madam? Daddy's got big ears.'

'Huge.' She nods, sending a splash of milk out from her bowl as she plonks her spoon into it. 'Not me. My ears small. Daddy's huge.'

'Cheeky monkey,' he says, stroking the top of her head. 'Now, what's so important that it stopped poor Mummy from sleeping, I wonder?'

He glances back at me. I feel my eyes hardening. A shot of pure rage pulses through me.

It's as though I am seeing everything clearly for the first time. Can our entire relationship really be built on lies? Can my husband really have stolen my money? Twenty thousand pounds of it?

But if it wasn't for the money, why would Kim have ever handed her daughter over to us? It doesn't make any sense.

Robin told me she was in debt, that she'd lived this crazy life, not looking further ahead than the next week, racked up credit card bills and overdrafts with no way of paying them off. That I could believe.

He told me that she'd threatened him with an abortion, saying she simply couldn't afford to have the baby. If she was pregnant she couldn't work, and if she couldn't work, she would starve. He said it was only right that we compensate her and that yes, twenty thousand pounds was a hell of a lot of money, but it was worth it to make sure that she was comfortable while she was pregnant, and that lots of people spent the same or more on IVF.

When I researched it online and discovered that surrogates in the UK are usually paid around seven thousand pounds, not twenty, he even made a joke about London weighting. He said that I shouldn't see it as buying a baby, rather helping out with Kim's living costs.

He told me that it was perfectly legal to compensate surrogates for their expenses. That we weren't doing anything wrong, even though morally it had always troubled me.

I watch him with Riley. This is what he always does, I think. And this is what I have always hated. Talking to me indirectly, through Riley, as though I am their pet dog perhaps, or some other inferior, incapable being. *What do we think Mummy would say about this? Who didn't put the lid back on the orange juice? Silly Mummy.*

I think of all the times I was the brunt of his jokes – the fact that I have always been material for his shows – how I laughed it all off, said it was flattering. What an idiot I was. What an idiot I have been.

'What is it?' Robin asks, again.

'It doesn't matter,' I say. 'It's boring . . . complicated . . . not something I can talk about in front of Riley anyway.'

She's not listening, she's too busy chomping on her cereal, but I still kick myself a little. I don't want her picking up on any of this. Not anything, not even the slightest whisper that any respect I once had for her father has been shattered.

Robin frowns at me, but then he does what he always does: he dismisses my feelings with a wave of his hand, and turns to something else. In this case, it's making his own breakfast, limping around the kitchen as though his foot injury wasn't self-inflicted.

He thinks I believe him. He thinks I've bought his lies, hook, line and sinker.

I almost feel sorry for him. His arrogance has always been his downfall. He has no idea what's coming. No idea at all.

ROBIN

It was surprisingly easy to get tickets to Sarah's new kids' show. Not the sell-out she was hoping for. But even I'll admit that it's not the best timing. Playing with fire again. It's going to get me burnt.

I sent Kim a long message last night telling her exactly what I thought of her little conversation with Esther. I told her Esther was confused about the money, and I laid it on thick about how selfish Kim had been, given Esther's condition and her post-traumatic stress disorder. Said she'd been seriously ill, that her mental health was incredibly fragile. I offered to meet her, to talk the whole mess through, but she hasn't replied.

The money.

God, yes, it was wrong, but at the time I was desperate. My debts were insurmountable; it seemed like the perfect solution. Esther had it; I needed it. She was my wife; technically it was my money too anyway.

Plus, it made her feel better about taking on Riley – she thought she was saving her from a mother who'd happily flush her down the toilet, and the thought that she had handed over money gave her some sense of proprietorship.

And anyway, she would never have understood how I'd got myself into all that mess. She's had a steady job and a reliable pay cheque ever since she left university. She has no idea what it's like when you're self-employed, how you live one day to the next, how hard it is when you get dropped by your management and everyone stops working with you and you end up spiralling into debt, spending every spare pound you have on coke. Self-medication to numb the pain.

Esther couldn't possibly understand how desperate I was. How humiliating it was, to have to steal from my own wife.

Not for the first time, I have no idea how this situation is going to sort itself out. But I can't think about it today. Today is so important. I just need to see Sarah, show her how I've changed, that I'm no threat to her now, and convince her to tell someone – anyone who matters – to take a chance on me, my stupid sitcom. It's my last hope. The only way is up.

Unfortunately, Riley had a bad night and now she's in a grump too. Esther said she felt sick this morning, that she wasn't going to go to work, and of course as soon as she said that, Riley wanted to stay with her.

They say kids can sense tension, and she's a smart cookie, my daughter. In the end, I told Esther that I'd booked theatre tickets, that it was too late for a refund. She looked surprised, but she let us leave without much comment, and I dragged Riley out of the house screaming that she wanted to stay with Mummy.

Perhaps I was being an idiot – perhaps she's too young for the theatre. The website said it was perfect for those age three and up, and Riley's only two. But she's clever, it's her favourite

265

book and she has a pretty impressive attention span for her age. So hopefully it will be OK.

The show's only an hour long anyway.

The reviews have all been raves, of course. Lots of chat about Sarah's broad appeal and versatile talent. '*It appears she can switch effortlessly between smutty* Fleabag-*esque humour to winsome childish charm – a force to be reckoned with on a comedy scene where women are finally coming into their own.*' So declared the *Guardian*.

She would have loved that one.

For once she's starring in something she hasn't written herself, and I'm curious. When we were together she always told me she would never do that. She was too proud.

But children change everything, don't they? As the *Guardian* interview with her revealed, she longed to do something that her children would appreciate. So far, so clichéd.

It's a matinee performance – as they all are – and I suppose that probably also appealed. An hour-long show twice a day in the West End for three months, not much of a challenge, really. Home in time for a nice curry and bath before bed. Plus there's the added fact that she's getting tons of extra press and good karma points for doing something so unexpected of her. Her management are smart.

Her management.

My old management.

Saul Webster and Larry Bernstein. Dropped me like a ton of bricks when Sarah and I broke up.

And yet here I am, in the queue outside her show, waiting for some spotty wannabe thespian to rip my ticket and direct me to my seat, having shelled out more than forty-five pounds for the privilege. Surely she'll take pity on me? It's been years now.

But this is Sarah, after all.

'Who's the mug here?' I say to Riley. She stares back at me. She's wriggling in my arms, complaining to be put down. 'Me, that's who.'

'Snack, Daddy,' she says. 'I hungry.'

I roll my eyes and pull out a breadstick. I've stocked up on food in case she kicks off during the show. I want Sarah to see us, but not if Riley's being a total brat.

'If you're a good girl and behave yourself, I'll get you an ice cream afterwards.'

Her eyes light up, and the doorman ushers us inside.

After the show ends, we step out on to the pavement. Clearly there's something in her genes. Riley loved it, sat mesmerised throughout. I watched her, wanted to see if she would notice Sarah, or pay her more attention than the rest of the cast. But even though Sarah was playing the lead role of the witch, Riley was far more interested in the poor sods sweating inside the dragon and dinosaur costumes. I have to admit it made me smile.

She loved the show. And of course, she loved the tub of chocolate ice cream I bought her even more.

I lean down and laugh.

'Oh, monkey,' I say, ineffectually attempting to wipe the brown smears from her cheeks with my thumb. 'You're covered in ice cream. Silly billy.'

She giggles, her round eyes scrunching up as she curls her little hand around her mouth and laughs along with me. She's so flipping cute sometimes. She makes everything feel all right again. It's all simple, when I look at her.

'Right, sweetie, now, would you like to go and meet the people who were in the show?'

'Yep, yep, yep!' Riley replies, but she's not really listening.

'They're called the cast, and they're the people who dressed up as the dragons and dinosaurs, and . . . of course, the lady that played the witch. We can go round to the secret door at the back, and wait for them to come out. And if we ask really nicely, then they might sign our programme. What do you think?'

'Yes, Daddy!' says Riley, in the non-committal way of a distracted two-year-old. She's staring at the colourful rickshaws that have pulled up outside the theatre.

'Great, come with Daddy, then.'

I take her by the hand and we walk round the side of the theatre. I've never done a show in a venue like this, of course – a proper, West End theatre. I wonder what the dressing rooms are like. Rumour has it that all these posh theatres are horribly run-down backstage, that the dressing rooms are damp and filled with mice.

Sarah was scared of mice, if I remember rightly.

There's a huddle of other cold parents already standing at the stage door, so I hang back a little. The kids range in age from tiny tots like Riles to monstrous seven- and eight-year-olds giving their parents lip.

Eventually the cast emerge. A dinosaur first, and the kids have a good laugh about the fact that the actor still has his

268

green face paint on. He scribbles his signature on the programmes, smiles and accepts the compliments, but his eyes are tired. No one wants to do kids' theatre – the pay is shit, the recognition non-existent.

Three years at drama school studying Chekhov, only to end up playing a monosyllabic dinosaur in a sweaty foam costume. At least I've never gone there, never sunk that low.

Riley stares up at him as he chucks her under the chin, but she doesn't say a word. She's a deep thinker.

Then more of the cast start to come out, and some of the band and tech crew too. Sarah's taking her time. I think of her, backstage, timing it carefully in order to make the most impactful exit.

Is that where it all really went wrong for me? Was I just too unwilling – no, unable – to play the game?

Eventually, the scuffed black stage door opens and there she is. Wearing dungarees and a huge brown teddy bear coat. Her hair is tied up with a headscarf and she's wearing her Buddy Holly glasses. They were conspicuously absent during the show, but with them on she is instantly recognisable. My heart begins to pound.

She doesn't spot me at first. Of course not, she's too busy sucking up all the praise from the gathered sycophants like a dried-out sponge. But then her head rises from scrawling her signature on the last programme waved in front of her, and I see the flicker of recognition as she spots me. The way her eyes widen, the little swallow to try to ground herself.

I smile broadly, to show I'm no threat, hoisting Riley into the air and taking a step towards her.

'Look, Riley,' I say, still grinning. 'It's the lady who played the witch! Look how different she looks now she's not in costume.'

Now we're closer, I can see the fine lines around her eyes. She's still staring at us. At me. Is it anger there? Or shock? Or something else?

I can't read her. This woman I used to know so well.

But then something in her snaps. She gives a little shake of her head and beams at Riley.

'Would you like me to sign your programme?' she says, staring straight at Riley and ignoring me completely. 'What's your name?'

Riley looks back at me, unsure of whether to answer.

'Her name's Riley,' I say, but Sarah still doesn't look at me. I'm impressed with her ability to ignore me completely while still being professional.

She doesn't even look frightened.

I thought she was meant to be terrified of me; I thought I had caused her 'significant psychological harm'.

'She's two.'

'Two years old!' Sarah exclaims, still smiling at Riley, her shoulders turned away from me. 'Aren't you a big girl?'

She takes the programme from Riley's hand then scribbles her name across it, thrusting it back at her.

'Listen,' I begin. 'I know it's been forever. It's nice to . . .'

But Sarah turns – very deliberately, very decisively – away from me, and strides off into the Soho crowds, without looking back.

ESTHER

Now I know for sure that I can't trust my husband, everything is somehow a bit easier.

I look at my reflection in the mirrored cabinets above our new double basins. They're so new that there's still plastic film across them. I reach up and pick at one corner, pulling the plastic away from the glass. As I do so, the sensor backlights come on, illuminating my face.

I stare into my own eyes, willing myself again to think of something – some reason – why Robin might have kept that money. We've always had separate finances – our own bank account each, and then the joint account for bills. But of course I'm the only one who's paid anything into the joint account in the past few years.

So what has he done with the money? Has he been sitting on it? Saving it in case he ever wants to leave me? Apart from the odd packet of fags, he never buys anything for himself. I have to practically force him to get new clothes. It doesn't make any sense.

I lift my fringe away from my forehead. I have aged so much in the past few years. Underneath, the skin is marked with deep lines that run horizontally. I like the fringe, I like covering the lines up. It makes me feel a little less exposed, I suppose.

I blink slowly at the woman in the mirror and then I do what I always do: I clean my teeth. It's the one habit I'm not prepared to break. Sometimes I do it ten times a day, sometimes only four. Claudia told me to snap the elastic band on my wrist instead, but she doesn't understand how much it helps. I'm always gentle, so I don't see the harm in it. And it feels like I'm rinsing my mouth clean, like a mini fresh start.

After I have recovered, I have a strange sense of relief, and determination that I will find out the truth, and will protect Riley at all costs. First of all, though, I need to talk to Kim. I found her number in the paperwork from when Riley was born, and, with fingers that no longer tremble but instead pulsate with courage, I call her. The only nerves I feel are that she might not answer.

This is it. No more lies, no more pretending, no more putting on a brave face.

I'm a mother, and I am going to do the right thing for my child.

We arrange to meet in a cafe near Waterloo. Kim thinks it's too risky to come to me. I send Robin a text saying that I'm feeling better, so I've decided to go into the office for a few hours. I hate leaving Riley with him now I know the truth, but what choice do I have? And the one thing that I trust – the only thing that I trust, I think – is that he loves her. He would never hurt her.

But what if I'm wrong about that, too?

272

Kim looks even worse than last night – her skin is pale, and when I walk up to her I realise that she's not wearing any make-up.

'Sorry,' she says, noticing my surprise. 'I was . . . I was asleep when you called me.'

I nearly roll my eyes, but I stop myself. She's coughing again, and she looks out of breath.

'Have you got a chest infection?' I say. 'You don't look well.'

'Something like that,' she replies.

I buy myself a coffee and her an orange juice and then I take a deep breath.

'He texted me after Viv's party. He told me you're ill,' Kim says. 'He said I shouldn't talk to you; that it would be too much for you.'

'I'm fine,' I say, forcefully. 'I want to understand. What you agreed. With him. Tell me everything. He's pushed me out for so long. I'm fed up of being sidelined. I'm not weak and pathetic. I'm strong and I want to understand. How did it . . . how did it even happen? I've heard his side of the story. Now I want yours.'

'The night we slept together,' she says, her fingers wrapped around the glass of orange juice as though she might throttle it, 'he was off his face. I mean, really, really drunk. He was ranting and raving about you, and what you'd done. He was in a right state. His head was bleeding – God knows what he'd done. At one point he went outside and punched the tree in Viv's garden. Proper punched it. I thought he must have broken his knuckles, but he didn't seem to notice. He kept talking about his parents . . . and about his ex. Sarah.'

She pauses and I look at her.

Sarah.

Who is she and what hold does she have over him?

'He went on and on about what a joke his life was. How all women betrayed him. It wasn't that attractive, to be honest.'

'But you still slept with him,' I bite back.

'Yeah,' she says, shrugging again. 'What can I say, I'm a fuck-up. I'd had some pretty shit news myself that day. I was pissed off with the world, with what life had thrown at me. It was angry sex. Revenge sex. I guess I wanted to get back at you. The way you looked at me at the New Year's Eve party. As though I was just a stupid slapper.'

'What? But I . . .' I start, but then I shut myself up. She's right, part of me did see her like that, but after what she did, how could she blame me?

I press my fingers into my forehead, rubbing the skin under my fringe.

'Afterwards, when he'd sobered up a bit, he started crying. Going on and on about Sarah. How she'd ruined his life. It was only after a little while that I got her full name. Sarah Harrison.'

My head snaps up in surprise.

'Yeah, I know,' she says. 'Who would have thought it? Must be quite painful, given how famous she is now. I certainly wouldn't mind her career.'

'I . . .' I say, dumbstruck. 'But . . . but . . . we watched all the episodes of her sitcom together! He never said. He never said once that they dated.'

I'm burning with the humiliation of it – remembering all

274

the times that I laughed out loud at her acting, all the compliments I paid her as we discussed the show together.

He once said – actually said to my face – that he thought she was attractive! I lift my hand to my forehead again.

I even had a fringe cut in, just like hers. And he never said. *He never said.*

I squeeze my eyes closed, try to calm myself down. I have to hear this. I have to confront this. No more pushing it away.

'Oh, it was more than dating,' she says, and I wonder if there's a hint of glee as she breaks this to me, or if it's just my paranoia. 'Apparently they were together for years. Writing partners. Love's young dream. And then . . . she dumped him. Upgraded for Dean West.'

Kim pauses gazing off into the middle distance.

'I mean, to be fair . . .' she says. 'I would too.'

She gives a short laugh that turns into another cough.

'Anyway, he was blathering on and on for ages, full of self-pity. He started annoying me, to be honest. So his ex suddenly became uber-famous? So what? That's the industry for you. You have to just suck it up. It was about 4am by then. I gave him some more coffee and kicked him out. I didn't want him still there when Sean and Viv came back the next day.'

'He didn't get home until 5am that night,' I say. 'I remember because I laid awake all night waiting for him. I thought . . . I really thought he might just never come back.'

'It's hard,' Kim says. 'Because probably it would have been for the best if we had never slept together. But Riley . . . Riley is everything.'

I stare up at her. She notices my surprise.

275

'Don't worry, I know you love her,' she says. 'I know what a good mother you are. I'll be honest, Esther. I always thought you were a bit stuck-up. I never understood what Viv saw in you. Viv's so fun, so outgoing. And you were always there in the background, looking like you'd sucked on a lemon. Judging us all. One-drink-Esther. Never wearing bloody fancy dress. Never making any effort to join in.'

'I . . .' I start, 'I . . . I'm just not like that, that's all. I'm not a performer . . . I just . . .'

'Think you're better than us?'

'No!' I reply. 'Not at all. I just didn't know how to fit in. I was so intimidated by you all. You all seemed to be so good at having fun. I don't know how to have fun. I never have . . .'

I think back to my teenage years, the way I'd sleep with anyone who smiled at me the right way. Pretending I enjoyed it.

Kim frowns at me.

'You do know that no one feels like they fucking fit in, don't you?' she says.

I sit back.

'I don't understand . . .' I say. I can't read her. I don't know what she wants from me. 'It still doesn't explain . . . if Robin never gave you the money, then why did you give Riley up? If you wanted her . . . it doesn't make any sense.'

'I'm dying,' she replies, then gives a long, dramatic laugh.

I frown.

'I mean, we all are, but I'm on a faster course than everyone else.'

I stare at her, unsure whether what she's saying is a joke

or not. But then I look at her again, and suddenly, like the sun coming up and shining a light on the world, everything about her makes sense.

'Breast cancer,' she replies, taking in the expression on my face. 'I've got the gene. I first had it at twenty-three; it was treated, double mastectomy. Hence the good boobs – I got a new pair on the NHS and asked for an upgrade. I went into remission. But the day your charming husband came round was the day I found out it had metastasised. It's in my bones, my liver, and as of last week, apparently, my lungs. Hence my forty-a-day cough.'

I stare at her.

'Don't believe me?' she says, and then with one swift yank she pulls off her hair. Except it's not her hair. It's a wig. Underneath, her head is covered in a fine down.

'We gave up chemotherapy a while ago,' she says, stroking her head. 'But it's taking ages to grow back this time. I'm gonna be a nearly bald corpse – every girl's dream.' She laughs croakily again.

I look at her face, and then I look at her eyes, and I realise that the eyebrows she painted on were just that – paint, and nothing more. And her fake eyelashes, so ridiculously long and thick, were that way because there was nothing else there.

She replaces her wig, adjusting it so deftly that it's hard to believe it's not her real hair.

'I don't . . .' I say, scrambling to find some words to make sense of this situation. 'But when you had Riley . . . you . . .'

'I was about to start treatment, and then I found out I was

pregnant. It might have been stupid, but I thought it was some kind of gift from God . . . I knew it was my last – my only – chance at becoming a mum. It's all I've ever wanted.'

'But . . .'

'Robin stepped right in. The knight in shining armour. He said you guys could look after her for a bit once she was born . . . then when I got better, then . . .'

'You could have her back?'

'Exactly,' she says. 'We would have a shared custody arrangement. That was the plan. But as you can probably see, he's not kept his side of the deal at all.'

The enormity of Robin's lies suddenly dawns on me.

'Why didn't he tell me?' I say, pathetically.

'He said you knew. That you were fine with it. I always wondered . . . well, I thought you were a better person than me to agree to be a stepmother in this situation . . . but if I'm honest, I didn't have any choice. My mum died years ago, my dad's getting on – and anyway he smokes like a fucking chimney. I could never have left my baby with him. I had nothing, no support. Just mates who said they'd do their best for me, but there's helping out and then there's looking after a newborn while their mum is sick as a dog being treated for cancer. I was worried social services would take her away . . . but then Robin offered and . . .'

'I can't . . .' I said. 'I can't believe it.'

'He's her dad, after all. It seemed the best decision. No, the *only* decision. But it was never meant to turn out like this. Two years down the line, and I've only seen her a handful of times. Every time I contacted him he'd make an excuse – some pathetic reason why we couldn't meet up. And then . . . six months ago they told me that there was nothing more they could do for me. It's all come to shit. My time's nearly run out. It's kind of impossible to believe, you know? Impossible to accept that this is *it*.'

She starts to cry. I can't bear it.

'I *wanted* that baby, I wanted to hold my little girl . . . I've been trying so desperately hard to get well again so that I could have her back. But fighting your husband . . . I'm worn out.'

'I love her,' I say.

'I know you do,' Kim replies, pulling her bottom lip inwards. 'You've done a far better job than I could have done, considering. But I love her too. I'm still her mum.'

She purses her lips together, and I notice the skin around them is dry and cracked, as though she's been out in the cold for too long. It reminds me of my mouth, by week ten of my pregnancy. When it was so sore I could barely part my lips.

'She's my baby. *Mine*. He was nice as pie to begin with, telling me he looked forward to me getting better so we could sort out the arrangements properly. But then he started cutting me out. He stopped replying. Then he blocked me on Facebook . . . he said it was upsetting for you! I just wanted to see my daughter!'

'He told me you were away on a cruise ship,' I say.

'Did he? He fucking wishes. Ever since I was diagnosed I've mostly been staying with my dad in Stratford. He knew that. I've not been able to work, but on the days I wasn't seeing my consultant or being treated I've been talking to lawyers, trying to work out my rights. But they weren't optimistic. He's her dad, he's on her birth certificate, he's been looking after her since she was born. And now I'm dying. Game over.'

She pauses, her mouth set in a line.

'It wasn't exactly a fair fight.'

'I'm so sorry,' I say, reaching over the table and taking her hand. 'I'm so sorry you've had to deal with this.'

I stare at Kim. I thought of her as tough, carefree, selfish. But she's the opposite. She's done the most unselfish thing of all – given up her child, because she wanted Riley to be loved and cared for while she was sick.

I have hated this woman for so long, and now I find myself wanting to reach out and hug her, to thank her for putting Riley first.

'What should I do?' I say.

'I don't know,' she says. 'It's why I wanted to talk to you. I just want to make sure Riley is safe. That's all that matters to me now. For the last two years, Rob's made my life hell. And now I'm dying and I just want to make sure . . . fuck, I just want to make sure she has someone decent looking after her. Someone who really cares about her, not just themselves.'

'I do,' I say. 'I love Riley like she's my own.'

'I know you do. That's why I wanted to get this all out in the open. There's something about his relationship with this Sarah woman that he's hiding. I want to know what it is. He lies about everything. Like I said, he texted me, he was furious that I spoke to you. He said you're not well, that your mental health is shot.'

The rage bubbles inside me.

'I'm fine but . . . how can I stay with him now? And if I leave

280

him . . .' I say, my brain feeling as though it might explode. 'If I leave him . . . I'm not Riley's legal guardian. I haven't officially adopted her. I'll have no right to see her . . .'

'I know,' she replies, suddenly quiet.

'He has looked after her since she was born. He was so desperate to be a stay-at-home dad.'

The penny drops, but it's not just a penny, it's a great iron boulder, the size of a warship, crushing me completely.

'I've got parental responsibility but nothing else . . .' I say, my words tumbling out like sand. 'He promised me that I could adopt her, but he blamed you for holding it up. He said you were impossible to get hold of . . . You're both on the birth certificate, so you both have to agree to it.'

'He never even asked me.'

I sink back down, mired by my own absolute stupidity. He has been playing us both off against one another the whole time.

Robin, the perfect father.

Is it really possible that he has planned this all along?

ESTHER

Kim has to go back to the hospital, and I sit for a while in the cafe after she leaves. In utter shock.

I think of all the times Robin told me that he couldn't get hold of Kim, of all the lies he has told me. The hundreds of lies.

She's so unreliable.

I have no idea where she is. Somewhere on a cruise ship. Somewhere in the Caribbean.

I just can't get hold of her. She's not answering my emails.

Don't worry, it will all get sorted.

Meanwhile, Kim had been pleading, desperate to see Riley. To find out how her daughter was, to make the most of the pitiful time she had left. She had even turned up at our old flat, only to find out we had moved. And when she called him, Robin had refused to tell her our new address. How could anyone be so cruel?

For years Vivienne has told me that Robin is abusive. I've shrugged her off, telling her that he was the opposite – that he loved me. That he had never been violent to me, not once. That he had never said anything cruel to me. That everything he did, he believed was for the best.

282

But Viv, she had always been like a dog with a bone.

'He doesn't let you breathe,' she used to say. 'It's weird. He's there all the time, telling you what to think.'

'No,' I would reply. 'It's not like that. He's loving me, looking after me. He means well. It all comes from a place of love.'

I thought she was jealous. That Sean wasn't as attentive, that he didn't care what she did. I thought the only type of love that mattered was the one that was all-encompassing. I thought the rest of the world was wrong.

I leave the cafe as it closes, and walk for what seems like miles, until I find myself standing on London Bridge. Robin hasn't texted me to find out how I am, which is strange. I wonder if he'd even care if I didn't come home. It strikes me that if I died, he'd truly have it all. The house, the life insurance I'd meticulously organised, the child all to himself.

Is he capable of killing me? Is that part of his plan too?

I realise part of me is waiting for him to call, to ask me if I am OK, what time I will be home. Some stupid, conditioned part of me still hopes that if I speak to him, it will take me back to my old way of thinking. That just hearing his certainty about things will convince me that everything Kim has just told me is a lie. But he doesn't ring. And I don't ring him. Stalemate.

I stand on the bridge for a long time, watching the boats passing under me, and the people rushing past. They all have somewhere to be, but I have nowhere to go. I am rootless. I have no parents. Robin is my only legal family. I have responsibility for Riley, but no rights. Robin is everything.

I have built my whole world around him, but I know nothing about him. It's all based on lies.

What has he spent the money on? Will I ever find out?

I carry on walking, unsure where to go, when I see the green neon light of a budget hotel on the other side of the bridge. Unthinking, I ask them if they have a room. They are pretty busy, the woman behind the reception desk tells me. But there is one twin room available.

I buy a bottle of water from the vending machine in the reception and take the lift to the room. It's on the fifth floor, the views across the Thames partially obscured by another giant tower block, the one shaped like a walkie-talkie. But it's quiet, and I am alone. I have to get my head straight somehow. It's only 4pm, but I am exhausted. I lie down on the bed and try to sleep.

I suppose I must do, because a few seconds later, according to the red lights of the alarm clock radio by my bed, it's now 6.30pm and my eyes feel as though someone has tried to cement them together.

My phone is out of battery, so I can't check it to see if anyone has rung me. For a second I feel an amazing sense of freedom. I imagine disappearing from my life. Just taking Riley and getting on a train and going somewhere else. Anywhere else. Where no one would ever find us.

But even as I am thinking these things, I know it's not possible. I am tied to Robin, because he is Riley's father. For the past three years I have been desperately trying to persuade myself that our relationship was OK, that it wasn't toxic inside. That we could be a family, a good family, and bring up a child in a healthy, happy environment.

The way I felt when I first held Riley, that tiny little button of a baby, was indescribable. We weren't related by blood, but it didn't matter. The only thing that mattered was her, and her happiness. This tiny little baby I had thought was unwanted by her birth mother – how could I refuse to take her on?

But all the while I've been unknowingly keeping her from her birth mother.

And the guilt still lingers at the back of my mind. That I had thought I wanted to kill my own baby.

It was the ultimate rod to beat myself with. And oh, how Robin had let me do it. How he had manipulated and needled until my insides were mush.

In this moment of clarity, I feel sure that I actually hate him. In a way I have never hated anyone before.

I suppose he hates me too. But why keep me around at all? Just for the money? The house? The security?

What is the point of me?

I climb out of bed and go to the tiny bathroom, splashing water on my face. I have to gather my strength and resolve, and make sure that I am ready for what lies ahead.

Riley. Kim and Riley. They're all that matter now.

Back in the bedroom, I switch on the small kettle. My throat is burning in the same way it did after a particularly bad day of vomiting.

I remember the way Robin had looked at me when I was being sick – I interpreted it at the time as pity but it was actually more like disgust.

'You've never looked hotter,' he had said as he handed me a tissue to wipe my mouth. And I had smiled weakly along with him, my stupid confused brain telling me he was trying to

285

cheer me up. Always compensating for him, when the cerebral part of me knew that this was all his way of lording it over me, of belittling me, of reminding me that I was dependent on him.

I thought because he didn't hit me, that made him a good husband. How utterly low my standards have been.

I make a cup of tea and drink it while it's still scalding hot, looking out across the Thames. And then I find a packet of chewing gum in my handbag, and I sit at the tiny dressing table and I chew and I make some notes. Just the bare facts. I will keep them hidden in my handbag, to be re-read whenever I feel my resolve weakening.

Once that's done, I brush my hair through with my fingers and head for home. I know what I have to do. And I know how I'm going to do it.

ROBIN

Fuck Sarah then. I have bigger fish to fry.

Still no reply from Kim. I don't like it. I don't like it at all.

I log on to Facebook, unblock Kim's account and try to work out what might have happened to her. It occurs to me that if she died, no one would let me know. We have no mutual Facebook 'friends' – other than Viv, of course. Kim's father knows that I've got Riley, though. So I suppose I'd hear about it eventually.

But still, it might be days later.

Then again, she's not going to die, is she? She's not going to just go away like that, and solve all my problems for me. That would be too easy, and nothing ever goes my way.

I think I got away with it – I think Esther bought my story about the money. But there's no guarantee. And now I feel like I'm standing at the edge of a cliff that's slowly but steadily crumbling away beneath me.

I look down at Riley, who's sitting in her high chair at the island unit. She's scribbling on a piece of paper with a black crayon. Her scribbles are so hard that she's almost pushed the crayon through the paper.

'Steady on there,' I say, moving the paper upwards slightly. 'Why don't you do a different colour? Pink? Orange? Daddy's favourite colour is purple. Or mauve. Funny word, isn't it? Mauuuuvvvve.'

She shakes her head and picks up the black crayon again. I laugh.

'No, Daddy, black my favourite.'

'All right then, goth child. Black it is.'

I think back to the last time I saw Kim. Just before Christmas. She'd bought Riley loads of presents. I wasn't kind. We met at a soft play centre down the road. She was having a break from her treatment and had been pestering me for days.

'Hey,' she said, as she walked up to us. She leant down and stroked Riley's face. 'Hello, my little princess.'

'I not a princess,' Riley replied. 'I Riley Madison Morgan.'

Kim smiled, but her eyes were watery.

'You're right, princesses are rubbish. Riley Madison Morgans are *much* better.'

'Come on, let's get a coffee or something,' I said.

I didn't have the patience for her. For the situation. I just wanted her to leave us alone.

We sat in one corner of the cafe sipping weak tea while Riley was penned in the under-threes area.

'We need to sort this out, man,' Kim said. 'It's not . . . you can't keep pushing me away like this.'

'I'm just doing what's best for her,' I said. 'It's confusing. She's only two – she doesn't know who you are.'

'Well, whose fucking fault is that?' Kim said, slamming down her polystyrene cup.

'Language! It's no one's fault,' I replied. 'It's just the way it is. You've been ill, you've got nowhere to live, no job . . . you can't be what she needs right now. You can't just turn up whenever you feel like it and shower her with presents. That's not parenting. She needs a mother who has the energy to cope with her. Plus she's too young. She doesn't understand.'

'That doesn't mean I can't see her! You don't have to try to explain . . . just let me spend some time with her, so that when the time comes she'll at least know who the fuck I am.'

I glanced at Kim, my fingers twitching. Was she going to cause a scene here? This was why I should never have met her. She was too unpredictable.

'She knows who you are,' I said, smiling as Riley came back over to me and rummaged in my backpack for her drink. 'You know who this is, don't you, Riley?'

'Auntie Kim,' Riley replied, flicking the straw of her drink back into the bottle and speeding off.

I knew it was cruel at the time. I couldn't bring myself to look Kim in the eyes.

'Auntie . . .'

Her voice was a whisper.

'It's just easier this way,' I said, swallowing. 'We'll explain everything when she's older.'

I glanced up. Kim's eyes were red-rimmed.

'But there might not be . . . I might not be here when she's older,' she said, and I could see she was struggling to get a grip. She wasn't one for tears, this wasn't part of her persona, and it was obvious how uncomfortable she was feeling.

'Well then, if you think about it, it's probably better for

289

Riley that she doesn't get to know you,' I said. My tone of voice reminded me of my father. I felt a little sick. But this had to be done. Sometimes the right things to do are the most difficult. 'Don't you think? You don't miss what you've never had, after all.'

'How can you . . .' Kim began, but then she stopped, sniffed. 'Fuck this. You can't get away with this. You can't keep my daughter from me! I've got rights, you know, you absolute fucktard. She's mine!'

'She's ours. And you should have thought of that before you gave her up,' I replied, stunned again by how easy it was to slip into my father's rhetoric. He would be proud, if he could hear me.

'I didn't *give her up*!' she said. 'I allowed her father to look after her while I was being treated for breast cancer.'

I paused, sipped my tea.

'Listen,' I replied. I had to do the right thing for my daughter. 'I'm sorry, I know this is difficult. But I think for now, it's best if you concentrate on yourself. On your . . . treatment. And finding somewhere to live. A job. All that stuff. And then we can talk about Riley. What's best for her, going forward. I'm just protecting her. Doing my job as a father. You have to see that.'

She stared at me.

I couldn't decipher my own feelings. Was it triumph, that I had her exactly where I wanted her? Or disgust that I had ever had anything to do with her? Or was I genuinely trying to do the right thing? I didn't know. It was a mixture of all three. All I knew for sure was that Riley was happy, safe and secure with me and Esther. And that Kim didn't fit into this picture. Not at all.

I decided to change tack.

'I'm sorry that you haven't managed to get well as quickly as you'd hoped,' I said, laying a hand on hers. She glared down at it and I pulled it away again. 'I really am. I can't imagine how difficult it must be knowing that you can't be with your daughter.' I made it sound like she didn't have a choice. 'But you must know that Esther and I just want the best for her. We're looking after her – you can see how happy and healthy she is.'

Kim didn't speak, she just stared over to where Riley was carefully balancing huge foam blocks one on top of another.

'You've done the right thing,' I said, all the while wondering if I was doing the right thing. 'I know it must be incredibly difficult, but you've put Riley first. Like any good mother would have done. You should be proud of yourself for that. Leaving her with us while you . . . while you weren't in a position to be able to care for her properly. That was the right thing to do. That was what any decent mother would do.'

I paused, trying to examine her face for any sign of emotion. But it was a blank slate. Then, a single tear ran down her cheek. She brushed it away with the side of her hand, stood up and walked out.

I thought I'd done it. I sat back in relief. It sounded – although she hadn't been specific – as though Kim was going to die soon. Soon enough, anyway. As heartless as it was, there was no benefit in letting Riley get attached to her, only to have to explain why her Auntie Kim suddenly disappeared from her life.

It was horrible. It was fucking sad, of course it was.

I didn't want Kim to die.

But anyone could see that it would be for the best.

ESTHER

I leave the hotel, get home and slip back into the role I have played for years. Robin is in a mood, barely speaking to me. Once I would have worried, endlessly obsessed about what might be on his mind, what bad news he might have had that day, but now I'm relieved. It means he's too distracted to notice that I am behaving differently.

After dinner, I leave him sitting in front of the television and go upstairs. He's drinking more than normal – on his sixth bottle of beer already – but I don't care. Let him drink himself to death. In our new en-suite I clean my teeth.

As I leave the bathroom, I spot Robin's phone, lit up beside the bed. A text message. I read it.

It's from a number not stored in his phone.

I'll remind you that what you did today was a breach of the restraining order. Don't come near me again. Sarah.

Sarah.

What has he done? *Don't come near me?* Where has he been today? The theatre, he said. But I don't know what show. He didn't answer me when I asked.

Sarah Harrison. His ex. It's mind-blowing.

And then it comes back to me. I Googled her earlier – she's performing in *Dragons and Dinosaurs* at the moment. That's where he's been today. He took Riley to see his ex-girlfriend. But why? And what did he do to end up with a restraining order?

Kim's words echo in my mind: *There's something about his relationship with this Sarah woman that he's hiding.*

I leave the phone by his side of the bed and tiptoe down the hallway to Riley's bedroom. I have never been scared of Robin before, but now, suddenly, it's all-consuming. My heart is pounding in my chest – it feels as though I'm free-falling through my own life. Everything I know and trust has been turned on its head.

Riley's bedroom door is open and one of her legs is sticking out from under the duvet. I pad across to her, avoiding the toys and books that she's scattered across the floor, and gently reposition her in bed, so that she's completely covered by the duvet again. I stroke her soft blonde hair away from her head and lean down to kiss her, pausing for a few seconds to listen to the soothing sound of her rhythmic breathing. She is such a peaceful child when she's asleep.

'I love you,' I say and then I straighten up and tidy away some of the toys, thankful for the pink rabbit nightlight.

I try not to cry as I tiptoe out of the room. I am terrified.

I barely sleep, aware all night of the sound of Robin's breathing beside me. But by the time the sun comes up, I feel more positive. I'm lucky. One of my oldest friends is a lawyer. Jeremy. An expert in his field. I will sort this out, the fair and legal way.

I ask him to meet me before work but he's tied up with his own children, so instead he agrees to meet me at a cafe by my office at lunchtime.

He sits patiently as I work up the courage to speak.

'I need to leave my husband,' I say, because right now that feels like the only thing I know.

Viv's words when I told her about Kim and our plan for the baby ring in my mind.

'What are you trying to prove by staying with that arse-hole?' she said. 'You don't have to be ashamed to admit you've failed. You can walk away, you know. Sometimes walking away is the stronger thing to do.'

But it was her I had walked away from. I thought the stronger thing to do was to stay, to try to sort out our issues. But more selfishly than that, I wanted the baby. I wanted Riley, desperately.

Added to that, I took my marriage vows seriously. What Robin had done was a mistake, but it was a one-off. Extenuating circumstances. We had to make the best of it. For better or worse.

I was loyal. I was stubborn. I was an idiot.

'It hasn't been right for ages,' I say, noticing Jeremy's surprise. 'It's complicated.'

Jeremy nods, waits for me to continue.

'Riley is not my biological daughter,' I say, and the starkness of the words spoken aloud stings more than I expect. I have never said it before. Not aloud. I have whispered it to myself, when I have felt guilty for not being there, to punish myself for not being the mum I thought I should have been. But I have never told anyone. Not like this. 'I was pregnant once, but I had a condition that made me very sick.'

I shake my head. He doesn't know anything about my pregnancy. Not many of my friends do.

'Anyway, I had a miscarriage at ten weeks. Robin was devastated. He didn't cope ...' I say, then take a deep breath. 'After I lost the baby, he didn't cope well. He slept with this other woman – a friend of a friend. She got pregnant and ... I know any sane woman would have left him after what he did. But ...'

I pause again, searching Jeremy's face for any sign of what he's thinking, but it's professionally blank.

'We ended up taking on the baby. I know it sounds insane. It *was* insane. But ... it was complicated, and I was so desperate to become a mother. I was in such a dark place after my miscarriage. And I thought she didn't want the baby. Robin told me she would have an abortion if we didn't agree to take the child. But ...' I stop, breathless. I need to simplify this horrific situation somehow, to get across to Jeremy what really matters. 'We took Riley home when she was just two days old. But I've never officially adopted her. I wanted to, but my husband said she had to agree too – the mother – and he told me he couldn't get hold of her, that she was away with work and ignoring his attempts to get in touch. Robin's her biological father; he's on the birth certificate. I've only got parental responsibility for her, like a normal stepmum. We applied for that straight after she was born, so I could take her to the doctor, things like that. We did everything legally, bar adoption. So technically I'm not her parent, or legal guardian.

Just her stepmum. So if my husband and I break up, what happens to her?'

I start to sob. I so didn't want to cry. Jeremy reaches forward and squeezes my hand.

'I love her so much,' I say. 'My marriage is over, but I can't cope with losing her . . . I can't . . . please tell me there's something we can do?'

I frantically wipe at my eyes and nose with a paper napkin from the table. I need to stay strong.

'It's not as uncommon a situation as you might think,' Jeremy says, once I've pulled myself together a bit. His eyes are kind, and they give me some hope. 'There are loads of stepchildren out there. Quite often people marry and take on the children from their partner's previous relationship. Not realising that if they then break up, they don't have any legal right to see the child. The best thing you can do is come to some sort of agreement with him, Est. Surely he will see that it's in Riley's best interest to continue seeing you?'

I shake my head. He doesn't understand.

'You don't know Rob,' I say. 'I wish I could believe that he would, but . . .'

I'm about to repeat the words, but I realise that I don't know him either.

'If I left him he would hate me; he would use Riley against me. I just know it . . . And there's more to it. He lied to me. He lied to me about her biological mother. He told me she didn't want the baby, but it wasn't true. She's been sick. She's got cancer, and now she's dying. She was too ill to look after Riley when she was born, so she agreed to let Robin and me look

297

after her until she was better. He didn't tell me any of this. And there's more . . .'

I can barely believe that this life I'm describing is mine.

'He said she was going to have an abortion. Unless we gave her twenty thousand pounds to keep it.'

I swallow.

'Go on.'

'I know, I know, it was wrong,' I say. 'We didn't do it the right way – it wasn't an official surrogacy. I know you're only allowed to give surrogates money for expenses in the UK. I was just so desperate. But anyway, he never gave her the money. It was all lies – the whole story. She wanted the baby, she was just sick. And he never gave her a penny. He kept it. He kept it all. It was . . . it was my money, my life savings. I gave it to him to give to her and he kept it. I don't know what for – he doesn't have paper bank statements, so I can't find out where the money has gone. And there's something else. He has an ex. I don't know much about her, but she texted him yesterday. To remind Robin of a restraining order against him. I don't know what it means. He has so many secrets; he's kept so much from me. I can't trust anything he says anymore. I can't stand being around him.'

'God, Esther. I'm . . .'

'I know.' I laugh, through tears. 'It's fucked up. Completely. And now I don't know what to do. I literally don't know. I can't talk to him; I can't trust him not to lie to me again.'

'Are you scared of him?' Jeremy says, and he suddenly looks so concerned that it makes me want to cry.

I imagine Robin, what he would do, what he would say, if

I came home and told him what I knew. I picture him on the stairs the other night, cradling his foot with a bloody towel. What kind of person kicks a television screen? What kind of person ends up with a restraining order against them? I don't know what he is capable of. I don't know anything about him anymore.

'Yes,' I say, my voice as fragile as a bubble. I nod, staring down at my lap. 'Yes, I am.'

What I always loved about Robin – his unpredictability, his reluctance to conform – they are the things that now frighten me the most.

NOW

ESTHER

We have just closed the door to the Bad News Room on our way to Riley's ward when a doctor approaches us and gestures for us to stop. Viv squeezes my hand.

I know what he's going to tell me. His head is bowed, as though at a funeral. He's coming to tell me that Rob is dead. How will I cope? What will I say?

'I'm very sorry, Mrs Morgan,' he says. 'But I'm afraid your husband's condition has deteriorated. He sustained a serious head injury, and the swelling in his brain is not going down. We're doing all we can, but he's currently on a life support machine, and the next few hours will be critical.' He pauses, his eyes briefly flicking over to DS Tyler.

'I'm very sorry.'

I stare at him, unable to muster up any sort of feeling whatsoever for this news. I thought it would be worse news. I thought it would be *the worst*.

I realise, with a shock, that I am disappointed.

Out of the corner of my eye, I see DS Tyler staring at me, waiting for my reaction. I take a sharp intake of breath, try to work out what I should say, how I should feel. I think of Riley. I just want to see her.

'I . . .' I say, my eyes falling down to the floor. 'Is he in pain?'

'No. He hasn't regained consciousness since we brought him in,' the doctor replies. 'So he won't be aware of a thing.'

'Thank you,' I say, although I don't really know what I am thanking him for.

Viv puts her arm around me.

'We were just on the way to see Mrs Morgan's daughter,' DS Tyler says, and the doctor smiles.

'Of course.'

Mrs Morgan's daughter.

My heart begins to pound. Surely it can't be this easy? I wonder if anyone checks these things. If anyone does the kind of due diligence you'd expect and hope for when it comes to child safety, or if they'll just believe me, the wife, the mother of his child, and ask no further questions.

I can barely speak, I am breathless with fear that my whole world will collapse as soon as I say what I really want to say. That instead of putting her arm around me to comfort me, DS Tyler will pull out a pair of handcuffs and take me away with her. That she'll know that this situation was exactly what I have been hoping for.

'Would you like me to call any of your husband's relatives?' DS Tyler says.

'No,' I say, glancing over at Viv, who won't meet my eye. 'Not now . . . thank you. I can do that . . . I'd like to go and see my daughter first, please. I want to talk to the doctors, find out exactly what happened to her. And then . . . then I'll visit Rob.'

ONE WEEK EARLIER

ESTHER

It takes a lot of pride-swallowing to do this. But my pride is what got me into this situation in the first place.

I tell Anna I have a doctor's appointment and arrange to meet Viv at a bar in Balham. She's late of course and, as I sit there waiting for her, I sip a sparkling water and run over in my mind exactly what I have to do.

When she arrives, I order her a cup of ginger tea – the only thing she says she feels like drinking at the moment – and we sit opposite one another.

'How are you feeling?' I ask. 'Not too sick, I hope?'

'No,' she says. 'Just knackered really. And don't fancy my usual things.'

'Glad to hear you're OK,' I say, smiling at her. 'I'm so pleased for you.'

'Thanks, chicken,' she replies, sipping her drink and eyeing me through the steam evaporating from it. 'Are you OK? You look . . . I dunno. What was it you wanted to talk to me about? You sounded stressed on the phone.'

'I need to ask you something,' I say. 'And I want you to be honest with me. No protecting my feelings, none of that shit.'

Her eyebrows rise. I don't normally swear.

'Sure,' she says.

'What do you know about Sarah Harrison?' I pause. 'Or more specifically, what do you know about Sarah Harrison and Rob?'

She sighs, pulling her top lip inwards.

'Why?'

'I need to know,' I say. 'I now know that she's his ex . . . that something happened with them.'

'God, Esty,' she says, tilting her head. 'I don't . . . why don't you ask him?'

'Viv,' I say, my voice cracking. 'I'm your best friend. I need you to be honest with me. Please.'

She leans back on the leather chair.

'I don't know much for sure,' she says. 'It's all just rumour and gossip – you know. I know they dated for a long time. And it didn't end well.'

'What happened?' I say, my heart thundering with desperation. 'How did they break up?'

'I don't think it was anything that bad – they just grew apart and she dumped him. But he didn't take it very well. Got a bit obsessive. Stalkerish, you know. I don't know anything for sure—'

'What did he do?' I say, urgently. 'Just tell me.'

'It's all just rumours, Est,' she says. 'You should really talk to him.'

'Tell me. Please.'

She sighs, looks over my shoulder at the rain drizzling down outside.

'OK, but you have to know that this is just hearsay, stuff I've heard on the grapevine. I haven't got any evidence to back it up, and anyway it was ages ago. And I only found out about a lot of it a few months ago. Otherwise I would have told you before you got involved with him.'

'Told me what?'

She sighs.

'Someone I was working with on my last play said that he abducted her.'

'What?'

'Drove her off to the middle of nowhere in his car or something, and wouldn't let her out. Apparently, at one point he pulled over and banged his head on the steering wheel repeatedly, threatening to kill himself if she didn't take him back. She was terrified. I think he ended up crashing the car. But I don't know any more. Honest. And this is all years ago, like when they were twenty-five or something. It could all just be exaggeration.'

'She took out a restraining order against him,' I say. 'So probably not.'

'What?'

'And he's broken it recently. She sent him a text message warning him off.'

'Oh God, Esther,' Viv says. 'I'm so sorry.'

'I've been such an idiot, Viv. It's all such a mess . . .'

'What's happened?' she says.

'It's Kim. Rob lied about . . . well, everything.'

I tell her the whole sorry story – including the bit about the money. She listens with a far more sympathetic ear than I could ever have expected.

'It's a complete mess,' I say. 'Jeremy says my best bet is to persuade Kim and Robin to agree to me formally adopting Riley. And then I can leave him. I could fight him in the courts for access, but he would definitely oppose that. The stuff with the money is something, but it's so hard to prove. It's my word against his – and we're married, after all, me giving him twenty thousand pounds isn't that unusual, and admitting what I thought it was for doesn't exactly paint me in a brilliant light either. Plus, he's never hurt Riley, never put her at risk, never done anything that could be seen as damaging to her. God knows the lies he could spin if he was clever enough about it. He could claim that I never liked Riley, that I was only fighting for custody now to spite him.'

'But if you adopted her, legally, he couldn't stop you from having contact with her?'

'Exactly. It's just a piece of paper, just a technicality, but it's everything,' I say.

'We need to track down Sarah,' Viv says, her eyes lighting up. 'Surely with her testimony, you'd have a stronger chance? And with everything you went through – how could any court judge you for wanting to stop Kim from having an abortion? You were in a state, trying to do the right thing. I don't see how anyone could paint that in a bad light.'

'I hope you're right,' I say. 'But I don't know . . .'

'I'll make some calls,' Viv says. 'Don't worry. We'll find Sarah, and we'll nail that fucker once and for all.'

'I'll do bath time,' I say as Robin turns off *In the Night Garden* and reaches down to lift Riley up from the sofa. Her wide eyes are unfocused and she blinks slowly as I come towards her.

Robin straightens up.

'Oh, OK,' he says. 'If you're sure.'

'Of course,' I say, smiling at him.

I try to remember a time when I pursued him, when I was the gusher, the one making great statements of true love. They must have existed, once. But no matter how deep I forage, I can't find any traces of that woman – no, that girl. She's gone. All these years of our dysfunctional relationship have battered her beyond recognition.

'It's why I came home early.'

'You look tired,' he says, tilting his head to one side. 'Honestly, why don't you just relax? She's knackered today, she'll be a fusspot. Get a glass of wine. I'll do it. I know how busy your days are. It's important you have some downtime.'

'Don't be silly! I want to do it,' I say, turning my back to him and scooping Riley up.

I kiss her on the top of her soft blonde hair, holding her to me. She feels heavy on my hip, but she fits there, perfectly.

'Great,' Robin says, a spark of confusion in his eyes. I have to try harder to mask my true feelings. 'I'll get started on dinner then.'

Later on, once Riley is tucked up in bed for the night, I steel myself. I take my seat on the bar stool at the island unit and watch as Rob prepares dinner for us. Whatever was bothering him the other day seems to have dissipated. He's in one of his rather manic 'up' moods, and has decided to make pasta.

Cooking has been his obsession over the past few years. I think of all the times he has lost his temper because food has stuck to the pan, or he's overcooked steak by a minute or two, or his triple-cooked chips have burnt on their third cook, and I remember the way my heart used to pound with fear at his fury, at the unpredictable nature of it. *Why. Can't. I. Get. Anything. Right!* he would shout, at no one. What might he break this time? I always justified it as OK, because it wasn't directed at me. No matter that it consumed me, that it filled the air between us like toxic smoke.

'I need to talk to you about something,' I say, my voice trembling slightly. I cough, swallow some of the white wine I poured myself. 'It's about Riley.'

His ears prick up at that and he turns around, spatula in hand, an expectant look on his face.

This is how I get your attention, I think. This and only this. Is she the only thing you truly care about?

What does your version of caring look like, anyway? Possessing, controlling, *owning*?

'We need to get the ball rolling again with the official adoption process,' I say. 'Kim must have a price. If she wants more money, then that's fine. We'll fucking do it.'

I don't know where the swearing has come from, but Robin notices. It feels good to be using his own lies against him.

'What if her turning up at Viv's party was just a warning? What if she is planning to come and claim her?' I say, my heart pounding. I've never been a very good actress. 'She's *my* daughter. I've raised her, provided for her, held her when she's cried . . . But what if Kim decided she wanted her back?

We wouldn't be able to stop her. God knows what that woman is capable of. If she can lie about the money she's already received . . .'

Something unreadable passes across Robin's face, and he turns back to the frying pan, pushing the mushrooms around with the spatula. He's thinking about the fact that she's dying, that he won't have to worry about her for much longer. But he doesn't want to have to tell me that, doesn't want the whole ball of thread to unwind.

'I know,' he says lightly to the mushrooms. Then he pauses again and turns towards me. 'You're right. But we can't give her more money. I refuse to. And no court in the land would give Kim custody over us. You've got parental responsibility; Riley calls you 'Mum'. The adoption thing is just a piece of paper.'

It's not though, is it; it's your way of keeping Riley from me! I want to shout, but instead I inhale slowly and think of Kim.

She had texted him earlier to say she was happy to go through with the adoption. That she wanted to meet to discuss it. It was all part of our plan. To uncover his true motives.

Apparently, he didn't reply.

'It's not just a piece of paper to me,' I say. 'It's important.'

Robin shrugs, turning back to the cooking.

'Dinner's nearly up,' he says, as though he's created something amazing. 'Do you want to get some bowls out?'

I glare at his turned back as I lean down to take some out of the cupboard, placing them with meticulous precision on the island unit, adding cutlery and a wine glass for him.

He serves the food then sits beside me, making a big fuss

of how delicious it is, perhaps he's missed his calling as a chef, just five ingredients in this, don't I know? It tastes pretty bland to me, but I eat it slowly, hoping he can sense my mood.

'Cheer up, grumps,' he says, laying a hand over mine. His touch repulses me, but I don't move. 'Riley loves you. You're her mum. You have no reason to be insecure.'

'It's not just my insecurity,' I say. 'It's for the future. What if something happened to you? Or her. Kim.'

'Nothing is going to happen to me,' he says. 'And as for her . . . she was probably just bored that night, trying to put the wind up your sails. Looks like she succeeded. Honestly, I don't think you have anything to worry about.'

I squeeze my eyes shut. It's so difficult for me to ignore the urge to scream that I know he's lying, that I know she has been pestering him for months for access to Riley. That he blocked her on Facebook, ignored all her calls and messages, that he wants to erase her from our lives completely.

'Even so. I don't trust her. I want you to get in touch with her,' I say, lobbing my final grenade into his happy, relaxed evening. It feels good, even though there's an edge of danger to it. 'I want us to have a meeting. A proper meeting. I want to ask her face to face why she won't let me adopt Riley. Maybe I can change her mind.'

I hold my breath, hardly daring to look at him and see his reaction.

He has a chance now. To come clean, to tell me that Kim has been in touch.

There's a beat, and I imagine precisely what he's thinking,

the little cogs in his brain whirring to work out what's best for him.

'Sure, Tot,' he says, and he stops eating. He puts down his fork and stares directly into my eyes. 'I know how patient you've been with this situation, and I appreciate it. I know it's been tough. So, if that's what you want, that's what we'll do. I'll try and track her down. Now, tell me, what do you think of your pasta? Good, isn't it?'

ESTHER

I'm at my desk the next morning, staring at our campaign budget spreadsheet but unable to absorb anything in it, when my phone rings. It's Viv.

'Hi,' I say, picking up before the first ring ends. 'Everything OK?'

'I've been in touch with Sarah, and she's agreed to meet you,' she says. 'Are you free today? Lunchtime? She's got an hour before her show starts.'

'What? I . . . er, yeah, sure,' I say, looking up at Sarina sitting across the floor on the other side of the office. I wonder if she's noticed how distracted I've been lately. Ever since she promoted me. The irony. 'Of course.'

'I've already called Kim; she's on her way over to you now.'

'Fuck,' I say, and I almost hear Viv smiling on the other end. She likes the new, ballsy me. I just feel ashamed I kept her locked up for so long. 'I mean, great. Thanks so much, Viv. Really, I mean it. I'm so grateful.'

'It's nothing,' she says. 'I just wish I could join you, but I've got a midwife appointment. You better call me straight away though, as soon as you've spoken to her.'

There's a silence on the line.

'And Esther?'

'Yes?'

'Good luck.'

I make my way to the bar just by the Tate Modern that Viv suggested. Kim is already there, sitting in the window.

It's a shock to see her when I get closer. She looks bigger than she did at Vivienne's party, which was only a week ago, and most surprisingly of all she's wearing a tracksuit and trainers. I've never seen her in anything other than heels or boots. The change every time I see her makes me realise how little time we have left. I expected her to be wasting away, but instead she looks bloated. She's wrapped in a huge scarf, and glances up at me as I take my seat beside her.

'What are you drinking?' I say, gesturing towards the glass in front of her.

'Gin; it's the only thing I can stomach at the moment,' she replies. 'And yes, I know, I look terrible. Don't worry: in a couple of days once I've got my fake tan sorted I'll start to look human again. And don't mind the puffy face. It's the steroids – they make me look like a balloon.'

'You look beautiful,' I say, as it's the only thing I can do to help her, to cheer her up. I know how much she prizes her looks. I always used to find it vulgar, but now I realise she was making the most of what she had – her youth. I guess that's all you can do when you're handed a death sentence.

She pulls a face at me and tells me to get a drink. I do as

I'm told, my hands shaking as I pay the barman for a large glass of wine.

'Sarah should be here soon,' I say, looking around.

She nods.

'I sorted my will out,' she says, as I take my seat again. 'I've named you as guardian of Riley. But my solicitor said they would still see Rob as the statutory guardian, and you'd still have to fight him for access. So it doesn't really help us. It would all be so much easier if you were able to legally adopt her. Even then, of course, you'd have to challenge him for access, as he's been looking after her since she was born, but at least you'd have some rights. It's a bloody shitty system.'

'I know. My friend Jeremy said the same,' I say. 'Robin would claim he's been her sole carer, that he's the one who's brought her up, that I've had nothing much to do with her. I didn't even take maternity leave. At the time I thought it made sense for me to carry on working – we needed the money.'

'It's my stupid fault,' Kim says, slamming her glass down on the table. 'I should never have trusted him in the first place.'

'You weren't to know,' I say, reaching out and placing my hand over hers. 'You had no idea we'd end up in this situation.'

'I was an idiot. I should have asked more questions. I just went along with it, accepted everything the fucker said. When I think what you must have gone through, to have lost your baby like that, and then to find out that your husband had got someone else pregnant . . . you were so forgiving. So understanding.'

'I didn't want to face the truth,' I say, and even though I hear the words leave my mouth I still can't quite believe that it's me saying them. That I am sitting here in this bar with Kim, the woman I have obsessed over for so long. The woman I have judged, juried and executed so many times, both with and without Robin. 'And I still felt so guilty. About my own pregnancy.'

She pauses, looking at me.

'But it wasn't your fault.'

'No, but . . .' I stop. It wasn't my fault. She's right. 'I really wanted a baby. Somehow, I was able to separate it all – Riley, you, what Robin did. I just saw a baby that needed loving. It felt like fate. And at the end of the day, I might have been stupid and naive, but I don't regret it. I don't regret any of it. How can I? I am so lucky to have Riley in my life.'

'*I'm* sorry. For judging you,' she says, looking up at me. Her eyes are bloodshot but they're still the same as Riley's, and I look in them and feel the same love that I feel for my child. 'I have to be honest. While a part of me thought you were dull, a bigger part of me wished I was just like you. Sensible. Mature. Safe. Even if I wasn't ill, I knew you'd be a better mum than me. Someone who could offer her a stable life. Money. Loving parents.'

'That was all I wanted,' I say. 'And you know, I was forty last year, so I felt like my time was running out.'

'I know,' she says, twisting her scarf in her hands. 'I've been a dick. And Robin . . . he'd always intrigued me, you know? He just didn't give a fuck. We met years ago, when he was on the circuit. Got drinking in some bar late at night. I think he was already seeing you then – nothing happened anyway. He thought I was just some trashy dancer. At Viv's New Year's Eve party he didn't even remember me. But I remembered him. He was right, it *was* my fault. I kissed him. I was off my face that night. Facing the new year alone again, knowing that I was probably on borrowed time. But then I got pregnant and . . .'

'Everything changed.'

'I wanted her to have a different life from me,' she says. 'I saw the way you were – how self-possessed and together you seemed. I knew you'd be the kind of mum who'd make sure she had all the best stuff: shiny new shoes at the start of each school year, the must-have toy that sells out in days at Christmas . . . all the things I never had. I couldn't give her a future like that, even without the cancer. But I never thought . . . I never thought he'd just try to cut me out like that. To delete me from her life.'

Tears come to my eyes.

'Listen,' Kim says, leaning forward. 'I know I have no right to ask anything of you. But I've run out of options now. I don't have the time to mount a legal case against Robin for custody. And no judge would grant me it even if I did. But I can't bear to die and leave my daughter with just him as a carer. So either you have to get custody – somehow – or you have to promise me you will never leave him. I mean it. Never.'

I stare at her fiery eyes, and I find myself nodding. It's an easy promise to make. For once, Kim and I are firmly on the same page.

ESTHER

'Esther?'

The voice is instantly familiar. My stomach turns over again, but I swallow away the nausea. I've had enough of it debilitating me. I steel myself and turn to look at the voice.

'Hi,' I say. 'Sarah. Thanks so much for coming. This is . . . this is Kim.'

Sarah smiles and takes a seat next to us. She's smaller, slighter than she seems on television. And prettier. Delicate features framed by that heavy, impossibly glossy fringe and her huge black glasses. As she sits down I notice the couple on the next table whispering and pointing at her. She must have to deal with that all the time. What a peculiar life.

'Can I get you a drink?' I say.

'Water's fine,' she replies, helping herself to the jug I brought over earlier. 'Thanks.'

I clear my throat.

'I don't know what Viv told you,' I say. 'I'm Rob's . . . wife. But it would be really helpful – I mean, really, really helpful – if you could . . . just tell me a little bit about your relationship with Rob.'

She bites her lip. This is not how I expected her to be. Not serious like this. She's always so confident and energetic on screen.

'He came to see me a few days ago,' she says. 'At the theatre. He was waiting at the stage door. With a little girl. Is that your daughter?'

My eyes flick to Kim.

'Yes,' I say. 'Well, actually, she's Kim's biological daughter. I'm her stepmother.'

Sarah frowns, the fringe covering even more of her eyes.

'It was a shock to see him. He's not meant to come near me. He knows that. I . . . I don't know why he did it. He could get five years in prison just for approaching me.'

My heart lifts a little. Perhaps this is something we can use.

'Five years?' Kim says, clapping her hands. 'That's brilliant.'

I frown at her. Sarah looks confused. I'm suddenly terrified we'll scare her off.

'Sorry,' I say. 'I know it's probably horrible to talk about, but if you could let us know why you took out a restraining order against him, it would be so helpful.'

'Of course,' Sarah says, her voice suddenly more confident. I can tell it's a story she's told often. 'Rob and I met at drama school. It was a pretty intense relationship from the very beginning. Fiery. Passionate. Whatever you want to call it. My parents hated him.'

I smile at her.

'But you know, I was twenty-one. I thought he was amazing. We . . . clicked. We were inseparable, really. And we started writing together, and then performing, and eventually we

322

launched as comedy partners. Did all the usual venues. Edinburgh for four years in a row. Got rave reviews, lots of regional tours. It was all ... well, it was all great. A dream come true.'

'Go on.'

'But then ... Rob didn't deal with success very well. Some people don't, you know? It sounds ridiculous, but in many ways it's more difficult than failure.'

I frown but nod anyway.

'And I got approached by a producer – a woman – who wanted me to write something on my own. A sitcom pilot. It was fine. Rob was a bit miffed, but he said it was cool, to go ahead. So I did, and the producer loved it and ...'

'Was that *Holding Place*?' Kim asks.

Sarah nods, her face splitting into a wide smile. As it does so, I can see why Rob loved her. Truly the sort of face that lights up a room. There's a charisma about her, some indefinable quality that makes you want to never leave her side.

'I was so proud of that show. It was the first thing I wrote completely solo, you know? It did pretty well, the BBC picked it up. I got three series out of it, decent enough viewing figures. It was amazing. But Rob ...' She sighs. 'He couldn't handle it. He was jealous. It was all so predictable really. I was working all the time and he was left behind. I mean, he was writing his own scripts and stuff, but nothing was getting picked up. And I was getting recognised more, and getting lots of exciting phone calls ... he couldn't handle it.'

It's so hard to believe she's talking about my husband. This whole other life he had, before I even knew him. If only I'd

323

Googled him, would I have found all this out myself? When we met he told me he'd only ever done solo stand-up, that that was his thing.

'He was drinking a lot,' she says. 'Then there was the coke. Loads of coke. Everyone did it, it was part of the scene, but he was becoming a bore. We started to fight. By that point we were fighting all the time. I was pissed off with him, frustrated that he wasn't being supportive. And he thought I was leaving him behind. Couldn't handle my success. He couldn't be happy for me. Every time something good happened, it would remind him of how things weren't working out for him.'

'Sounds familiar,' I say, unthinking, and Sarah looks back up at me.

'Sorry,' I continue, 'it's just . . . well, ever since I met him he's been in and out of jobs. Not really working much, doing some stand-up but nothing really substantial. Whereas I've been lucky – no, not lucky, I've worked my arse off – and I've been promoted quite a few times. My job has always been so important to me; I work for a charity, and it's something that's, well, really close to my heart. It was becoming an issue, but then I got pregnant . . . and . . . well, he offered to be a stay-at-home dad. It seemed to be the best solution.'

'He always said he wanted to have kids,' Sarah says. 'That was another thing we fought about. I wasn't sure. And I certainly didn't want them in my early twenties, when my career was really starting to take off . . .'

'He just wanted to control you,' I say.

She raises her eyebrows.

'Maybe. Anyway, things came to a head. I said I wanted

a break. I said I'd move out of our flat and go and stay with friends for a bit, just to get my head together. I mean . . . don't get me wrong, I still loved him. Or at least, I loved the memory of us, the way we were in the beginning. He was very lovable then. Funny, charming . . . fit too. But there was something underneath it all that I didn't like. A nasty streak, which he was finding harder to hide.'

She takes another sip of water.

'He didn't take the break-up well. He was hysterical. It was pretty shocking, seeing him like that. He cried and begged me to stay, tried to barricade me in the flat. He said he couldn't live without me.'

I swallow. It still stings, despite everything. Would he have ever said these things to me? Was I always just second choice?

Would I ever live up to her? His beautiful, famous ex?

'I got out of there,' she says. 'Took my stuff and went to stay with a mutual friend. But it was awful. He would turn up all the time, off his face, and shout and hammer at the door to be let in. We called the police a few times, but they didn't really care. He never threatened me . . . he was just annoying: crying and shouting and begging. It wasn't fair on my friend. So . . . I told him I'd move back in. I was so busy with work, I just couldn't deal with the drama. But then . . . then I met Dean.'

'Your husband?'

Sarah nods, her face brightening again.

'He's my everything,' she says. 'I don't know how I could live without him. We were paired together by a production company who wanted us to workshop this idea they had. As soon as we met, I knew, I just knew, he was the one. But I handled it all wrong. Dean and I started sleeping together, but I was still technically living with Rob. Although he wasn't there most of the time. He was out, getting drunk. Or passed out on the sofa. He had some obnoxious friends – hangers-on. Drug dealers. We were like ships in the night. But then he came home one day and he was being really weird. Agitated. Said he wanted to take me out, to talk about our relationship.

'It was a Sunday. I was knackered, but I knew things had to get sorted, so I agreed. I got in the car with him. I didn't realise he was still totally off his face . . . I should have known, it was stupid. It was Sunday morning and he'd been out all night – nothing too unusual about that – but I thought he might have sobered up. Anyway, I got in the car with him and that's when it all went wrong. I thought we were going to our favourite pub by Victoria Park for lunch, but he locked the doors and just kept driving until we were out of London. I asked him what he was playing at but he wouldn't answer, he just kept driving. He had this look on his face. I'll never forget it. Just blank, like he'd checked out of his own head. I was screaming at him to pull over and let me out, but he wouldn't, and then, eventually, when we were in the middle of God knows where, he told me he knew all about Dean. That we were sleeping together. He started smashing his head on the steering wheel, screaming and ranting. He wasn't making any sense. Then he started driving again, going further away from London, talking about how he was going to find Dean and kill him. I couldn't get out of the car, he was driving so fast. I honestly thought . . . I thought he was going to kill us.'

'Oh my God,' I say.

'I didn't know what to do. I tried everything – denying it, being nice – I even said Dean . . .' She hangs her head. 'I even said Dean had come on to me and I didn't know how to turn him down. I know, it's just awful. But I was so scared, I was trying everything to talk Robin down. But nothing worked. He just got more and more angry and eventually, he was winding all over the road and I knew it wouldn't be long before he crashed. I resigned myself to it. I thought that was it for me. I was going to die.'

She laughs.

'I didn't die. And neither did he, obviously. But he did crash the car. I broke my leg in three places. I cracked my head open on the dashboard. I was in hospital for two weeks.'

She lifts her fringe away from her forehead and it's then that I see the scar – not just a scar, but a deep groove, as though someone has taken the top of her head off and put it back in the wrong place – that runs across it.

She takes a deep breath.

'He was fine. Arrested for dangerous driving initially, but they let him off. Some issue with the evidence. I don't know. I was in hospital. In no fit state to deal with it really.'

'Jesus Christ,' Kim says.

'He tried to make it up to me afterwards. He even came to the hospital. But my parents got involved and the court issued a restraining order against him. And I hadn't seen him since, until he turned up at the theatre this week. Still, I always knew, somehow, that he would come back into my life at some point. But I never expected to see him there, outside my show. And especially not with a child. I was shaking for hours afterwards. It was horrible.'

I reach out and take her hand and she smiles at me.

'Now, I've told you everything,' she says. 'It's your turn.'

ROBIN

Esther has never been very good at deception. I picked well when I picked her.

She's trying to hide something, but she's not succeeding.

Her behaviour last night really bugged me. The adoption thing. It's not going away.

I don't know what to do.

So I do what I always do when I've exhausted all other options: I phone my big brother.

As I listen to the phone ringing, I tell myself that if he doesn't answer then it's fate. I'm not meant to share this. But if he does . . .

'Bro,' he says, cutting through my thoughts and sending my blood pressure rising. 'Everything all right?'

He knows. He knows I only phone him when I've dug myself into a hole and can't see any way out.

'Yeah,' I say, and suddenly I'm thirteen again, and the bigger boys at school have stolen my lunch, and I'm pathetic and too scared of them to stand up for myself, and I come snivelling to him for what – comfort? A bit of his sandwich? Whatever. He loves it. It's his favourite role: the hero of the hour.

'You on your coffee break?' I say.

He laughs; his deep, masculine laugh.

'What's a coffee break?' he says, and my temper rises. *Yes, all right, Nick, we all know you work So Bloody Hard.* 'It's fine, I've got time to talk.'

'I've got myself into a situation . . .' I begin, and I hear him inhale. I picture him at his desk, pushing his hands into his eye sockets in exasperation.

'Not like last time, I hope?' he says. 'Not . . . Sarah?'

'No,' I say. 'No, it's . . .' The crushing weight of failure strangles my ability to speak.

'Well, that's something at least,' Nick replies.

I take a deep breath myself.

'It's Riley's biological mum.'

'The surrogate?'

'She . . . she wasn't a surrogate,' I say. A perverse tingle of pleasure runs through me and briefly I wonder if I have been doing this all my life. Just trying to get attention by shocking people. 'Not exactly.'

'What do you mean?'

'She was someone I . . .' I say. 'We had a thing. It was complicated.'

'Go on,' Nick says. The tone of his voice has dropped.

'You have to promise never to tell Dad. It wasn't anything, just a brief . . . Esther and I were having a hard time. But anyway, she got pregnant. And after what happened with Esther . . . we decided to take on the baby.'

I pause. There's no way of explaining this so that I come out of it looking good. No way at all.

'Esther wanted to,' I say. 'I know it sounds mad, but she did. And the other woman . . . she was ill. She's got cancer. I said we could take care of the baby while she was getting better, then, I don't know. We'd see. She's a bit of a train wreck. Fuck, that sounds bad. It's not her fault. I just really wanted to be a dad, you know. I really, really wanted that. And it was my baby too. Plenty of single mums bring up babies without their biological fathers, why can't dads? I thought it was for the best if we took the baby on and . . .'

'Stop,' Nick says. 'Just back up a minute. Let me get this straight: Riley's mum is someone you had a fling with. She got pregnant, but she has cancer, so she gave you the baby . . .'

'Yes, but . . . she thought, I guess she thought she'd get better, and one day we'd share custody or something. But I couldn't tell Esther that, could I? She would never have agreed to it if she thought she might have to give Riley back one day.'

'Right . . . so you lied to Esther.'

'The other woman . . . her life's a mess. I guess I thought she'd just . . . move on. Get over it.'

'Move on? Are you kidding me? So what's happened now? She wants her baby back?'

'No,' I say, scrunching up my fists. I hate when he does that patronising thing. 'No, it's not that. She's still really ill. She's in no position to take her back. It's Esther. She's . . . she's totally obsessed with the idea of adopting Riley. Officially. She never . . . she never did. Of course we couldn't do it when Riley was first born because the other woman would never have agreed to it. I thought Esther would just drop it. But lately she's like a dog with a bloody bone.'

'So what's the problem? The other woman still won't agree to it?'

'No . . .' I say, exasperated. 'No, I mean, I don't know. Maybe she would, now. She's not getting better. But even if she dies, I can't risk it. I looked into it. If we apply for Esther to officially adopt Riley, someone has to come and assess us as a family, even though I'm her biological father. I temporarily have to relinquish my rights, and make Riley a ward of the state, and then "reclaim" her . . .'

'That just sounds like legalese,' Nick says. 'If you're her biological dad . . . I don't understand the problem.'

'Think about it,' I say. 'Think about the idea of social services poking into our lives. What if they find out what happened with Sarah? There's no way I'm going to risk them taking Riley away from me, or trying to claim she might not be safe with me.'

'Jesus, bro. I don't know how you do it, but just when I think you've started to sort your life out . . .'

'All right, I know,' I say. 'I don't need a lecture . . . I just thought – I don't know – maybe you could help. My head . . . it's a wreck.'

'You don't have many options,' he says. 'You'll just have to come clean with Esther. Explain about Sarah . . . why the adoption thing is off the table.'

'I . . . I can't,' I say. 'She won't get it. I've been fobbing her off ever since Riley was born. And you know how it sounds . . . the Sarah stuff.'

'Listen, Rob, I don't know what you want me to say,' Nick says, sighing. 'For once in your life, do the right thing, not the easy thing.'

'All right, Mr Moral,' I say. 'Thanks for nothing.'

I hang up. He immediately rings back but I mute my phone.

As always, I'm alone.

I think about Esther, the way she was last night. Something's changed. She knows something ... or she's planning something.

I heard her throwing up the pasta in the downstairs loo after dinner. She thinks if she runs the cold tap hard, I won't hear her. She thinks I'm so stupid, so useless and disorganised and hopeless that I don't notice these things. But I notice everything. The fact she still cleans her teeth about forty times a day, the elastic band she wears on her wrist, the little heaps of hair she leaves on the arm of the sofa, after she's spent the evening pulling them out of her head one by one.

I don't know exactly what's wrong, but I do know something isn't right.

I decide to play I Spy. I drop Riley off with Lovely Amanda, who lives next door with her short, but not particularly sweet, husband Martin. They have two children under four. Amanda's blonde hair is always tied up in a ponytail, her pale skin spotted with freckles. She's really into yoga, and organic food, and looking after Riley at short notice. She's literally the neighbour of dreams.

I head to Esther's office, and check the 'Find My Friends' iPhone tracking. She is in there, as she should be. So far, so normal. I sit outside her office on a metal bench in the freezing cold and watch the world go by. Perhaps I'm getting paranoid in my old age. It's all Sarah's fault. She messed with my head all those years ago, and I've never got it straight again.

At a little after twelve, Esther emerges from her office building, squinting into the sunlight. It seems early for her to be going to lunch, but perhaps she has a meeting at lunchtime, so she's had to go out beforehand and 'grab' something. How *wonderful* it must be to be so important. So busy.

I'm strangely furious with her. It's unsettling.

I follow her, a baseball cap pulled down low over my forehead, like some poor man's Bond. And what do I find?

Kim.

Again.

It's all my fault, of course.

Kim. I underestimated her. I got her all wrong. I thought she'd get over Riley. I sent her photos that first year, I kept her sweet. I met up with her in Tooting and let her hold the baby. I thought she'd be busy with her illness, then find someone else and move on with her life. I thought she'd understand that it was better for Riley if she just stayed with us.

But no, I should have kept a closer eye on her, it seems. Because here they are, the two of them. Heads together. Thick as thieves.

I watch them, trying to work out what they might be saying. They're not shouting, not arguing. No uncomfortable body language.

And then someone else arrives. I almost fall over in shock.

Sarah.

She joins them at the table, and they sit listening to her as she undoubtedly tells them what a horrible, horrible man I am. But she won't tell them that it was all her fault. That she was cheating on me, screwing her writing partner behind my back. Or that she'd abandoned our projects to work on stuff on her own, leaving me sitting around twiddling my thumbs like some trusting loser.

I'm tired of this. I'm so tired of being the mug, the one who suffers, when all I've ever tried to do is be a loving partner, husband, father.

And there they all are, slagging me off together. Three women. Thinking they can get one over me again.

Not this time.

No way.

I simmer with anger throughout my journey back home, chain-smoking as soon as I get off public transport.

How can I shake it off before Amanda drops off Riley? I should have joined a boxing club or something. Right now, I wish someone would knock seven bells out of me. Right now, I wish my brain would die and never work again.

Nick has left me four messages since this morning. I haven't listened to any of them.

Seconds after I get home, the doorbell rings. I can hear them babbling away on the step outside. Just metres away. So innocent. So full of life. My toddler daughter and her little friend. My heart lifts. At least she loves me.

The low winter sunlight seems unbearably bright as I open the door. Riley is holding something out to me.

'Daddy,' she says, and I lean down and take what she's offering from her. The fragments of a brown leaf that has been squashed together in her palm. 'For you. It's a leaf.'

'Thank you,' I say, staring at my little daughter, then back up at Amanda. 'It's just what I always wanted,' I say, breathing out slowly. 'Everyone needs a dead leaf. Everyone. What shall we call him? Sid? Marguerite? Jamelia?'

'Looks like a Marguerite to me,' Amanda says and I look at her and she winks. Just winks, like that, as though all is right with the world.

I manage a smile.

'Well, we'll be off then,' Amanda says, and her face suddenly blurs as I struggle to concentrate. 'Leave you to it. Madeline's got swimming this afternoon.'

'Yay!' The little girl jumps up and down on the spot. Riley grins.

'Thanks for having her,' I say, hoping that the words will mask whatever non-verbal communication I'm clearly leaking all over the place.

Amanda smiles.

'No problem,' she says, and she turns away, taking Madeline's hand as she leads her down our front path.

I close the door. Riley is sitting on the bottom stair, waiting for me to take off her shoes. That's what we do. Routine.

Think!

But whatever way I look at it, I realise that there's no way back from this. No way out. Not now Esther knows what I've done. Sarah will have told her everything.

Riley is staring at me with her huge grey eyes.

I will lose her. That's for definite now. Five years for breaching the restraining order. They'll take me to the cleaners. They'll take her away from me. And then there's the business with the money.

I did it all for the best, but it's all gone wrong. So horribly wrong.

I will never see her again.

'Don't take your shoes off, Riles,' I say, leaning down to her level. I hold her in my arms and pull her towards me. She wriggles and pushes me away, confused. That same puzzled stare on her face.

On the radiator cover next to me there's the little bowl we keep our keys in. It's not a solution, but it's something. If we can just get away so that I can get my head straight.

'We're going out,' I say, and I grab the car keys. In the kitchen I rummage in the drawer for our passports.

Then I turn and open the understairs cupboard, groping around in the dark to find the safe. I open it, take out the pile of fifty-pound notes I've kept there ever since Esther gave me the money. It was all that was left of it once I'd cleared my debts.

For once I am grateful to Past Me for his foresight. My emergency funds.

Well, this is an emergency.

'Where we going, Daddy?'

The words stick in my throat. Wherever I'm going now,

there's only one thing I'm sure of: I'm going to take her with me, and I'm not coming back.

'Never you mind, sweetheart. Just a little adventure with Daddy.' I bend down and squeeze her cheeks. 'Go grab little Lammy, she'll want to come too.'

ESTHER

Back in the office, I find it impossible to concentrate on anything.

My head is spinning with what Sarah told us. In a way it's positive, but it still seems like an uphill battle. There's so much I need to sort out before I can actually leave him. When Kim dies, he will be the only one who has to give me permission to adopt Riley, and he will never give her up. But if we can persuade Sarah to be involved somehow, to give evidence against him or something – surely there's a chance the court will let me adopt her? *Surely* there's a chance.

My head is killing me. I sit at my desk and type an email to Jeremy. I hope he can help me. It's such a complicated mess. Who knows what a court would think if I made a challenge for custody? Would they believe that I had no idea about his past, all this business with Sarah? Would they judge me for handing over twenty thousand pounds, thinking it was going to Kim?

After I finish the email, I pull out my notebook and start to write down everything I can think of that might be of use. All the times Robin has behaved strangely, or aggressively. For now, I have to stay with him, to protect Riley. And he has to

339

stay with me, because I provide the security, the finances, the cosy family set-up he always wanted.

When I look at Riley it's impossible to imagine a world without her in it, and if you gave me a million pounds and the opportunity to turn back time and keep my own baby, I wouldn't do it. Because it would mean my darling, delightful, unique and surprising Riley would never have been born. And that would have been the greatest tragedy of them all.

Blood is not thicker than water. Love is thicker than everything.

I pick up my phone. For now, I have to go back to how things were, before Kim's revelations threw a bomb into my life of denial. I have to go back there. To pretend that I never found out any of this stuff about his past. Just play my part, until I have everything in order to mount my case.

Whatever happens, Robin mustn't suspect that I know anything.

I open WhatsApp. It's just gone 3pm. I do what I always do in the afternoon – check in for an update. Robin sometimes sends me a picture – some little snippet of their day together that warms my heart and makes me green with jealousy all at once.

Hope you two are having a lovely day and keeping warm. Send us a pic? X

The message is delivered straight away, and then the app tells me Robin is online. I exhale. It's always a relief.

One of my more irrational fears is that he'll have a heart attack while he's looking after her, and that she'll be left alone in the house until I come home. He told me a few years ago he had a scare, that his heart was found to be inflamed. A side effect of his past lifestyle, clearly, although he didn't elaborate at the time.

The word '*Typing*' appears at the top of the screen. It seems to last for ages, as though he's being interrupted, or changing his mind about what to write.

But eventually, when the message comes through, it's just a single word. Nothing more.

Sorry.

And then he goes offline.

My hand flies to my mouth. I grab my handbag and race to the door, leaving Sarina and Anna open-mouthed as I ignore their shouts asking me where I'm going.

NOW

ESTHER

Riley is asleep in the bed on the children's ward, and I stand over her, stroking her soft blonde hair. She looks fine, but the doctor tells me that just to be safe they'll be keeping her in overnight for observation.

'I'm sorry about the delay in getting the information to you,' the doctor says. 'There was some confusion about next of kin as she was brought in in a separate ambulance from your husband.'

'We didn't find the car straight away,' DS Tyler says to the doctor, looking down. 'It had rolled into a ditch.'

She turns to me.

'Your husband had walked quite some distance to try to get help before he collapsed on the road. We found his mobile phone on him, but it was broken, likely in the accident. Riley was fine. She was just confused, but her car seat protected her well from the impact.'

'Nothing more than a few bruises,' the doctor says, giving me a smile. 'She will be absolutely fine.'

I stare at the doctor as she tells me, trying to take it all in.

DS Tyler told me they found their passports in the car.

Clearly Robin was planning on kidnapping Riley, but where was he taking her?

I think about the road where he was found. Epsom. I have a vague recollection of it being the home of a racecourse, but other than that, I know nothing about it. I take my phone out and search for the name of the road on the maps app. It's one of the main roads out of London. But it doesn't help – it doesn't provide any context, or tell me where he might have been going.

'Why did he crash?' I ask. I think about what Sarah told me; about him ranting and raving and terrifying her with his erratic driving, and can't bear to imagine how frightened Riley must have been if she had to experience the same.

'We're not entirely sure yet,' DS Tyler says. 'But there will be a thorough investigation. You'll get all the answers you need, I promise you.'

I'm burning with anger that he put our little girl's life at risk like that.

Vivienne holds me for what feels like hours as we sit by Riley's bedside. I can't face going home, back to that empty house, so eventually I go to Viv's flat and she makes up the spare bed for me. She hands me a cup of tea and a piece of pizza, and we sit together on the sofa, and I think about how close I came to losing Riley.

'I can't believe he would just take her like that,' I say, staring out at the patio beyond Viv's huge folding doors. The patio where I first saw Robin kiss Kim. The patio where it all began. It seems ironic that I have ended up here. 'Where was he going to go? Did he even have a plan?'

'I guess if he wakes up you can ask him,' Viv says, rolling her eyes. 'Sorry. I don't know, Esty, I don't know what to make of that man. I just . . . I just wish you'd never met him.'

At 10.30pm I make my excuses and go into Viv's spare bedroom. Whatever happens now, I have to protect Riley. She's the only thing that matters. And I need to get hold of Kim, to tell her what's happened.

I pick up the phone and wait for her to answer, but it goes straight to voicemail, as it has done every other time I've tried to ring her. I leave her a message, telling her she needs to call me urgently.

Eventually, I fall into an unsatisfactory sleep, punctuated with dreams of Riley's wide eyes and tear-stained face, trapped alone inside that car, and Robin collapsing on the roadside, leaving a pool of blood around him.

I wake the next morning to the sound of my mobile ringing. It's the hospital.

'They're letting her come home,' I tearfully tell Viv after I hang up.

'I'll come with you,' she says. 'Then we can go back to the house together.'

Rob's parents and Nick were with him last night. They arrived just after I left. I'm dreading seeing them, trying to explain it all.

Before we collect Riley, we go to visit Rob. He's lying immobile on his hospital bed, surrounded by machines. It's surreal to see him so still. He was always jumping about, fizzing with energy.

There's been no change in his condition. The doctor didn't sound hopeful. I wonder if this will be my new existence? Suspended in limbo, waiting to see if my husband will live or die. And if he lives, what then? Will he be arrested? Is it possible to kidnap your own child? I'm too frightened of the answers to ask the questions.

'His head is so swollen,' I whisper to Viv. 'And look at all the grazes on his cheek.'

'I guess from where he fell on the tarmac,' Viv says, shrugging. Her voice is flat but when I look up at her, her eyes are bloodshot.

'I suppose I should tell Sarah,' I say, softly. 'But I need to get hold of Kim first.'

'I'll try calling her when we leave,' Viv says, wrapping her arm around me. 'Come on, there's not much point in us sitting here staring at him. I'm so sorry, chicken, what a bloody mess.'

I give a half-hearted smile and we make our way to the children's ward.

Thank God for Riley. When she's around it's impossible to focus on anything but her. She's her usual cheerful, cheeky self, fascinated by the nurses' uniforms and the fact that the bed she slept in is on wheels.

I hold her so tightly that she pushes me away, telling me I'm squashing her. I smile and kiss the top of her head.

On the way home Viv makes her laugh singing songs from *Frozen* in that impressive belt of hers. Once we're back at the house, we all spend a few hours getting things straight, and then we go for a long walk round Wimbledon, waving Viv off at the bus stop.

It's a frosty day and Riley tells me the trees look as though they're sparkling. I cook her favourite dinner – fish fingers and potato waffles – and she only asks about her father once.

It's a little taster of how simple, joyous and happy life could be, if only she was mine alone, but I know it won't last.

The next morning, I am back sitting next to Robin's bed in the hospital. Despite the fact he's gravely injured I can't bring myself to even touch his hand. I stare at his face. My mind is a complex mess of feelings, and I can't even begin to untangle them.

'Mrs Morgan?'

I look up. Robin's consultant is standing behind me.

'Yes,' I say. 'Hello . . . hi.'

'We've had the results back from your husband's latest tests,' she says softly. 'I'm afraid they're not particularly encouraging. The bleed to his brain was significant and at present, he's still unable to breathe for himself. That's why he's on the ventilator. He's also on medication to keep his blood pressure elevated. However, his condition doesn't seem to be improving . . .'

'What . . . what does it mean?'

'At present,' she says, 'the machines and medication are keeping your husband alive. Without them, his body would not be able to function. Also, I see from his history that ten years ago he had a heart attack brought about by prolonged cocaine use. As a result his heart isn't as strong as we would hope, and it's not coping as well as we'd like for someone his age. I'm very sorry.'

A heart attack?

'I didn't know that,' I say, sniffing. 'I thought he'd just . . . had a scare. I didn't realise he'd actually had a heart attack.'

The consultant looks uncomfortable.

'It was before I met him . . . Sorry, what were you saying?' I ask.

'Your husband is very poorly,' she says, smiling sympathetically. 'And at the moment, unless something changes, I'm afraid he is unlikely to recover from his injuries. We're doing everything we can, and he's stable for now. It's just a case of waiting to see if he fights back.'

I nod and try to imagine what would happen if he did recover. Would he be confined to a wheelchair? Would I have to be his carer? I am his wife, after all. I'm his next of kin. He's my responsibility.

'Thank you,' I say. 'If it's OK, I'd like to sit with him for a little bit longer.'

'Of course.'

She leaves the room, but seconds later the door opens again. I look up. It's Kim. Her face is so impossibly pale I almost don't recognise her.

'Kim!' I say. 'I tried calling you.'

'I know, I got your messages.'

'Where have you . . . where have you been?'

'On the sixth floor,' she says, smiling grimly. 'Visiting old friends. It's where I've been having my treatment.'

She walks over to me and pulls a chair up beside me, staring at Robin.

'God, the hours I've spent in this place,' she says. 'I might as well get my post redirected here.'

I laugh. The break in the atmosphere is a relief.

'I'm sure.'

'Where is Riley?'

'Rob's parents are looking after her,' I reply. 'Don't worry.' She nods.

'Shit, man,' she says. 'He looks worse than me, and that's saying something.'

'They think he's going to die,' I say, and I don't even care if he can hear me, if he understands. 'The doctor just told me. Well, not in so many words but . . . He's very unlikely to recover from his injuries. Without the ventilator, he can't breathe. Also, his heart is weak. He had a heart attack years ago. He's stable for now, but what happens long-term? I can't actually . . .'

I start to cry.

'I mean, I don't know what to think,' I say. 'After everything, everything I've found out about him . . . and now . . . this. I mostly just feel anger. I'm so angry that he's done this, that he's put us in this situation. I don't even get the chance to have it out with him. To sort it out. It's not fair. This isn't a level playing field. How am I supposed to feel? What am I supposed to think?'

Kim says nothing.

'I loved him so much,' I say. 'For so long. And then . . . I don't even know what he thought of me, in the end. Did he ever love me? Was he just using me? And what . . . what will

351

happen to Riley if he dies? She adored him. He was so good to her. He loved her so much . . .'

'Listen to me,' Kim says, gripping my wrists and twisting me round to look at her. 'You're a good mother. Riley loves you. You will get through this. And you will be fine. I promise you. I wouldn't . . . I wouldn't leave my daughter behind unless I knew she was going to be OK. And she will be, with you to take care of her.'

I bite my lip.

'And as for Robin . . .' she says, her voice softening slightly. 'You can still love him. He was your husband. And he cared about you – of course he did. He was a messed up man, but he loved you and he loved Riley. You can still grieve for him, you can still be sad.'

I sniff again.

'It's just hard . . .' I say. 'On the one hand wishing . . . no, not wishing, but just knowing how much easier it would all be if he went away. But on the other . . . how can I think like that? How can I *want* Riley to lose her father? What kind of mother does that make me?'

I rub my face with my hands.

'God,' I say, pulling myself together. 'I don't want that. Of course I don't. I'm so sorry. I haven't slept well . . . Robin's parents were very, very upset last night. It was hard, they expected me to be too but I just . . .'

Kim frowns and gives a short sigh.

'Listen,' she says, leaning forward. 'Why don't you take a quick break? Go to the loo and wash your face. Then get us both a strong coffee. I really need one. And you just need a few seconds to get your head together. I'll sit here with him until you come back.' She glances over at Robin. 'He's not going to care, is he?'

I nod and stand, looking back at her.

'Thanks,' I say, and she smiles, and she shoos me out of the door.

There is a queue at the coffee machine. I feel agitated as I wait, even though I'd give anything not to have to go back in that room.

Ten minutes later, I stop short, two coffees in hand, as I approach Robin's room. Kim is standing outside the door, peering in through the glass in the window.

'What's happening?' I ask, rushing towards her. Through the window I can see four or five people huddled around his bed, fiddling with machines, shouting commands at one another.

'He just . . .' she says, staring at me with her huge wide eyes. 'The machine stopped working. Then the alarm started and they all rushed in. It was . . . weird.'

I frown at her, staring through the pane of glass as I watch the medical team at work. It feels like I'm watching a scene from a television show. How can this be me? How can I be standing here, watching these events unfold?

'But it doesn't make sense! He was on a ventilator . . . They said he was stable!' I say.

She shrugs, looking down.

'I don't understand!' I say. 'He was . . . he was just fine.'

Through the window I see the consultant lay a hand across

her colleague's arm. He gives a brief shake of his head and she stops what she's doing.

'Perhaps he didn't like being alone with me, after all,' Kim says, her voice so quiet it's almost inaudible.

My head snaps round to stare at her.

'Can't blame him, I guess,' she says.

And then she looks down at the floor and shrugs again, refusing to meet my eye.

Afterwards, I go back to the house. I give Kim our address before I leave, tell her to come over and see Riley whenever she likes. They have missed so much time together. When I get home, Robin's parents are sitting at the kitchen island. They can tell by my face what's happened.

'I'm so sorry,' I say, 'he had a massive heart attack. They said there was nothing they could do.'

I feel numb as I watch Sandra's face collapse in front of me. Mike looks shell-shocked, but he puts his arm around Sandra as she leans on his shoulder.

'It's my fault. It has to be. I just don't know where we went wrong,' Mike says, and I see him for what he is: a father, unable to understand his son. Just like I was a wife, unable to understand her husband.

'He was always so troubled,' Sandra says, and her eyes well up again. 'But he was a good boy! He was a *good boy* deep down!'

I stare at them. Sandra sobs.

'Where's Riley? I ask.

'She's having a nap,' Mike says. 'She seemed very tired. I suppose being at the hospital was a lot for her to process.'

I nod.

Later when Riley wakes, we tell her together that Daddy has gone to heaven, all sitting round her in the living room like some strange committee. She doesn't really know what's going on, but she understands our tears and she hugs us all in turn, bringing us each one of her soft toys as a comforter. I am stunned by her empathy. For someone so young, she's so wise.

I am so very proud of her.

ESTHER

Sandra offers to stay for a few days to help with Riley, but I tell her it's not needed. I can see she's relieved. I know she wants to be back in her own home, to grieve in private. Of all of us, she seems to be finding it the hardest.

I wave them off at the door, Riley in my arms, wondering when I'll see them again. They've never felt like family, not really, but they are Riley's grandparents, and I know they love her.

I watch their car pull away at the bottom of our road and I turn to go back into the house, closing the door behind me. But before I've made it back to the kitchen, the doorbell rings.

I put Riley down as I go to answer it, assuming Robin's parents must have left something behind.

But it's not Sandra and Mike.

'Kim!' I say, surprised.

'Is it OK if I come in?' she asks. 'I was . . . waiting for them to leave.'

'Of course.' I swallow. She looks down at Riley, smiling, and my heart begins to pound.

'Hello,' she says, crouching down until she's at Riley's level.

'I don't know if you remember me, little one. I'm your Auntie Kim.'

Riley stares at her for a few seconds, then throws her arms around Kim's shoulders, almost sending her toppling backwards.

'I like your hair,' Riley says, patting it. 'Like Moana's.'

Kim laughs.

'Shall I tell you a secret?'

Riley nods.

'It's not my real hair. My real hair is yellow. Like yours.'

Riley gasps and Kim cuddles her again. When they break apart, I see Kim's eyes are damp with tears.

In the living room, we sit on the rug and play with Riley's favourite toys: her ever-growing collection of musical instruments. Her particular obsession at the moment is a tiny keyboard, and she presses each note in turn, watching for Kim's reaction as they sound out.

'She's really musical,' I say, smiling. 'The second she hears music she starts bopping about and trying to sing. We were hoping . . . I mean, I want to get her lessons as soon as she's old enough. Piano, probably, to start. Or maybe recorder. I'm not sure exactly, I'll ask what's best.'

Kim nods. Despite the smile on her face, she looks so tired.

'Can I make you another cup of tea?' I say.

'No thanks,' she says, 'but I better just shift position. Sitting still for too long makes various bits of me ache. I'm sorry. I might have to head off soon.'

'Of course.'

She rolls onto her knees, wincing slightly at the movement, then stands slowly, reaching for the sofa to pull herself up.

'You have a lovely house,' she says, looking around.

'Thanks. We only just finished doing it up.'

'Aren't you a lucky girl Miss Riley?' Kim says, 'living in such a nice house?'

'In the summer Mummy said we get a padding pool,' Riley replies, still focused on her toy keyboard. 'For the garden.'

I laugh.

'Yes, I did,' I say. 'She remembers everything.'

Riley looks up.

'Will you come Auntie Kim? In the padding pool?'

Kim smiles and strokes Riley's head.

'I would love that,' she says. 'If I can. Let's see, shall we, poppet? Let's see how things work out.'

I look away, blinking back the tears.

The next morning Amanda from next door takes Riley to her favourite softplay, while I stay at home and try to come to terms with everything. I try to remember what my last words to Robin were. The man I had married, the man I had loved, the man who had broken my heart.

My phone buzzes on the island in front of me as I stare out at the frosty garden. It's been buzzing repeatedly with sympathetic messages from friends, but this time it's different. The message simply says,

Meet me on Putney Bridge at twelve. Don't bring Riley.

I stare down at the phone. Kim's given me twenty minutes to get there.

I shove my feet into a pair of trainers, pull on my coat and wrap a huge scarf around my neck before heading out. My hair is wild and my face unwashed and blotchy with crying. People are staring at me as I trudge through the snow to the Tube but I don't care.

At Putney Bridge, it takes me a few minutes to spot her. She's leaning against the concrete, hunched.

'Hi,' I say, as I approach.

She turns to face me and as our eyes lock together, I stare at her.

'How's Riley today?' she asks.

'Fine,' I reply. 'A bit confused, but she's OK. She talked about you non-stop after you left last night.'

'I wish I had asked you to bring her now. But it wouldn't have been fair on her. It's so cold.'

She turns her head to look across at the river.

'You can come and visit her again tomorrow,' I say. 'She would love that.'

Kim shakes her head. Her eyes are still fixed on the Thames.

'No,' she says. 'No, I don't think so.'

I stare at her.

'What's the matter?' I say. 'Why . . . why did you call me all the way out here?'

'I wanted to explain,' she says, turning her head back and meeting my eyes again. 'I wanted to explain why I did what I did.'

I frown.

'What do you mean?'

'I'm sorry,' she says. 'I had no choice. I couldn't leave

359

knowing everything was in limbo like that. I did it for her.'

'What are you saying?' I ask, my voice rising.

'Robin. I helped him on his way,' she replies. 'Like I wish someone would be brave enough to do for me. You get to learn quite a lot of stuff about the machines when you spend as much time in hospital as I have.'

My hand flies to my face.

'What are you telling me, Kim?'

'It doesn't matter,' she replies. 'I did what I had to. I did what was right.'

I can't speak. There's no appropriate response to this confession. I feel utterly wrung out, exhausted, as though every emotion I ever had has been sucked out of me.

'I never told you how my mum died, did I?' she says, leaning against the side of the bridge. I take a step closer to her. The wind is brittle in my ears. I wish I had a hat.

'No,' I say. 'You didn't.'

Of course you didn't, I barely know you.

'She was great, my mum. The life and soul. A real character. But she had her problems. Bad taste in men.'

'Oh.'

'She met my stepfather when I was thirteen. I hated him from the start, but she wouldn't listen. He was a bully. Controlling. Violent. She loved him. He could be funny and he was handsome, but he was also an insecure twat. I moved out just before my sixteenth birthday, went to live with my dad. I couldn't stand the way he treated her. But she wouldn't leave him. She wouldn't listen. Anyway, he killed her when I was seventeen. Stabbed her in our kitchen. Then tried to claim it was an accident, that he didn't "mean to do it".'

'I'm so sorry.'

'That's why I had to do it, you see,' she says, staring at me. 'I couldn't go, I couldn't leave her, risk it.'

'He would never have hurt her,' I say. 'He wasn't like that. I mean, not with Riley . . .'

Kim stares at me, her lip curling.

'That's what they all say. That's what my mum said. The truth is, you don't know. You don't know what he was capable of, and you don't know how his brain injury might have affected him, if he'd got better. Too many risks. Too many unknowns. And the pressure of you having to take care of him, if he'd been stuck in hospital or needed full-time care for the rest of his life – where would that have left Riley? With one stressed-out parent? Trust me, kids need more than that. Kids deserve more than that. I'm sorry that it had to be this way. But it's for the best.'

'He texted me, just before he died,' I say. '*Sorry.* That's all it said. I'm so angry with him. I'm so, so angry. I wanted to know, Kim. I wanted answers.'

I shake my head.

'I'm sorry,' she says. 'I'm sorry that you're in pain. But I had to put Riley first. Just promise you won't tell her about me until she's an adult. She'll idolise her dad for not being there. She doesn't need that bubble bursting, doesn't need to know what a mess we all made of things.'

'But the lies, Kim,' I say, my head shaking forcefully. 'I'm so sick of the lies. I don't know if I can do it.'

361

She turns and stares at me again, hard in the face.

'You can and you will. Because you're her mother. And you'll tell her whatever hurts her the least. Won't you? Promise me that. I trust you, Esther. I trusted you from the start. I watched you with her yesterday. I know how much you love her. You're all she has left. You can't let her down.'

'But what will happen to you?' I say, and I suddenly have this certainty that this will be the last time I see her. 'Where will you go?'

'There's something I didn't tell you. At my last appointment, they gave me three weeks. I'm done, now. I've left behind something more precious, more valuable, than anything. My girl. I've made my mark on the world. I'm happy to leave it. And now I know for sure that I'm happy to leave her with you.'

'Don't say that,' I say. Angry, hot tears are rolling down my face. 'Come over tomorrow, we can go somewhere nice with Riley . . . you should get to know her properly . . .'

'Don't,' Kim says, and she holds her hand out as if to push me away. 'Don't talk about her anymore. Just give her this.'

She presses something into my hand. It feels cold and hard in my fist but I can't tear my eyes away from her face.

'And tell her I love her. And I'll see her again someday.'

I stand frozen as she turns and walks away. I can't move, so I just watch her figure departing, growing smaller and smaller as she crosses the bridge. I keep my eyes fixed on her as much as possible, but people keep obscuring my view. She disappears from sight for a few seconds, and when I locate her again, my mind struggles to process what I'm seeing.

Kim is carefully climbing over the low stone wall on the other end of the bridge.

'No!' I scream, and I race towards her, pushing past the lunchtime office workers in my desperation to reach her. But it's too late. She doesn't even turn to look back at me. There's not a moment's hesitation as she simply leans forward over the river, and lets go of the wall.

My scream seems to freeze time.

I peer over the edge of the bridge at the black Thames below, but she's already gone.

AFTER

ESTHER

Thankfully, everyone who matters – Robin's parents, the courts and social workers – all agree that Riley should stay with me. Finally, she is my daughter in the eyes of the law, as well as in my heart.

By the end of the adoption process, I am a shell of a woman, but I am a tiger of a mother. When the official papers come through, I sit on the sofa and sob. It's so hard to believe something I wanted for so long has actually happened.

Through my tears I see Riley approaching. She snatches the paper from my hand and puts it on the coffee table.

'No work now. Play, Mummy, please?' she says, shrugging, and I laugh at the expression on her little face. There is no time for tears with her around.

The police investigation concludes that the cause of the crash was a blown tyre. Robin did exactly what you shouldn't do in that situation: he braked hard, and the car spun off the road. Something so simple, but so deadly when driving at speed.

In some ways, it makes me feel better. It really was an accident. He didn't mean to hurt her.

Robin's and Kim's funerals are held within two weeks of each other. I don't know how I get through them, but whenever I feel myself begin to break, I look down at my daughter's wide eyes and I remind myself of Kim's last words to me.

Sometimes, it is as if Kim is here with us. They are so alike.

I go to Kim's funeral alone, uninvited. I slip in at the back of the crematorium, and thank the woman who gave me everything, and then I leave before the rest of the family and friends file out. The chapel of rest is packed with people and the songs are loud and celebratory. It feels at odds with how I feel, but I know she would have liked it.

We were always at odds with one another. But I am coming to terms with what she did. It wasn't right, but I understand why she did it. I respect her. I respect everything she did for us.

March rolls into April, and suddenly the winter has gone, and the weather has switched to baking hot, and I am beginning to feel there's some light at the end of the tunnel; that the future will be better.

We are in Riley's bedroom, having a 'spring clean'. It was her idea. She saw it on her favourite children's television programme and begged me to let her do one.

We're sitting surrounded by piles of her stuff on the carpet.

'Come and sit next to me, Riles,' I say, touching her on the arm.

She stops looking through her books and gazes at me, obediently trundling over and climbing on to my lap.

'I've got something for you,' I say, and I unfurl my palm to reveal a silver locket on a long chain.

'Oh,' she says, taking it from me and looking at it. 'It's a neck-less.'

'It's very old,' I say. 'I think. Auntie Kim gave it to me to give to you.'

Her little fingers struggle with the mechanism as she opens the locket. Inside, there is a picture of her as a baby, and another of Kim.

'Look, Mummy,' she says, pointing at the two tiny photographs. 'Here's a baby. And that Auntie Kim! She coming for the padding pool?'

I swallow back the tears.

'Auntie Kim is very special,' I say, staring down at Kim's face, the wideness of her smile. 'She's your guardian angel.'

'A guardian angel,' she says, proudly. 'Like a unicorn?'

'Sort of,' I say, smiling. 'But she can't come when we get the paddling pool, I'm afraid. Because she lives in heaven now.'

'My daddy lives in heaven,' she says. 'That means I can't see him.'

I swallow.

'Yes, yes, that's right.'

I think of my father. How much he would have loved this quirky, entertaining and wise little girl.

'There are so many people in this world *and* in heaven who love you, Riley Madison Morgan.'

Riley beams at me and I fold her in my arms.

And then I glance down at the tiny picture of Kim, squeezing my eyes shut as I make a silent vow to protect our little girl for the rest of my life.

ACKNOWLEDGEMENTS

A massive thank you as always to my agent, Caroline Hardman, for all her support and guidance, alongside her brilliant team at Hardman & Swainson. I couldn't have done this without you.

I'd also like to thank the wonderful team at Quercus: my editor Cassie Browne as well as Rachel Neely, Stefanie Bierwerth, Ella Patel and everyone else who has worked so hard to make this book happen. I really couldn't ask for a better publisher.

I'm so grateful as always for my many author friends – thank you all! – but must give special mention to Caroline Hulse, who has saved my sanity on many an occasion; and Rebecca Fleet, who has been with me since the beginning. You should immediately buy and read their books if you haven't already, because they are both amazing writers.

I want to say the biggest thank you to my dear friend Sophy Greenhalgh, to whom this book is dedicated, for sharing her story of hyperemesis gravidarum with me. Not enough is known about this horrible condition – so few women want to relive the horrors after they have come out the other side

– and so I hope to raise a little more awareness of it through this book. I could not have portrayed the condition so authentically if it weren't for Sophy taking the time to share with me this most difficult period in her life. Soph, I think you are an absolute superwoman!

I'd also really like to thank my mum, who read this book countless times, giving a much needed 'reader's perspective' and helping me so much with some of the more challenging parts of it. Thank you too to my sister for telling everyone she meets about my books – I really appreciate your support! And thanks to my dad for checking my Amazon page more often than me. One day I'll have as many reviews as Lee Child.

Oli and Daphne – you are my two favourite people and you make me smile every day. Thank you both for being so supportive of this unusual career.

Finally, of course I must say a huge thank you to all the readers who have enjoyed my previous books – I still can't quite believe that strangers actually read my writing. What a dream it is, and you make it possible. I hope you enjoy this one too.

Loved *The Perfect Father*? Read this next . . .

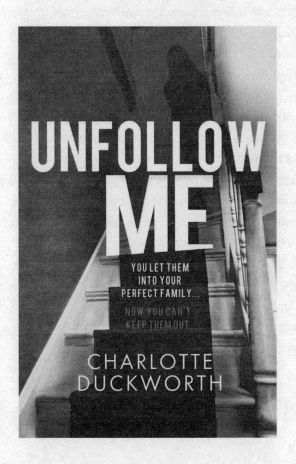

Out now in paperback, eBook and audio

Quercus

More compelling suspense from Charlotte Duckworth

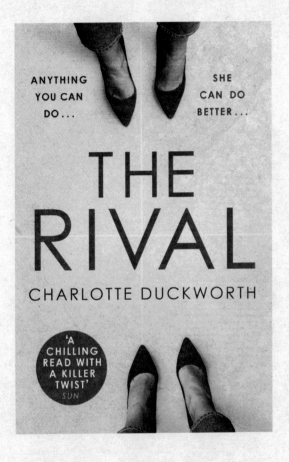

Out now in paperback, eBook and audio